COVENTRY LIBRARIES

Please return this book on or before
the last date stamped below.

To renew this book take it to any of
the City Libraries before
the date due for return

Coventry City Council

Celia Kyle is a *New York Times* and *USA Today* bestselling author, ex-dance teacher, former accountant and erstwhile collectible doll salesperson. She now writes paranormal romances for readers who:

1) Like super hunky heroes (they generally get furry)
2) Dig beautiful women (who have a few more curves than the average lady)
3) Love laughing in (and out of) bed

It goes without saying that there's always a happily-ever-after for her characters, even if there are a few road bumps along the way. Today she lives in central Florida and writes full-time with the support of her loving husband and two finicky cats.

Learn more at:
@celiakyle
Facebook.com/authorceliakyle
www.celiakyle.com

Wolf's Mate

Shifter Rogues Book #1

CELIA KYLE

piatkus

PIATKUS

First published in the US in 2017 by Forever, an imprint of Grand Central Publishing
First published in the UK in 2017 by Piatkus
This paperback edition published in 2018 by Piatkus

1 3 5 7 9 10 8 6 4 2

is available from the British Library

ISBN 978-0-349-41680-9

Printed and bound in Great Britain by
Clays Ltd, St Ives plc

Papers used by Piatkus are from well-managed forests
and other responsible sources.

MIX
Paper from
responsible sources
FSC® C104740
www.fsc.org

Piatkus
An imprint of
Little, Brown Book Group
Carmelite House
50 Victoria Embankment
London EC4Y 0DZ

An Hachette UK Company
www.hachette.co.uk

www.littlebrown.co.uk

*To my husband, for believing in me when
I wasn't ready to believe in myself*

CHAPTER ONE

A few minutes past eight and Declan Reed couldn't take his eyes off the windows in the building across the street.

"You remember our shift ended two hours ago, right?" Cole drawled. The pain-in-the-ass tiger shifter was his partner for this operation. Eh, the dick was his partner in most operations. Declan ignored the man.

Their shift had ended at six, and the other men on Shifter Operations Command Team One, Ethan and Grant, had taken over, but Declan couldn't force himself to leave. He couldn't force his *wolf* to leave.

Not while *she* still occupied the building.

Abby Marie Carter. Twenty-eight years old and five feet eight inches of tempting cougar shifter. She had long golden hair with a hint of a curl at the ends, bright blue eyes, and curves that made his palms tingle with the need to stroke every one of them.

"Not that I'm against keeping my eyes on a nice ass," Cole continued. "But since neither of us is getting in her panties, I don't see the point."

The tiger was a good ally in a tight spot and handy with a block of explosives. Declan would trust him at his back on any assignment. But having faith in the man didn't mean his wolf was okay with Cole thinking about Abby *or* her panties.

"Fuck off, Cole."

"We've been watching this place for four days and you've barely slept. Do you want to go through another psych evaluation? Because 'obsessive behavior'"—Cole formed air quotes with his fingers—"is a sure-as-shit way to end up on the doc's couch."

"Do you feel like being thrown out a window?" Declan pulled his attention from the building across the street and leveled a glare on the tiger shifter. "Because 'dickish behavior'"—he formed air quotes, mimicking Cole—"is a sure-as-shit way to end up hitting the pavement headfirst."

"Play nice, kids." A third voice joined their conversation— their team alpha—his order transmitted through the com device each member of the team wore in their ear. "Tighten up."

Declan glowered at Cole and his partner did the same to him, but they kept their mouths shut. Birch was a hard-ass bear shifter, and when he spoke, they all did their damnedest to listen. Sometimes it happened. Sometimes it didn't.

The men of SHOC Team One weren't known for their respect for authority, and they sure as hell hadn't been re-cruited because they played well with others.

"Aw, Birch. He started it..." Cole whined in his best impression of a five-year-old. Declan rolled his eyes, tuning out his partner's voice while he refocused on Abby.

Technically, their target was FosCo, the multinational company headquartered across the street. Except from the moment Abby walked into FosCo's lobby four days ago, he'd had a hard time tearing his attention from her. Staring at the cougar shifter was a lot more fun than watching the other staffers.

No one else popped in earbuds while they worked. They didn't get up from their chairs to stretch and add a little shake of their ass. They definitely didn't kick off their shoes and dance when the building emptied and no one was watching.

Abby did. She appeared professional when she walked into the office building every morning. Her blond hair was usually twisted in some girly knot that he wanted to run his claws through, and she wore a tight skirt suit with a pair of low heels. She fit right in with all the others in FosCo's headquarters.

Even if she wasn't a FosCo employee...or even human.

According to the file they'd compiled, she'd been employed by the accounting firm Ogilve, Piers, and Patterson for six years, landing the job straight out of college after earning her bachelor's degree. She still worked toward her master's as she studied for the CPA exam. Smart. Dedicated. A hard worker if her schedule was anything to go by. In at seven thirty every morning and out at nine thirty every night. In bed by eleven. His knowledge of her sleeping habits wasn't something he shared with the others.

"Obsessive behavior" and all that shit.

The team still wasn't sure what she was doing at FosCo, but Declan found he cared less and less about the reason as each hour passed. He just liked looking at her.

"Declan, you listening?" Cole's deep growl pulled his attention from Abby *again*.

The asshole wanted to lose his tongue before Declan threw him out the window.

"What?" he snapped.

"Guys." Cole groaned. "He's already pussy whipped even though he's never gonna get any."

Declan would tell the man to fuck off—again—but he

figured more was called for at this point. He didn't let his attention stray as he reached to his left and wrapped his fingers around an unopened can of soda. His next action was a blur—a single fluid move—as he whipped it at Cole's head.

Unfortunately, Cole's reflexes rivaled Declan's, and he snatched the can from the air. The tiger popped the top and guzzled the soda down in a couple swallows before crushing the container in one hand and tossing it over his shoulder.

"Thanks, man. I was thirsty." Cole grinned, but there was something else in the tiger's gaze. The man's body language said he was at ease, but the flicker of yellow in Cole's eyes revealed the feral beast just under the surface.

"Cole..." Birch growled over the com.

"I'd like the record to show that Cole is the one causing shit today." Grant, the other werewolf on the team, broke in. "It ain't me."

The crunch of chips and the smack of Grant's lips followed his words. The wolf was eating *again*. The man's stomach was a bottomless pit. Grant claimed junk food kept his mind sharp, which was a necessity as the team's tech operative.

"Or me." Ethan, lion shifter and genius with transportation, spoke up as well. Then he popped his gum, which had Birch growling some more. Ethan had what the doc called an "oral fixation." Declan knew better. Ethan just liked annoying Birch, and someone popping his gum while talking over the com pissed him off.

The alpha bear liked them to at least pretend to be professional like the goody-goody council Trackers, but that wasn't SHOC Team One. Declan wasn't sure why the bear shifter even bothered. Their backgrounds were varied, but they all shared a few traits—they were loners, reveled in pissing people off, and had a penchant for breaking the law.

All right, *laws.*

Violate enough of 'em and the council would send their Trackers after a shifter. Break those guys *well* enough and a shifter was given the choice between council punishment or "using their evil powers for good" with SHOC.

Declan's team was the best of the bad.

"Can someone remind me when I get to shoot someone?" Declan broke into their bickering.

"Or blow something up?" Cole added hopefully.

Birch sighed, and Declan pictured the big bear shifter closing his eyes and pinching the bridge of his nose in frustration. "Does no one remember the mission objective?"

Declan grunted and repeated the words from memory. "Observe. Confirm rumors. Eliminate the threat."

They were supposed to report in to SHOC headquarters, too, but in their tight group, they tended to get things done first and tell higher-ups about it later.

Right now Declan was ready to skip to the elimination step. After he got Abby out of there, of course. His wolf bristled at the idea of anything happening to the little she-cat.

"Get paid," Ethan tacked on. "I've gotta pay for that new Porsche in the garage."

"Exactly," Birch reminded them. "Right now we're still observing."

Cole grunted. "Observing is boring as fuck."

"We can't go in there and shoot everything to shit until we can definitively tie FosCo to Unified Humanity," Birch reminded them.

Unified Humanity was the oldest, largest anti-shifter organization in existence, bent on seeing shifters destroyed, even though the general population didn't know of their kind. Declan couldn't remember the whole story of its formation. It had something to do with a shifter wanting to mate a human woman back in the 1700s. Her transition had gone sideways, and when the dust had settled, she was dead and her family was out for blood. That one event was the catalyst for Unified Humanity's existence and the destruction they constantly wrought on his people.

"We could sneak in there and pop off a few rounds..." Declan's wolf yipped at the possibility. It'd been a while since they'd gotten to enjoy some large-scale destruction.

"No." Birch's voice was hard and deep, the bear's presence pushing forward to make its wishes known. "Quit whining like a bunch of teenagers and—"

"Looks like our kitty is about to get up and shake her tail." Grant sounded way too excited about Abby's nightly office-dancing habits.

Declan pushed to his feet, giving his left ear a double tap to shut off the com and silence the chatter of his team. He didn't want their voices filling his head. He was off duty.

"I'll see you later," he murmured to Cole, and ignored the tiger's cackling laughter.

Declan strode from the room, steps silent on the worn hallway carpet. They'd set up in an empty building across from FosCo. It'd been repossessed by the bank and sat empty for months. He and Cole watched from the top floor while Grant and Ethan had settled in on the seventh. Ethan had a thing about the number seven. Declan had a thing about being on top.

This time of night he liked the roof—cool air, soft breeze, and a better view of Abby.

He pushed open the exit door at the end of the hall, tromped into the stairwell, and took the concrete steps two at a time until he reached the door to the roof. He nudged the security door, broken panel swinging out, and trod onto the graveled surface. His boots crunched over the small rocks and debris, leaves and sticks dropped by birds snapping beneath his feet.

The night air rushed forward, the chilled breeze bathing him in the briny scent of the nearby ocean. He'd been locked up in that room for more than fourteen hours and it felt good to be outside.

And a little closer to Abby.

Declan followed the same path as he had the four nights prior, moving carefully over the flat roof to the brick railing. He threw one leg over the side, straddling the twelve-inch-wide concrete, and settled in to watch the one bit of brightness in his life.

Abby.

She kicked off her shoes, black pumps tumbling across the worn carpet and into the darkness beneath the desk. Then she pushed to her feet and nudged the office chair away. Her hair was next—she tugged on whatever held that uptight knot in place. Golden strands tumbled down her back, a little bounce now that they were freed. She shrugged, and her midnight jacket slipped down her arms to reveal the pale, snug blouse underneath.

All those curves…

Curves he dreamed about when he managed to convince himself he wasn't a violent piece of shit who didn't deserve to even think about her.

CHAPTER TWO

*A*bby's cougar tolerated being stationary during working hours—cats were nocturnal creatures, after all. At night her cat was ready to play, hunt, chase... basically, anything *but* sit on her ass and stare at numbers.

Which was why she had her evening playlist that included "O.P.P." by Naughty by Nature as well as "Stayin' Alive" by the Bee Gees. She popped in her Bluetooth earbuds and snatched her smartphone. A few button presses and the opening beats of one of her favorite songs filled her ears.

Then came a shake of her hips, a little *jiggle, jiggle, jiggle* of her ass, and she belted out the opening lines of "Wannabe" by the Spice Girls. She sang about friends, a lover, and *zigazig ah*... There were also a couple lines about lovers and *giving*, and she decided she'd like to have someone giving her something...

Something naughty and dirty and—and Abby's cat swatted at her, the inner animal hissing long and loud. Her cat didn't want Abby's mind to stray to sex if she refused to do anything about their dry spell. The feline knew her human half wouldn't leave work for at least another hour.

The cougar didn't project any other thoughts or emotions. She merely rose to her feet, presented her back to Abby, and then plopped back down on her ass. Natural house cats knew how to ignore their owners, but those kitties had *nothing* on a shifter's inner animal.

Nothing.

Abby ignored the animal and shook her ass a little more. *Shake, shake, wiggle, wiggle, jiggle, jiggle*... She even did a little "raising the roof," followed by a spin just before she stumbled and finally collapsed in the nearby office chair.

"Whew." She panted out a quick breath and then another before drawing air deep into her lungs and releasing it slowly. She slumped in her seat and nudged the ground, pushing and jerking until she was back in place in front of her laptop.

"It's Friday. You just have to make it through tonight," she murmured to her cougar, and it replied with a low grumble. "I'll let you play a little on Palm Island this weekend and then Monday it's back to regular hours at O.P.P."

Not to be confused with one of her favorite songs. This O.P.P. referred to the accounting firm—and her employer—Ogilve, Piers, and Patterson.

The cougar huffed, still a hint annoyed, but Abby also sensed the little flick of the cat's tail and the tremor of excitement that flowed through her furred body. The small island just off the coast of Port St. James, South Carolina, was a nature preserve—no humans allowed and nothing but natural animals running wild. Abby's cougar could safely stretch her legs, take a swim, and chase the island residents.

She leaned forward in the chair and grasped the edge of the desk, pulling herself back into place in front of her laptop. She popped out her earbuds, tossed them into the bottomless pit of her purse, and turned off her music, ready to focus on her job once more.

A job she loved...most of the time. While her cat reveled in the hunt for live prey, Abby's human half enjoyed the puzzles that came with accounting. She checked and cross-checked transactions, hunted for unbalanced entries, and scoured records for improperly supported payments.

Accounting was Abby's kung fu, and it was strong.

The cougar snorted at her butchered movie quote.

Brushing off the cougar's flare of anger, she snatched her pencil and the stacks of printouts she'd gathered, diving back into her audit. Her—not *their*—audit. A company the size of FosCo needed a double-digit team, not one woman, but apparently a surface audit was enough to appease the private shareholders. It wasn't her place to ask. It was her place to work and get paid. Abby ran her finger down the nearest page, comparing it to the spreadsheet displayed on her monitor.

That's there. And that's there. And that's...

She stopped and stared at the printout—a copy of a recent bank statement—and swallowed hard while she replayed conversations she'd had with the FosCo president recently.

"It's nothing but a small account we haven't taken the time to close," Eric Foster had said. "Don't even bother with it. It's nothing."

Abby gulped and kept her eyes on the account's activity.

In Abby's world, two plus two equaled four. Adding, subtracting, multiplying, and dividing...there were *rules* in numbers. As an accountant, she lived and died by them. Mainly because if she didn't do her job right, she didn't get paid, which meant she couldn't eat. It was amazing how things strung together like that.

Two plus two did not equal five hundred million dollars.

Five. Hundred. Million. Dollars.

Poof. Gone.

She stared at the screen, the digits swimming before her eyes.

It would have been fine if she'd found any type of notation in the client's files, but there was nothing. When money shuffled through accounts with nary a mention *anywhere*...

This was bad. So very, very bad. So many bads in so many languages, and it made her wish she'd taken a few foreign language classes in high school just so she could use them now.

Abby's fingers flew over the laptop's keyboard, entering the password that granted her access to her accounting firm's server. She navigated the file structure with ease, digging deeper into the electronic system. After each audit, every piece of paper the staff scribbled on was scanned and uploaded. Ten years from now the partners at Ogilve, Piers, and Patterson did *not* want to have to question an employee and hear the words "I wrote it on this yellow sticky..."

Apparently, yes, that'd happened. Coincidentally, it'd been Abby's predecessor, who was now retired and sunning herself in lovely South Florida. *But* the moral of the story was...

"Martha, where the hell did you save your notes?" Abby murmured, hunting through folder after folder until, "*Bingo.*" She'd found Martha's chicken-scratch scrawl—on a scanned yellow sticky, of course—listing every password the president of FosCo used, both personal and professional. The money had to be sitting somewhere, right? "You are a goddess among women, lady."

It didn't take long to bring up Gold Key Bank's website and even less time to log in and find...

Her missing five hundred million dollars. And then some.

She also saw where other large amounts came in and went out to...She clicked on the details for one of the most recent wire transfers—the name of the destination account holder was required when performing wires—and discovered...

She read the words. Then read them again. She skimmed them a third time and still couldn't wrap her mind around what she saw.

The cougar did, though. At least enough to push its way forward and fight for control.

Goose bumps rose along Abby's arms, and her cheeks stung while her fingertips throbbed with pain. To a casual observer she was immobile, but her inner cougar was going batshit. It paced in her mind and snarled, urging her to get the hell out of the high-rise office building.

The beast recognized something was *wrong* and they needed to *go*. Now. They needed to flee before *they* became prey.

Which was a possibility considering the information displayed on the screen.

The shifter world had their suspicions about FosCo. When conversations surrounding *that organization* came up, there were also murmurings about where *that organization* got their funding.

FosCo was one of the names bandied about—a supporter of *that organization*.

She shook her head and scrambled to find some sense of calm. This wasn't a kid's book about wizards, and *that organization* wouldn't suddenly appear if she thought of its name.

Eric Foster, holder of the controlling interest in FosCo, was funding Unified Humanity, the organization that had a hate-boner for all shifters. Abby was the first to admit that everyone could rock on with their own inner ball of loathing—Abby wasn't a huge fan of the president of her homeowners' association, after all—but Unified Humanity was bad.

No, *bad* didn't quite cover UH's actions. They killed pups and cubs without hesitation, entire families gone with a single bomb. Death and destruction to shifters were their modus operandi. And when the smoke cleared, shifters couldn't exactly call on human authorities, or the rest of the world would know about their existence. Their secret would be out.

Abby's breath rushed in and out of her lungs, her heart racing and threatening to burst from her chest. The cougar yowled and scratched, demanding she run.

But...

The cat didn't want to hear anything about "but" or "first they should" or "it would be a good idea to..."

It. Wanted. To. Run.

Abby assured the cat they would absolutely race from the building, *but* first... She shoved at the cougar, pushed it to the back of her mind and built a mental wall between her and the beast. The feline would break through at some point and overpower her human half, but the barrier would delay the animal's possession.

Delay it enough to give her time to dig deeper, find more, and make copies of everything she unearthed.

Unified Humanity had destroyed her life twenty years ago. Now she'd take every snippet of data she could so the shifter council could destroy them.

CHAPTER THREE

Something was wrong with Abby. Declan felt that certainty down to the center of his black heart. Still sitting on the brick railing, he kept his gaze focused on her. He skimmed her body with his eyes, noting the tension she now carried and her rapid-fire typing. She'd been a diligent worker from the moment she entered FosCo, but this was...different.

Methodical yet hurried.

Her pencil skated over pages, fingers dancing over the keyboard faster than Grant when he'd decided to try to hack the FBI. Her stare intent on the computer screen, she continued typing with her left hand, reached for her laptop bag with her right, and withdrew a cord. Abby diverted her attention just long enough to plug the computer into her nearby tablet.

Declan narrowed his eyes and let his wolf pull forward to assist his vision. The details of Abby's features—body—came into focus with the animal's help. The sharper vision allowed him to see the determined expression on her face and the panic lurking in her eyes.

Further proof something had gone sideways in her world. Whether it was personal or professional, he wasn't sure. He simply knew that his wolf demanded he go to her. The beast didn't know how to calm a woman or soothe her, but the asshole wanted to do *something* for her. Yes, the wolf reveled in the fear of others, enjoyed the scent of panic from their prey, but it hated *this*. Whatever had caused Abby's terror needed to die. Now.

A soft tone filled Declan's ear, his com reactivating—probably at Birch's order. The rest of the men had to see the change in Abby, too. That was the only reason the assholes would turn the device on after he'd gone off duty.

"Guys," he murmured to the team before anyone else could speak. His wolf's howl consumed his mind. "There's—"

Grant didn't let him finish. He released a harsh cough and cleared his throat. "Uh, remember how I didn't have approval to bug any FosCo offices and/or vehicles because we didn't want to risk the devices being found?" Grant chuckled. "And then remember how I did it anyway?"

"Grant..." Birch's growl rolled through the com, the rumble accompanied by the bear's heavy stomps and a hollow echo.

The team alpha was in the stairwell. Coming up to Declan or down to kick Grant's ass?

"Yo, Birch, it'd save you a lot of frustration if you didn't issue orders you know he's gonna break. You stopped telling me I couldn't bring experimental, untested explosives on ops. You're a lot happier now, am I right?" Declan could imagine the feral smile Cole wore.

"The point is..." Grant added his own snarl to the mix. "There's movement. Eric Foster leaves the office every day at five—"

"In his slow-ass SUV," Ethan muttered. "More money

than God and he drives a vehicle fresh off the assembly line with no modifications."

"—goes home and stays there." Grant continued talking as if Ethan hadn't interrupted. "Except right now he's in his SUV with four other men and they're headed back to the office."

Declan didn't like the sound of that. "Can you hear what they're—"

"Hold." The other wolf's voice snapped through the com, and they all fell silent. Tension vibrated in the air, the change in pattern putting them all on edge.

Declan's wolf leaped forward. His skin stretched and stung, the beast aching to push through.

Abby's tension...Eric's return...

The wolf wanted her out of there. Now. He tried to remind the bastard about their mission, but it just told him to fuck off. Something was *wrong*, and they needed to kill whoever needed killing to set things *right*.

And for the first time Declan realized he'd come to the roof without a weapon.

His wolf told him he was an idiot.

Declan couldn't really deny the accusation.

Grant spoke again. "They're coming for Abby."

Declan's gut clenched, and his wolf howled its objection. Adrenaline flooded his body, pumping through his veins and suffusing his muscles. The animal slipped its chain and shoved forward, wrenching enough control to change his body. Not fully, but enough to appease the anxious beast. His hands became claws, blunt human fingertips darkening and sharpening to deadly points. His gums burned, fangs straining against the flesh in his mouth until the razor-sharp points broke free.

As for the rest of his body, his muscles swelled, strength

from the wolf encompassing him from head to toe. He was power and strength personified.

Grant's words replayed in his mind, his thoughts alternating between his logical human half and the crazed wolf that fought for dominance. *They're coming for Abby.*

"No," Declan snarled, the word more growl than human speech.

"She stumbled onto something, and Foster must have gotten an alert." Grant ignored Declan.

"Hold your positions." Three words from Birch. Three words that had Declan's beast frothing at the mouth.

The wolf growled and barked at Declan, shoving at his mind while it issued its feral demands. *Go to her. Save her. Kill them all.* Declan probably should have let the animal hunt before this op. It was more bloodthirsty than usual.

"Birch..." He swung his other leg over the edge of the railing, both feet dangling above the sidewalk.

"I said hold."

Grant kept reporting on what he heard from the SUV. The joking wolf was gone, replaced by the no-nonsense SHOC agent. "Two blocks out. Weapons confirmed. Intent to use unknown."

The mere presence of the weapons was enough for Declan and his wolf. Five humans were returning to the FosCo building, armed and prepared to confront Abby. Unacceptable.

Declan planted his palms on the wide rail and pushed off, letting gravity yank him toward the ground. He twisted in midair, moving like a cat rather than a wolf.

Now he could dig into the small cracks of the building's facade and grasp window frames while he climbed down the side.

"Declan, what are you doing?" The team alpha's words

were followed by a harsh snarl over the com, and Declan couldn't help but grin.

"Out for a climb." He grunted and pushed off from the wall, allowing himself to drop a few feet before grabbing hold once again. He jumped and swung from handhold to handhold, his grip sure and firm with every flex of muscle.

"You're killing this op."

"But she'll still be breathing." Declan leaped, but his nails didn't get deep enough into the crack he'd aimed for, and he slid two feet before finding another hold. Man, he loved the rush—the danger—of free climbing.

"Declan," Birch growled again. The other guys might be afraid of a grizzly bear shifter, but Declan wasn't. He'd experienced a lot worse than a beatdown from an overgrown teddy bear. "Are you kidding me with this shit?"

"Nope." Declan didn't joke. Didn't Birch know that by now? Fight. Kill. Never joke. Hell, most times he didn't smile...unless he was about to go into a fight or kill someone.

Psychopath thy name is Declan.

Nah, one of those SHOC psychs said he was as normal as a twisted ass like him could be.

Declan made it down another ten feet, not bothering to look beneath him. He'd scouted the building before the op began. He was an experienced climber and knew what his body could take before it collapsed. Even then the wolf would help him, get him on the move within minutes. Minutes that had saved his life more than once.

He'd been grateful for the wolf *that* day. Five body shots had sent him down, but not dead thanks to his shifter nature. When he'd regained his feet, he'd hunted and taken out his own client. The bastard had sent two guys after the same target, and the other assassin had decided getting rid of the competition—Declan—was a good idea.

Declan had decided taking out the client and other assassin was a *better* idea.

He released the wall and fell the last ten feet, thumping to the ground in a crouch. He stayed in the building's shadow and scanned his surroundings. A pair of headlights came from his right, high off the ground. The wolf's hearing picked up the rumble of the approaching engine—Eric's SUV.

They were closer than he liked and that fact spurred him into action. He bolted across Broad Street and slipped into the alley between two buildings, the blackness swallowing him whole. His inner beast lent its assistance, allowing him to see in the dark.

"Grant, disarm the alarm." Declan ran down that narrow corridor and didn't stop until he reached the building's emergency exit.

"Done." Grant's confirmation came a split second before Declan punched through the solid metal barrier between him and Abby.

"Stand down, Agent." The team alpha tried, he really did, but Declan's wolf was too far gone. He took the stairs two at a time, racing past floor after floor in his bid to get to Abby before Eric and his men reached her.

"They left the SUV running at the curb. They're in the elevator." Cole joined the conversation.

"They know she's a shifter. They've got a hard-on for the kitten, Declan. Get moving." Grant's voice buzzed with agitation.

"Fuck," Declan spat, and pushed his body harder. His human mind cursed him for not having a weapon, but the wolf assured him a gun wasn't needed. They had claws. It would be enough.

"Did you bug the damned building?" Birch roared, but

Declan wasn't sure why the bear sounded so surprised. "God dammit. Declan, if you get your ass captured—"

"You'll let them turn me into a stuffed toy." He grunted and snared the door to the tenth floor. He yanked it open.

A long, dark hallway stretched before him, the soft glow of safety lights barely illuminating his path. A bright light fifty feet away beckoned him—Abby's office.

Unfortunately, a group of five human men—guns out and the thirst for violence on their faces—were bathed in that glow.

CHAPTER FOUR

A rap of knuckles on wood—two quick knocks that shattered the silence—announced Abby's visitor. Adrenaline surged and yanked the cat even further forward. It wasn't a single visitor, but *visitors*.

With Eric Foster front and center. Four others filed into the space behind him, forming a half circle of overgrown thugs at his back. Each man wore a tailored, midnight suit, but something told her the men were anything *but* mere business associates of Eric's.

Abby licked her lips and left her mouth slightly open, just enough to draw in air and sample the flavors now consuming the room. Human. Anticipation. Unease. A fury that had to come from the man in the middle, and the heavy scent of metal, an aroma her mind connected to guns. Normally that meant police officers were near, but these guys didn't look like humans intent on protecting and serving.

They seemed like the "killing and burying" type, with torture tossed in for good measure.

"Ms. Carter." A sharp voice wrenched her attention to Eric.

"Mr. Foster." She drew her lips into a gently curved smile, one that didn't expose her rapidly growing fangs. The cat was prepared to act, ready to do whatever had to be done to protect them. "How are you?"

Abby was thankful her voice didn't waver. Much.

He smiled at her, and yet it wasn't a smile. It was a violent promise. He knew something. Knew that *she* knew something. Or he'd discovered the truth about her cougar and no longer wanted a furry in his building.

That was what Unified Humanity called shifters— *furries*.

When they weren't being called dead.

"Better now that I'm here," he purred. Or rather, he tried to. She'd had a lion purr to her before, all sensual and sweet. That was not what filled her ears, but there were bigger problems than whether the human man could purr like a cat shifter.

The scent of his anger and the sticky sweetness of suppressed violence surrounded him in a whirling cloud. She knew those aromas, the hint of impending pain. Abby swallowed hard and pushed those distant memories aside. Now wasn't the time to let the past intrude on the present.

"Is there something I can do for you, Mr. Foster?"

Eric clicked his tongue. "Such formality. Call me Eric."

Abby forced her fangs to retract. No sense in revealing her inner cat and poking the crazy person.

"Is there something I can do for you, Eric?"

Other than die, of course. She smiled wide and tried to portray the innocence and sweetness everyone told her she possessed.

Her cougar snorted.

I am sweetness and light. Sugar wouldn't melt in my mouth, and you don't need to throw me out the window.

"Actually...you can." Eric moved around the desk, his

footfalls slow and easy as he neared. When he drew to a stop, he was in the perfect position to see her screen.

Her fingers tingled, desperate to hide what she'd discovered.

"You were instructed to ignore a specific account, Ms. Carter." He lifted his hip and sat on the edge of the desk. "And yet I was informed you disobeyed that simple directive."

"Eric, I..." Abby swallowed hard—she was doing that a lot lately—and fought back the rising bile in her throat. She wasn't going to puke all over the desk. For one thing, *ew*. For the other, it'd slow her down when she finally grew a set of brass ovaries and ran.

Because she was *so* running. The second she had the chance. At five eight and more curvy than lean, she had her bulk and her cougar's strength behind her, which meant she'd be a match for him. Maybe.

She licked her lips, mouth dry. "I didn't get a chance to look things over. I just opened the site and logged in. I didn't realize I was in the wrong account." She chuckled and tapped her forehead. She kept her eyes on Eric and reached for her mouse, intent on closing the Internet browser. "Sometimes I should be called a dumb blonde. I haven't really—"

"Do you know what else I learned?" A crazed light filled his eyes, a sharp edge of madness. Another wave of panic and adrenaline entered her blood. "I learned your secret."

"I—I—I don't have a secret." She shook her head and battled to suppress the trembles attempting to shake her from the inside out.

"Liar." He hissed the word. Again with the animal references.

"I just..." *Discovered your company funds an organiza-tion intent on exterminating my kind. That's all.*

"You're a shapeshifter." He spat the word.

Abby kept shaking her head. "I don't know what you're talking about. You mean, like werewolves? Mr. Foster, I'm hu—"

"Human?" He snatched her wrist in a punishing grip, squeezing muscle and bone. "You're still lying, but I know that pain breaks your kind."

Agony could shatter a shifter's control. Hell, it often did snap her kind's restraint and release the animal.

The cat thought freedom was a wonderful idea. She'd bust out with fur and claws, take a few bites out of the men in the office, and then run for safety.

"Eric..." She pushed the two syllables past gritted teeth, hissing as the pain grew. It spread from her wrist, tendrils of pain crawling through her veins and scraping her nerves. "I'm not a—"

"It took one phone call and now I know what you are." He bared blunted human teeth, as if the expression would frighten her.

The guns the others carried? Yes, they were scary. His sneer? Not so much.

He grasped her throat with her other hand, fingers curl-ing around her neck as if they were claws. He'd accused her of being a shifter, but he couldn't be sure, right? She had to cling to her skin. It was illegal to reveal herself to hu-mans. His hold tightened, gradually cutting off her air, and she fought to draw oxygen into her lungs.

"You're a furry who poked her nose where it doesn't belong. Now you're going to pay." Menace filled his ev-ery word, hatred evident in his voice. "But first we'll have some fun."

Abby didn't want to have any kind of fun with Eric Foster *or* his minions. Her cougar yowled, the cry consuming Abby's mind. It surged, giving her strength—enough that she should be able to overpower a single human man. At least enough for her to break free. Except the longer he kept hold of her throat—cutting off her air—the weaker she grew.

The beast's horror joined the terror consuming her human body. It blanketed her in a layer of blind alarm until she was hardly more than an animal driven to live. The cougar's emergence began with her whiskers, the flick of one thick strand after another pushing past the skin on her cheeks. *Pop. Pop. Pop.*

Her inner animal knew it'd fucked up by pushing free, but the deed was done and she hadn't finished. Fur came next, a golden layer of short strands that slid along her forearms. It led to her hands, fingers coated in her cat's coloring. Her fingertips burned, and she knew that her human nails were giving way to off-white claws.

"Boss, she's got claws." A deep murmur from one of the thugs, and Eric's attention flicked to her hands before returning to her face once more.

"You still want to tell me you're not a furry?" More disgust on Eric's features, and the stench of his hatred filled her nose. He shoved her away and rose from the desk. He stepped back, putting space between them before he spoke once more. "Tie her up. We'll transport her to—"

"Unfortunately"—another man rounded the corner, dressed in black from head to toe; he looked just as deadly as the others, pure danger etched into every line of his body, but something told her he wasn't part of this shifter-hating group—"Ms. Carter is otherwise engaged."

Then he became a blur of motion, whipping into action

before the goons could draw a weapon. The newcomer struck first, punching one attacker before kicking another. Each assault was quicker than her eyes could track and all followed by the snap of bone. She'd heard her own bones break each time she shape-shifted. There was no mistaking that sound for any other.

Grunts and groans filled the air, warring with the *thud*s of flesh striking flesh.

The newcomer caught someone's fist mid-punch and twisted his grip, turning until the human's forearm hung loosely at his side. He followed the action with an elbow to the face that sent his opponent stumbling back into the wall.

"Who the—shoot him!" Eric's voice joined the sickening echoes of the fight.

One of the remaining three reached into his jacket and withdrew a handgun, pointing it at Abby's savior.

Abby swept her gaze over the desk, searching for something to... Her eyes landed on the ancient ten-key calculator to the left of her laptop. Five pounds of plastic and metal that had to be more than ten years old.

She wrapped her hands around the device, yanked it until the cord ripped free of the wall, and launched it at the gun-holding goon. The calculator flew, a trail of calculator paper streaming in its wake, and slammed into the side of the human's head. The adding machine sliced into his flesh and tumbled to the ground, and her target swayed in place. He turned slowly, his dazed eyes locking on to hers for a split second before he collapsed.

Two bad guys down; three to go.

Assuming her savior didn't want to hurt her after he defeated the others.

"You bitch!" A fist collided with her cheek, knuckles

striking flesh with a solid punch that had her head whipping around.

She fell forward and caught her weight on the desk, slumping over the furniture. Pain blossomed in her face and quickly spread, expanding until the ache throbbed through her head. The room spun, reality swaying with a wave of dizziness that had her stomach lurching.

The punch was followed by a kick, Eric's designer shoe slamming into her leg, and another splash of agony filled her. "You *fucking*—"

"I'm not a fan of men who hit women." That dark voice slithered over her, almost emotionless except she thought she heard a soft thread of rage in the syllables.

Abby shoved the pain away and regained control of herself. Yes, she was grateful for this stranger's interference, but did she want to be around when he had no men left to fight?

She drew air into her lungs, moving beyond the dizziness and pulsating aches, so she could focus on escaping. Her plan hadn't changed—it had merely been delayed.

She pushed herself upright and swung her gaze to her computer and the tablet still connected to the device. The fight continued behind her, and she spared a quick glance for the battling men. The stranger split his attention between the three remaining humans, aiming more painful blows at Eric than the other two.

The stranger *really* wasn't a fan of men who hit women.

That didn't mean he wouldn't pick up with Abby where Eric had left off.

Abby snatched the tablet and yanked it free. She crawled over the desk and slipped off the other side, stumbling over the human she'd knocked out. She snapped her gaze to him and met his glassy stare, pupils wide and gaze unfocused.

Mostly.

He recognized her. He narrowed his eyes, hatred surging in his stare, and went into motion. He extended his arm, hand seeking his weapon, and she decided waiting around for him to find it wasn't the best idea.

She scrambled to her feet, tablet still clutched in one hand, and ran for the door. She gripped the doorjamb and used the hold to swing into the hallway.

But not before the loud *pop* of a gunshot reached her ears.

CHAPTER FIVE

*T*he shot didn't stop Declan's attack. Nah, it was the scent of Abby's blood followed by a sharp cry that was a mixture between cat and woman.

Abby had been shot.

"You about done playing with the humans?" Birch's drawl reached him through the com in his ear. "Because the cat is escaping."

Escaping and hurt.

Which meant Declan didn't have time to play with his opponents any longer. He didn't have time to kill them either. When these five died, it would be slowly, painfully. He'd settle for broken bones and blood for now. The wolf wanted Declan's promise that they could hunt them later. They'd scared Abby—*hurt* her. The beast decided they deserved to die.

Declan allowed the wolf to strengthen him, giving him the power to end the battle with a few more punches. Though he did make sure he broke noses while he was at it.

He finally turned to the office door and laid eyes on the shooter, the human slumped in the doorway, gun still in hand. This was the one who'd attempted to shoot Declan—stopped by Abby's insane intervention.

He leaped over the prone body at his feet, eyes not straying from his target. He couldn't eliminate them all, but he figured this enemy was on his way out the door anyway.

The human turned his gun on Declan, but a quick grab and twist ended with the weapon in Declan's palm. He quickly tossed it out of reach and continued his forward momentum. His speed didn't falter as he bent and wrapped his hands around the human's head. A harsh yank was followed by a ripple of bones snapping in rapid succession, and then he was in the hallway, racing down the long stretch of darkness and back toward the stairwell.

Drops of blood—Abby's blood—stained the ground, and his wolf urged him to go faster, push harder. She was bleeding and they weren't with her. The scent of her pain filled the air, and it pushed his wolf to the edge of savagery.

He burst into the stairwell, and the beast lent its assistance once again. He leaped down the steps, following the trail of Abby's blood. With each new drop, the beast became even more enraged, and it was torn between the chase and returning to finish the human males.

"She's on the ground. Heading east," Cole murmured.

"Declan, stand down. We'll—"

"Mine."

"*Declan.*" Birch's growl was filled with every ounce of dominance the man could exert, and Declan's wolf...

Didn't give a fuck. It didn't encourage him to at least stop and listen to the bear. No, it pushed him onward. He hit the bottom stair and emerged into the cool night. Abby's scent still filled his nose, and he let his inner animal direct him. Cole said go east, but she wouldn't remain visible to his team for long.

Declan rounded the corner of the building and took off

after Abby, his fury growing with every droplet of blood on the ground. His feet pounded on the concrete, boots thumping in time with his heartbeat. "Cole. Her status."

"Gunshot wound to the side. Slight limp. Not wearing shoes, so her feet will be torn to hell if her cat doesn't help."

"Her cat will help." Declan didn't doubt the she-cat's desire to survive.

"Break it off, Agent." Birch tried again.

"*Fuck off*, Agent." He wasn't stopping.

"North on Bay Street." Cole again.

"I've got eyes on her—tracking her with street cameras." Grant annoyed the hell out of him, but it was good to have the rule-breaking asshole on his side.

"Got the van purring and ready to go," Ethan drawled, the lion looking for any excuse to get behind the wheel.

"I didn't authorize—"

"Birch, give up. I'm taking her." Declan couldn't stop the wolf now. Not after it'd been teased with her scent, the flavors of her fear and blood.

The team alpha just sighed, and Declan could imagine the big bear dropping his head forward with resignation. "Grant, keep eyes on her. Cole, monitor the shit-storm across the street. When the live ones are out of that office, take care of cleanup."

"I've got these new guns I designed that alternate C-4 pellets and detonators that have a timing trigger, so—"

"Cole," Birch growled, and they all knew what that particular grumble meant. *I don't care. Just get shit done already.*

"Yes!" Cole shouted, and he imagined the tiger punching his fist in the air before he bolted.

Birch just sighed. "Ethan and I will rendezvous for a pickup once Declan has her in hand."

Declan grinned and took a sharp left onto Bay Street, still following the bloody trail. "See how easy that was?"

Birch grunted. "Move out."

The sounds of his team bursting into action filled his ear, but he focused on one single voice—Grant. The other wolf fed him directions, giving him a play-by-play of Abby's movements.

"Heading for the pier, Declan."

The fucking pier. A bullshit tourist attraction and family-friendly hot spot. Crowds filled the area every night, and their stench would overlay Abby's.

"Crowd won't hide her," Declan muttered, and increased his speed. Or rather, the crowd wouldn't hide her *for long*. Short-term, though, it could make tracking difficult.

Then she came into sight, those golden curls streaming out behind her and that ass he liked so much jiggling with every pounding step. It was fucked up that he was turned on by her while she ran for her life, but he couldn't stop himself.

"I have eyes on her," he told Grant. He'd been distracted when she'd bolted—trying to save his own life tended to do that—but now he noticed she clung to a tablet, grip so tight as if it held the secrets of life. What was so damned important that—

She reached the very end of the pier, bypassing the families and teens who lined the railing. She shoved them aside and climbed the safety rail.

That was when it hit him like a baseball bat to the kneecap: she was pulling a jumper.

Nah, no way. She couldn't be *that* dumb. She wasn't going to jump. More than one stupid-ass kid had lost his life against the maze of a pier's support beams. Good place to hide a body or two, perhaps, but that wasn't currently on the agenda.

She balanced atop the eight-inch-wide slab of wood. The one that was supposed to keep people safe, not act as a diving platform. She placed the edge of the tablet in her mouth.

"Abby!" He shouted her name without thought, the word erupting from his lips in a roar. His beast aided him, made his voice boom through the air, and it silenced everyone.

She glanced over her shoulder at him, reflective golden eyes—cougar's eyes—meeting his as they widened in surprise only to be replaced by fear. Why the hell was she afraid of him, dammit? He'd saved her. After beating a few others to shit, sure, but still ...

"Abby." He took another step forward, hand outstretched. "Wait." Then she was gone. She spun in place and leaped over the side. He stood there a moment, immobile, and tried to get a handle on his riotous emotions. "I lost her," he rasped. "She went wet."

"What the—"

"Say again."

"You're joking."

The men on the team mirrored his thoughts, and he didn't reply. Not until he knew more. He raced to the edge and searched the sea for her just like everyone else on the pier. He ignored the humans' cries for help while he plunged through the crowd. It wasn't until he reached the spot where she'd stood only moments ago that he knew she'd be okay.

Abby delved beneath the surface of the black water, the darkness swallowing her whole, but not before he recognized the change that rippled over her. Skin as pale as moonlight shimmered, to be replaced by fur golden like the sun.

Slipping quietly away, far from the shouting tourists, he ducked into the shadows and made his way back to solid land. Chatter from the others filled his ears, invading his mind. He kept his voice low but firm when he cut through them all. "Ethan?"

"One block south of your location."

Declan increased his speed when he hit the sidewalk and turned left. He wove through the crowd and broke into a jog when he spied the van. The side door slid open, Birch holding it wide, and the moment Declan was inside, the vehicle went into motion.

He glanced at the team alpha, noting the man's black eyes and the layer of dark brown fur on his cheeks. Birch's bear was right at the surface, just shy of busting free and tearing them all to pieces.

"Declan?"

"You can kick my ass later." He turned his attention to Ethan. "Get us to her place. Grant, what else do we know about her?" Yeah, she'd escaped, but why would a *cat* take a swim in the sea? He thought maybe desperate times called for desperate measures, but there'd been so many other ways to escape that wouldn't have gone so completely against her natural instincts.

"You read the history. My shit is thorough," Grant snarled at him, and Declan's own beast growled back.

"Hit him for me, will ya, Cole?" Declan's question was followed by a *thump* and a grumbled *ow* from Grant. "We know she's an orphan. Where'd she end up when her parents died?"

A silent pause, and then Grant spoke again. "Seals up in Alaska from eight to eighteen."

"Okay." That gave him the explanation he needed. Sure, Abby was a cougar, but she'd been raised by seal shifters. Her inner animal did okay with water and her foster family taught her familiarity with the ocean. "She'll use the water to travel. Won't come to shore until she's forced to. Grant, keep an eye out for her on the cams. Ethan, get us to her ASAP."

"You think I could lead the fucking team?" Birch's glare slammed onto Declan's shoulders, and he turned his attention to the bear. "What makes you think we're gonna keep chasing her?" Birch raised a single brow, black-eyed stare boring into him.

Because Declan couldn't *not* go after her. He couldn't exactly say that to Birch though.

"When shit went sideways, she stopped long enough to grab that tablet," he pointed out. "It's got something on there worth risking her life over. We want it."

Birch shook his head. "It won't last through the swim. We'll regroup at the office and try to salvage this op. Let's call in a team to tail her. You know the newbies need field time. Let them chase her down."

A flush of rage attacked Declan. The wolf didn't want anyone else near Abby.

Declan grinned. "You think her shit isn't going to be water resistant? It's gotta be instinctual by now." He shook his head. "Ten will get you twenty that our girl makes sure her gadgets will make it through a dip or two. A new toy came on the market not long ago."

"Our girl?" Now Birch raised both eyebrows.

Declan ignored the bear—*and* his knowing smirk. Asshole.

CHAPTER SIX

So. That happened.

Holy fuck a duck with a truck that happened.

Abby's heart pounded so hard it threatened to break through her rib cage, but she didn't have time to die. She was too busy trying to swim to safety. As in, somewhere very, very far from Port St. James.

Abby jerked and twisted, muscles and bone stretching and contracting. Familiar pain assaulted her, an experience she'd endured for years, as parts of the cougar overtook her human body. When she'd first shifted, her screams could be heard throughout the state. Now she reacted with no more than a small shudder. Her new shape ripped her clothes; bits of thread and cloth drifted from her body, portions of her skirt suit lost in the ocean's currents.

She pushed harder, flexed, and spun. Rather than fighting the flow, she moved with it, allowing herself to be dragged down the coast.

The tablet clenched between her teeth wiggled, and she tightened her bite. She couldn't lose it now, not after what she'd gone through to get it out of the building. The shifter council needed to see it, look over the evidence, and then send in their bogeymen to do whatever it was they did. She didn't want to think about how they did their jobs. She just wanted FosCo and Eric Foster to not exist any longer.

Buh-bye.

God, her fear was making her even more sarcastic than usual.

Fear of being caught. Fear of being killed. Fear of the tablet not getting into the right hands.

Fear of that blue-eyed stranger who'd saved her. The one who'd known her name.

And if he knew her name, he had to know where she lived.

She couldn't get caught. Not with the device in her possession. She had to hide it before she ventured onto land.

Abby twisted and bolted away from the beach, racing for Palm Island. No one would think to look there. It would be safe. It *had* to be safe.

Her destination came into sight, and she put on a last burst of speed, racing to the rocky gathering of coral and stone. Less than ten feet from the outcropping, she dove beneath the rolling waves, down and down until she reached the opening she sought.

She ducked into the pure darkness and used her claws to climb the interior walls of the small cave. Cool water enveloped her fully, the black encroaching on her like a monster from her nightmares. Her cougar pushed the panic aside, reminding her this was a safe place, a welcome place. Her cat loved the cave or running on four paws across the island—a place closed to humans.

Abby burst past the surface of the water, sucking in a breath of air. She placed her palms on the stone edge surrounding the cave opening and heaved herself onto a small ledge. She rolled to her back, laid one arm across her eyes, and pulled the tablet from her mouth with her free hand.

She fought to recover from the mile-long swim to the middle of the bay, preparing her body to do it all over again and get her home. Her cougar wanted to wait for a little while. It wasn't ready to venture back into a world of being chased.

They didn't have a choice. The tablet was safe. Now she had to nut up or shut up. It was one of her foster father's favorite sayings and one he'd often repeated when she'd hesitated to dive into the frigid waters off the coast of Alaska. "I don't have a thick layer of fat like the rest of the family" was not a good excuse for avoiding swims with the other seals. Neither were the polar bears that had tried to eat her. Or the killer whales. Or the bull moose. Those suckers didn't play.

Abby squared her shoulders and huffed, taking a deep breath before diving headfirst back into the inky sea.

Now she needed to swim home, get clothes, and disappear. Go somewhere and call someone, and when things weren't so hot, she'd come back and—

Look at her, sounding all gangster and like a criminal. *When things weren't so hot...*

Some of her fear floated away with her swim back to shore, exhaustion replacing the rapid race of panic and terror. The adrenaline that'd powered her every move no longer filled her veins, and her heart gradually slowed to a regular beat. Which, yay for calming down, but she needed the panic to keep her going. Abby dug deep, refusing to let the adrenaline crash sap all her strength. She'd do this. Home. Run. Call.

Abby lifted her head and scanned the beach, searching for landmarks, and sighed in relief. She was home. Or as close as she could get with the hundred yards of sand separating the waves and her building.

The hundred yards she'd have to walk half naked.
Great.

The night was just fan-fucking-tasmagorical.

Abby gulped and breathed deep, preparing herself for her cat's retreat. It was bad enough she'd come limping out of the ocean. She couldn't sport claws, fangs, and fur as she emerged. Then she repeated the slow, deep breathing for good measure, bracing herself as best she could.

Right. No screaming.

Her fur retreated first, her bones snapping and reshaping at the same time. The claws retracted and fangs receded. Her muzzle and whiskers were last, gold and dark brown replaced by her pale skin.

She was back to her human form, and she reached for her side, hand slapped over her wound. It hurt like a killer-whale bite—firsthand experience at sixteen, don't ask—but a quick glance told her it wasn't all that bad.

The cougar disagreed. Between the bullet wound, her black eye, and her limp, it believed it was dying—*dying*.

Chest deep in the water, she eyed the shore once more, searching for any hint of someone watching her. She stared into the shadows, trying to see past the darkness that filled the corners. She didn't see anything, but…

Abby had no time for "but." She had to get her ass moving.

She trudged through the water, feet sucked down by the sand, as if the ocean was trying to keep her. Like it knew what stupidity she was walking into and wanted to save her from herself.

With the water at her knees, she stumbled forward, falling to the sand and catching herself with her free hand. She shoved herself to her feet once again, strength all but gone. When she looked down at her injury, she was kinda thankful for the sea water. The blood didn't stand a chance against the waves, brushed away before she could realize the wound was a little worse than she'd originally decided.

The ocean lapped at her feet, and then she stood on dry land, the sand shifting beneath her soles. She was close now. The glowing lights of her building loomed, and she forced herself forward. Her body tightened and jerked with each step, muscles and skin around her injury pulling with her movements.

Thanks to the awesomeness of spandex, at least her bra and panties had survived the impromptu swim.

It hurt to breathe, to think, to do anything but hopefully trudge in the right direction. She knew her cougar worked to heal the damage, but she'd been logging long hours at the office—leaving early and coming home late—and hadn't been eating properly. Her body was tired before she even got out of bed in the morning, and with the injury ...

The cat was doing the best it could, but it couldn't do much.

The entry to her building came into sight, the glowing door a beacon to her exhausted body. She pushed herself, determined to do this.

She could.

She would.

Suddenly fabric enveloped her head and wrapped around her body, swallowing her in darkness. Strong arms kept her in place, holding her immobile. A large body aligned with hers, her captor's front against her back.

"Got you."

CHAPTER SEVEN

*A*bby was dead. Done. Ex-living, un-living, once upon a living, and now heaven and hell fought over her soaking-wet, shivering, miserable corpse. Apparently, her soul wasn't worth having because she still seemed to have *that* along with parts of her deluded mind.

Wait. It wasn't heaven and hell fighting over her wretched body. It was a couple of men. Maybe three? It could be a hundred for all she knew. The scent of the sea, briny and tinged with a hint of *eau de fish*, filled her nose. It obscured the different flavors in the air, and she couldn't figure out who—what—surrounded her. She could only go by voices and sounds coming from her captors. The baritones, scratchy rasps, and deep breathing echoed around her, bouncing off the metal walls.

She frowned and tilted her head, urging her cougar to come forward and give her a hand, er, paw. The persnickety feline hissed at her, reminding Abby *she* was the reason they were in this mess and *she* could be the one to get them out.

As if they weren't one and the same. She mentally groaned. Stupid, *stupid* cat.

Giving up on her cougar, she focused on the world

around her. Her vision was masked by the thick blanket over her head, but she could tell she was in a vehicle, large and heavy. She sniffled, but only inhaled seawater.

The cat released a wheezing chuckle.

Bitch. Just see if she ever bought catnip at the pet store. *Just see.*

That assumed she made it out of the hot mess alive so she could go to the pet store. If she had a Magic 8-Ball, her fortune would be "outlook not so good."

The voices echoed in the space, muffled by the blanket and too low for her to figure out what they said. So she focused on the tones, the tiny variances in speech patterns and pitch.

And heat. There was one man close to her, utterly silent but warm. A warmth that chased away the cold and made her forget about the bullet hole in her side. The vehicle swayed, tires rumbling over uneven ground, and she used the rocking motion as an excuse to ease closer to him.

The van rocked hard to the left and then right. The sudden movement threw her forward and then back, slamming her head against the unpadded wall of the vehicle. A soft whine escaped her.

A low rumble, no words, just a rolling sound, reached out to her, and a large hand cupped the back of her head. It rubbed her gently, touch easing the throbbing ache, and as quickly as the caress came, it was gone. But it reduced her panic just a little. That meant he cared, right?

Could she develop Stockholm syndrome after just five minutes?

She needed to focus on how the hell she was going to get out of this mess. Three men had kidnapped her. Oh, it'd been only one guy to toss a blanket over her head and shove her into the vehicle, but she heard two others. When she got free, they'd all go down and get carted off to jail.

When. Not if. She had to stay positive. She'd be free and they'd be gone.

More murmurs, one voice snapping, another snarling, and one that was soft and hard at the same time. One the rest listened to without question.

The van swayed, and she rocked forward with the rolling motion, losing her balance. She tensed, waiting for the inevitable pain from slamming into the floorboard. But it didn't come. A thick, strong arm wrapped around her waist, hand settling on her hip as he pulled her closer. His touch slipped from her waist to her shoulder, and a soft tug pulled her against him—Hot Guy.

"Rest." The low murmur reached out for her, and Abby was torn between doing as he said and refusing whatever comfort he provided. This had to be some sort of good cop/bad cop scenario. Except his actions had been a mix of the good cop/bad cop behavior. Maybe he didn't know how to play the game.

Regardless, resting seemed like a great idea. As adrenaline fled her body, the ache in her side grew, agony increasing with each passing second. She lowered her head to his shoulder and slumped against him, giving her captor her weight. There was no harm in relaxing and conserving her strength.

Abby beckoned the cat once more, needing its help to heal her wound. If she saw a chance to escape, she'd take it, but her bid for freedom would be hindered by the injury.

The animal grumbled but pushed forward, the beast's rapid healing swirling and surrounding her wound. It tingled, a warm rush sliding over the area, followed by the burning itch of knitting flesh.

She gritted her teeth and trembled against her captor, the pain snatching her control. He tightened his grip, tugging her even closer until their bodies were aligned. They fit together like two pieces of a puzzle sliding into place. As if they were made to complement each other.

And wasn't that a screwed-up thought? Exhaustion, pain, and fear were making her crazy.

"Six minutes out." A low murmur filled her ear—Hot Guy again. His voice was soothing, and somehow it drove away the sharp edge of pain. Her cat responded to his deep tenor, releasing a low, trilling purr of her own.

So. Fucked. Up.

Instead of replying, Abby swallowed hard and nodded. She needed to focus, dammit. These might be the last six minutes of her life.

The van slowed, rolling to a stop for a moment, and the mechanical hum of a window rolling down filled the space. A few beeps and the sound repeated, window going back up as the vehicle rocked back into motion. Then they were going around and around in what seemed like a never-ending spiral.

The squeak of tires and the roar of the engine echoed around them, and she took a little comfort in that. The space they drove through sounded empty, a large cavern that only held their vehicle. Maybe she'd only have to face the guys that currently held her and not some big team of baddies.

The van took one last sharp turn and rocked to a stop, gears thumping when the driver put the vehicle in park before he turned the key and cut the engine. It dropped them into silence for one beat and then two before her captors burst into action. Metal grinded against metal, someone yanking open the side door. That was followed by the heavy *thud* of boots on a hard surface. Concrete?

Metal clanged, cloth rustling but not cotton—something else. Nylon? The rasp of Velcro and then a heavy weight *thump*ed beside her. She squeaked and jolted with the sudden sound, and followed that up with a moan. Her wound pulled, what little healing she'd managed now undone by her thoughtless movement.

Everyone fell silent with her groan, and the heavy weight of their gazes settled on her shoulders. She didn't know how she knew that they stared; she just *knew*.

And didn't like it one bit.

Abby bit her lower lip and swallowed any other whimpers and moans that threatened to break free. Being the center of her captors' attention could never be a good thing.

Soon their movements picked up again, the jangle of buckles and the metallic rasp of zippers with the occasional grunt and low whispers. They spoke, they moved around, and they left her alone.

Which was great as far as Abby was concerned.

Then a large, strong hand wrapped around her biceps, holding her in a punishing grip, and yanked her to the left. She scrambled to gain her feet, silently cursing when her captor jerked and she scraped her knee on the sand-covered, uneven van floor. Now her knee throbbed in time with the pulsing ache in her side.

Her captor pulled her out of the van, further tearing her wound, and blood flowed free of the cut. What little clothing she wore had dried during the ride and was now soaked in blood.

"Careful, asshole!" The deep, chocolatey baritone boomed through the cavernous space. It was tinged in rough fury that felt more like a caress to her cat. And hell, she wasn't sure how a voice could sound like chocolate, but his *did*.

All chocolate and smooth and sweet with a hint of hot and...*Ahem*.

The tight grip on her arm eased a little. She'd be bruised by the rough handling, but if she had bruises to bitch about, it meant she was alive to do the bitching.

She'd take it.

She listened for everything, counted every step as they led her to what felt like a smaller area. Their footsteps were now muffled—by carpet? The buzz of lights—fluorescent—reached her as well. An office of some sort? With an attached parking garage?

The three men remained silent during their trek down hallway after hallway. They turned left, then right, then left and two rights? Why did she have to be a number person and not some amazing Tracker chick?

Soon their pace slowed before they stopped altogether. At least for a moment. Just long enough for one of her captors to...unlock a door? And if it was *un*locked, it could then be *re*locked.

She might be blind, hurt, and exhausted, but she wasn't stupid. Okay, maybe a little stupid because she'd already let them take her to a secondary location. Statistically, that meant she was *for sure* going to be killed.

Abby was taking a hard pass on going into that room though.

The man holding her tugged and she tugged back, leaning away and digging her bare heels into the carpet. She shook her head, the blanket still blinding her, and it swung with the rapid movement. A whimper escaped her lips, terror stealing her ability to speak.

Had she mentioned hard pass?

The grip on her arm tightened, a growl following the squeeze, but she was already too scared to be even *more* frightened by the man. "Move."

She moaned, fear still forcing her to be silent.

"Let her go." The voice was louder, but familiar—Hot Guy. That order was followed by the disappearance of the other man and a deep grunt. Then she found herself lifted from the ground and cradled high against the stranger's chest. "Got you."

The first time he'd said those words, a wave of panic had overtaken her. This time a blanket of something else drifted over her body—calmness. A calmness she didn't expect to experience again manifested with his touch and murmured words. There was something wrong with her.

The cat snorted and wondered if her human half had always been so slow.

Hot Guy took two steps into the room and paused; then a hard *thud* was followed by the squeak of hinges.

"Dec—" The man's voice was cut off by the slam of the door.

There was the familiar scrape of a lock, and her captor growled low, "Keep out!"

When no one opened the door once more, he seemed to relax, shoulders dropping though he still held her securely. He carried her across the space, five long strides, and then he slowly bent, placing her on a hard surface before withdrawing.

Abby stayed in place, huddled beneath her blanket—cold, bleeding, and in pain—while she waited for whatever happened next. Questioning? Torture? A game of Uno?

The blanket was swept away, exposing her to the room's bright light, and she blinked against the harsh glow. Bright splotches filled her vision, and she squinted while she fought to bring the room into focus.

A man towered over her—dark hair, blue eyes, heavily muscled body, and black clothing.

"You," she whispered. He'd saved her once, but was it only to kill her now?

CHAPTER EIGHT

*M*e," Declan grunted, and stopped himself from saying anything else. She feared him—face pale, eyes wide, and the stench of her fear nearly overwhelming the coppery tang of her blood.

Blood that soaked into her clothing and turned her pale top a deep red. A fact that enraged his wolf. The beast paced in the back of his mind, snarling and growling with every step. For an animal who normally enjoyed the scents of fear and blood, it was pretty pissed about both coming from Abby. And Declan wasn't going to question why. At least, not yet.

He couldn't help her fear of him, but he could handle tending her wound. He'd patched up himself—his team— enough over the years.

Declan dropped to a crouch and slipped his knife from the sheath strapped to his side. He tugged on her shirt with his other hand, lifting the bottom edge to expose her side. "Take this off."

He expected her to listen.

He *didn't* expect her to shove him away with flailing hands.

"No." Abby even went so far as to push the fabric back into place. "I'm fine. Thank you for your concern."

"You're fine?" He moved her shirt out of his way *again*, pointed the tip of his knife at her seeping wound, and then met her stare. "That's a bullet hole in your side."

"I have no idea what you're talking about." More tugging down while he wanted the cloth *up*. "I'm perfectly fine."

More like perfectly delusional. Declan didn't remember chicks being so difficult, but it'd been a while.

He closed his eyes and sighed while he prayed for patience. "Lift your shirt."

"No."

"You know, most people would try to be accommodating after they've been kidnapped," he drawled.

"Why should I make killing me easy on you?" She clenched her jaw and tipped her chin up, a stubborn gleam in her eyes.

Her arguing made his dick hard. Her words made his wolf growl all the louder.

"I didn't save your ass to kill you." He yanked her shirt up and held it in place, ignoring her when she tried to wrench it free again. "I rescued your ass..."

Because the wolf hadn't let him stay on that damned rooftop, and he still wasn't ready to examine why his beast had been so determined. It hadn't cared about orders from the team alpha and his responsibilities to SHOC. It'd needed to keep Abby from harm. Period.

He changed tactics. "You've been working for FosCo all week, but something changed tonight. What was it?"

"Who are you?" she countered.

"A concerned citizen." He rolled his eyes and placed his knife between his teeth. He used his free hand to press on her side. The bullet had entered her back but hadn't popped out the front. Which meant he had to dig it out before her cat got too far in her healing.

Extracting a bullet after the wound closed was a pain in the ass.

He felt along her waist, fingers pressing her soft flesh, and he pretended not to notice the silken feel of her skin beneath his hand. He'd spent days fantasizing about Abby, but none of his imaginings included her bleeding all over him.

Declan ignored her harsh inhale, the way she stiffened, or the fact that she'd stopped breathing altogether. He knew he hurt her—he'd been shot more than a few times, and that shit never got easy—but it couldn't be helped.

He finally worked around to her front, still searching for that bullet, and... He withdrew his touch and pulled his knife from between his teeth. He gestured at the vague shadow beneath her milky skin.

"There it is. Hold your shirt for me and don't move." He released the cloth, and it fell back into place. Declan closed his eyes and begged for patience. Again. "Do you know how to follow directions? Or do you ignore hired killers for shits and giggles when they give you an order?"

Abby's swallow was audible, and a new wave of her fear slipped into the air. He could scent her sweat, the flood of adrenaline that filled her body, and the stark panic that followed in its wake. He hated that he could sense the changes in her—that she even experienced the riot of emotions—but he had to admit it was useful.

She surged, throwing her weight forward while she struggled to gain her feet. Struggled because he easily reached across her, his hand finding the curve of her hip, and pushed her back into the chair. She flopped against the seat, and a long, low groan eased past her lips.

The wolf snapped at him for causing her pain. Apparently, it thought he could have been gentler. Declan was getting real damn tired of the animal. If it wasn't demanding he jolt into action no matter the consequences, it was bitching at him.

"You done?" he drawled, and she glared at him. At least she still clung to her spunk despite the pain. "Because this is happening. You can sit still, let me take care of this, and get your inner cat working on healing you, or you can fight me."

"Inner cat?" She licked her lips, small pink tongue darting out. "I have no idea what you're talking about. Who are you? Are you crazy? They have hospitals for that. And drugs."

He snorted. "Abby, you're a cougar shifter. You know that, I know that, and the guys outside that door know that. I'm gonna tell you again—sit still and let me treat you. Then you're gonna answer some questions."

"Then you'll kill me?"

"For the love of..." He growled, and his vision wavered, the wolf snatching control for a split second before Declan managed to wrestle the beast back.

Abby gasped, eyes widening with her shock. "You're a..."

"Wolf," he snapped. "A very pissed-off, annoyed wolf." He waved his knife, drawing her gaze. "One who's trying real hard to do this the easy way, but I'm losing my patience."

His beast told him he'd cling to his patience and his human half would be happy about it, dammit. For some reason, the animal bounced between the need to take over and dominate the curvy cougar and the desire to give her the time and space she needed.

Contrary wolf.

Voices outside snared his attention, and he split his focus between Abby and the world just outside that door. His team—Birch and the others—were near, but too far away for him to make out their words. His animal told him they weren't important. Nothing was more important than taking care of Abby.

Declan sighed. "What do you need to hear so that I can do this already?"

"Who are you?"

"Declan Reed." He bit off the words and reached for her for what seemed like the thousandth time.

She leaned away. "I wasn't done."

"Of course you're not," he grumbled.

"Why did you help me at FosCo? Why did you chase me? Why did you kidnap me? Who—"

"I should have just gagged you and tied you down. It would have been easier." The wolf told him he would have *tried*, but the beast wouldn't tolerate restraining her...unless she asked nicely. "I'm with Shifter Operations Command and we're on assignment."

"To rescue me from Eric Foster?"

"Sweetheart, while your death would have been a devastating loss to the hot-blooded men of the world, you aren't the reason for this op."

She shook her head. "I don't understand. Then why...?"

Declan didn't understand either. As for the why...he shrugged. "Felt like it."

He also felt like he was done with their back-and-forth. Pain etched Abby's features, and the scent of her blood made his stomach churn.

Deciding to act without her help, he kept her shirt raised with one hand and pricked her stomach with the other, not giving her a chance to object. She screamed. Just a quick shout followed by a deep inhale, which she held in her lungs.

Blood welled at the new wound, and he placed his knife between his teeth once more before pinching the flesh around her cut. He rubbed back and forth, encouraging the ball of metal to rise. It moved up, up, up, and then popped through the slice. He caught it with ease, the silver slug coated in her fresh blood.

The moment he released her she gripped her side, but she didn't make a sound. Not a single breath passed her lips.

But she didn't need to yell or cry out for him to know she was in pain. The woman who'd chattered and questioned him was pale and trembling, giant tears pooling in her eyes—silent tears.

A twinge of regret needled his heart. "Sorry," he mumbled, and focused on the tip of his blade. He wiped the flat of the knife on his pants, cleaning it of her blood, and then slid it back into its sheath. Declan pushed to his feet. "I'll get you some protein so your cougar can heal you, and I'll see what kind of clothing we've got around here."

Clothing? A whole lot of nothing, probably. An abandoned office building wasn't exactly a place that had an overflowing lost and found.

My clothes...

Nah. They'd be too big and might give his team the wrong impression. Like he claimed her or something. Which he wasn't. Even if he'd already disobeyed orders for her. Probably would again before the night was through. Not much to be done about it though.

"You could let me go home." Her voice was tiny, more a rasp than anything.

"Abby," he huffed, ignoring how good it felt to say her name. Damned good. "You think you can just walk away now? After that mess?" He shook his head. "FosCo—their *associates*—aren't going to let that happen."

Golden eyes zeroed in on him, the woman's cougar staring out. "You mean Unified Humanity."

He narrowed his eyes. "What do you know about it? Them?"

"I—"

Two heavy thumps, the door shaking in its frame, cut her off, and Birch's shout came through the thick wood panel. "Declan. Get out here."

The wolf bristled, snarling and growling while it shoved forward. It recognized Birch as its alpha—of a sort—but it didn't like taking orders when they clashed with the animal's desires.

Birch's tone had an edge that usually came when the man was getting ready to tell the team something they wouldn't want to hear. Which was why he didn't want to leave Abby even if she needed food and clothing.

"Declan!"

CHAPTER NINE

*W*hen Declan joined Shifter Operations Command there'd been some give-and-take during negotiations. Declan got a pardon for his past and future "extracurricular activities" if he limited his freelancing to humans. In exchange, he'd agreed to abide by SHOC hierarchy and commands. There'd been a big ceremony and everything.

So when Birch demanded Declan leave Abby, he did. Eventually. He made sure her cougar stopped the bleeding first. His wolf couldn't stand the idea of her waiting for him to return while blood continued to seep from her wounds.

Once the cat did its job, he pushed to his feet with a murmured, "I'll be right back."

And he would be *right back*. He'd made it only two steps toward the door before his wolf whined and pulled against Declan's mind. He wasn't going to give in to the animal's desires. Yet. He'd see what had Birch's dick in a knot first.

He tugged open the door and stepped into the wide hall. Birch stood in the center of the passageway, arms crossed over his chest and fierce glare in place. Ethan leaned against the opposite wall, legs crossed at the ankles and his attention on his cell phone. He wondered what game the lion was obsessed with now.

Declan pulled the door closed once more before he spoke. "Where are the others?"

"Cole's focused on cleanup." Translation: blowing up the offices next door. "Grant's keeping tabs on emergency services. He also said we're having difficulty contacting headquarters."

"Really?" He lifted his eyebrows. "*Grant* is having problems—"

Ethan snickered, and Birch's glare snapped to the distracted lion—waste of a scowl in Declan's opinion—before returning to Declan once more.

"Grant doesn't have tech problems." Ever. The other wolf might appear to be more obsessed with his stomach than his job, but there wasn't anything he couldn't handle.

"Yeah, well..." Birch sighed and glanced at the lion. "Ethan, keep an eye on her. She doesn't leave. Declan, you're with me."

Declan didn't want Ethan to keep an eye—or anything else—on or around Abby. So when Ethan pushed away from the wall and moved toward the door, Declan shoved him right back into place.

"You can watch the door from where you're at."

The lion pulled his lips into a knowing smile. "No need to get your tail in a twist, wolf-boy. Just thought I'd keep the kitty company."

"She doesn't need company." And she sure as hell didn't need some pretty-boy lion near her. "She prefers to be alone."

Ethan snorted in disbelief. "Uh-huh."

Yeah, Declan didn't believe himself either.

Birch spun on his heel and stomped down the hall. "Move it, wolf."

He turned to follow his team alpha, his inner animal howling, urging him to remain and guard his territory. The beast didn't get that people couldn't be territory. His wolf told him he was an ignorant idiot and to just watch how quickly Abby turned into . . .

Declan tugged on the wolf's mental leash. He didn't have time to deal with the whiny bastard. Not when a sense of unease permeated the air.

The set of Birch's shoulders and the tension in the bear's fingertips put Declan on edge. He wasn't gonna like what came out of his team alpha's mouth next.

Birch led him down the hallway and around the corner, not stopping until they reached the inner stairwell. Then the team alpha turned, face an expressionless mask. He tried to hide his thoughts, but Declan wasn't sure why. They'd stared down death together too many times to have many secrets.

Declan mirrored Birch's stance, an appearance of relaxation while ready to burst into action. "Just get it out."

"You blew the op."

"We got most of it done." Declan shrugged. "We confirmed FosCo's part of Unified Humanity."

"No. We verified that Eric Foster is a member of UH based on what Grant picked up on his wiretaps. We have nothing on FosCo or their dealings. Like I said"—Birch pointed at him—"you blew the op."

Declan shook his head. "Can you bitch at me later? I need to get Abby something to eat and new clothes."

The wolf's growls grew louder with each passing second, and he wasn't sure how much longer he could resist the animal's demands. There was just something about the cougar that gave the beast a strength he hadn't experienced in a long time—nearly fifteen years. Back then—on *that* day—he'd lost control and...

Yeah.

Declan huffed. "Fine. We'll get the bitching out of the way, but make it quick. Which lecture do you wanna go with? There's 'Shifter Operations Command put their faith in you and you swore to blah, blah, blah...' or would you prefer 'As your team alpha, I expect my orders to blah, blah, blah...'?"

Birch dropped his chin to his chest. "I could save myself a lot of aggravation if I just killed you now."

"True, but I'm good at what I do, so you won't."

The bear grunted and lifted his attention to Declan once more. "Not today. The director might have different ideas when he knows the details."

"He doesn't need to know everything. Just leave the worst out of the field report." It wasn't like they hadn't done it in the past.

"Not an option."

Declan jolted and furrowed his brow. "Why not? Ethan totaled a million-dollar *Lamborghini* on SHOC's dime and you conveniently 'forgot' to tell headquarters. I only killed a guy. It wasn't like he was an innocent."

It wasn't like it was the first time he'd doled out a little justice while on the job, either.

"No, they weren't, but that's not why this can't get swept away. The director already knows."

"Knows...?" He lifted his eyebrows in question.

"The director knows about the fight *and* Abby."

"How? Did fucking Grant report in while—"

"No, he didn't." Birch sliced his hand through the air,

and Declan snapped his mouth closed. "I'm not sure how they know about Abby and what went down tonight. Headquarters com'ed while we were on our way back with her. Grant got the initial orders, but our systems have been 'down' since."

"Initial orders?"

"The director is en route to the southern field office. A team has been dispatched to take custody of Abby and bring her to him for questioning. As soon as we transfer custody, we're ordered to return to headquarters for debrief."

His wolf growled, and Declan did nothing to suppress the beast. The rumble rolled through the air, his animal making its displeasure known. His fingertips burned, the wolf's claws attempting to push through his human skin. His fangs strained against his gums, the sharp points piercing his flesh and slowly dropping into place.

SHOC was taking Abby from him.

"No." He sounded more wolf than man.

"You don't have a choice." Birch pointed at him. "You created the mess. You brought her to the director's attention. She'll have to deal with the consequences."

Declan shook his head, still unwilling to accept Birch's words. "She's not involved."

Birch dropped his voice, tone grim. "That's not for us to determine." A growl slid into Birch's words. "It's our job to follow orders, Agent."

"He'll..." *Hurt her. Break her.*

Normally Declan didn't care. Whoever ended up in a room with the director deserved the punishment—usually. Not Abby though. Never her.

The SHOC director was cunning, unbending, and often

violent. And everyone was damn loyal to the asshole. Kinda made sense since he was the one who made sure agents didn't end up hunted by council Trackers. Or worse— imprisoned by the council.

Declan's skin stretched, the wolf scraping him from the inside out. It gnawed on him, punishing him for the situation.

"Yeah, he probably will." Birch's look layered a heap of guilt on his shoulders. The man's brown eyes turned black with the presence of his bear. He rolled his shoulders and cracked his neck.

"It's not happening." Declan pushed the words past his wolf's teeth.

Birch snorted. "No choice, remember? Disobeying orders brands you a rogue."

He simply shrugged. Declan had been called worse by better men.

"Bottom line, a team is inbound and you'll hand her over. Now isn't the time to enter a dick-measuring contest with the director. There are whispers coming out of headquarters—shit that doesn't make sense—and it's making me damned twitchy."

No one liked it when a grizzly with a short temper got twitchy.

"We done?" Declan was afraid to say anything else. His animal had him riding the edge of control, and now wasn't the time to shift and destroy everything within reach. They could go feral and vent their anger later.

"We're done."

Declan spun on his heel and strode down the hallway, the need to get to Abby pushing him onward. He split his attention between his path and Birch at his back. He listened to the slow, rhythmic thumps of the bear's boots on the stairs, the team alpha probably returning to Grant.

With each step closer to Abby, a plan began to form. One that'd cause a fuck-ton of trouble, but it sure as hell would be fun.

And it started with Ethan.

CHAPTER TEN

*A*bby concentrated on remaining calm. She breathed deep, meditated—complete with *ohm*—and added a prayer to any available deity for good measure. Anything to keep her body relaxed and loose while her cougar did its thing.

Declan hadn't returned with any protein to help feed her cat, so the animal made do with what little strength remained. Then again, even if he *had* brought her food, should she have eaten it? Her Stockholm syndrome–infected brain said, *"Of course I would because he would never hurt meeee."* It even added a little trill on the end.

She was losing her mind. It was bad enough she had to balance her human mind with her cougar.

She took a deep breath and released it slowly. She emptied her mind of the cat and the part of her that decided her captor's eyes were sexy. She beckoned the animal forward, nudging it to focus on her wound. Well, *wounds*. Declan had given her another one, but at least now she was metal-free. The cougar grumbled, both appreciative and annoyed in equal measure. Now it had *double* the work with *no food*. *None.*

Food was a big thing the cat kept circling back to. It was

hungry, dammit. They'd run and swam and then there'd been a lot of panic and... Was it too much to ask to get a burger or something?

Focus. She spoke to the she-cat, and it hissed at her.

But at least the beast did as she demanded. The wounds on her side burned and itched, skin and flesh drawing closer as the animal encouraged healing. It worked from the inside out, repairing the deepest parts of her side before moving closer to her skin. Nerves and veins pieced back together, muscle merging until it was once more whole.

The cougar whined and huffed, swaying on her paws due to exhaustion. She hung her head low, spine curved and snout nearly brushing the ground. Even the animal's tail drooped, the tip not flicking an inch.

The holes in her side still throbbed, the healing not complete, but it was better than it'd been.

Rest.

The cougar whimpered, soulful golden eyes flashing in the darkness of Abby's mind.

You did good. Rest now. You can try more after we eat.

If they ate. She hung her prayers on Declan—that he told the truth—but he could have simply been telling her what she wanted to hear.

SHOC were the good guys—ish. They were the monsters in the dark who hunted and killed the bogeyman— by any means necessary. Lying, cheating, stealing, killing... They did it all without guilt.

At least, those were the rumors passed around. *"SHOC keeps us safe from humans who want to harm our kind. Just don't make them angry because they know how to hide bodies."*

The shifter council monitored and policed shifters. They got accolades and awards. SHOC got looks of pure fear and a wide berth. But Declan had been nice, right? The niggling doubt nudged her once more.

The sound of someone's approach reached her, muffled by the solid wood door but still audible. She'd call on her cat for assistance, but it'd already done so much for her—them. If the newcomer was entering, she'd find out what he wanted when he appeared.

Low murmurs followed, one voice tinged with an animal's growl while the other remained slow and calm. The growl drew her attention most. She might not understand the words, but she recognized the rise and fall, the pitch and tempo.

Declan had returned. Which thrilled her cat a little too much, a delicate purr sliding through her mind. One that also gathered in her chest and threatened to break free. She wasn't going to purr for her captor—she *wasn't*.

The voices rose, Declan's snarl deepening, and then his rumbles were countered by the other man's. Their volume grew, growled words gradually becoming clearer, and then...

The voices snapped off like a switch followed by a low *thump*, a door-shaking *thud*, and the brush of fabric on wood. One of them hit the other and sent him collapsing against the door.

If one was on the floor, who was left standing?

Please be Declan. Please.

It was better to have the devil she knew-ish, right?

The knob turned, near silent until the latch fully disengaged with a soft *click*. The panel gradually swung inward, revealing the hallway as well as the man collapsed in the doorway—blond with tanned skin and deep brown eyes.

Wait, what?

Declan stepped over the fallen male and strode to her. "Time to go, Abby."

"I think you cracked a tooth when you hit me, asshole," the man on the floor growled.

Declan didn't respond. Hadn't he heard the guy snarling?

"Declan, he's awake." She pointed at the guy, who looked to be getting comfortable. He reached into his pocket and tugged a cell phone free, attention on the device rather than them.

Declan glanced at the other man and then back to her and shrugged. "I only kill other agents on Tuesdays."

Abby wasn't sure if he was joking and was too afraid to ask.

"Declan had to make it look like I tried to stop him." The man tilted his head and met her eyes. He gave her a wink and a smile. "He hits like a declawed house cat—all paws, no claws."

"Ethan, shut the fuck up," Declan snarled, but his touch was gentle as he pulled her from the chair. He wrapped his hand around her wrist and led her to the door, holding her steady while she stepped over the other man.

Ethan snorted. "You're just mad that I'm right."

"Can you run?" Declan stared at her, his gaze heavy and intent.

"I . . ." The way he stared at her, the way his wolf peeked out from behind his blue eyes, told her that her answer was very, very important. "Yes."

She didn't think she had any other choice.

"You realize that the moment you hit the garage, the alarm will sound, right?" Ethan lifted his head and quirked a brow.

"I'm aware." The heat of Declan's glare warmed the area around them.

"And that the van has a global positioning tracker? If you think stealing it will help..."

"Ethan, spit it out already."

Ethan frowned. "Cranky." The man turned his attention to her. "You really want to go with him, kitten?" He waggled his eyebrows. "Once you go lion..."

"Ethan..." Declan's grip tightened, nails digging into her flesh.

"Fine," Ethan grumbled, and dug into his pocket, yanking a set of keys free. "It's on the second level of the garage." He tossed the jangling keys at Declan, and he caught them with ease. "Be nice to her. She's a delicate piece of—"

"Machinery." Declan grunted and tugged on Abby, pulling her to the right and leading her down the hallway.

"I don't get a thank-you?" Ethan called after them, but Declan simply kept walking and Abby had to jog to keep up.

He didn't slow until they reached a solid metal door, and a peek through the small window showed a dimly lit parking garage on the other side.

He paused, his gaze on the garage while he spoke to her. "We're going out this door and down two flights. Birch is above us on seven with Grant. Ethan will take his time joining them, which will give us a few extra seconds."

Declan turned his attention to her, stare intent and unwavering. There was a tension in his jaw and determination in his eyes. As if getting her away from the building was the most important thing in his world at that moment.

"Why are you doing this?"

"I can't let you stay here." A different set of emotions flittered across his face. Something she couldn't read, but she didn't imagine it was anything good.

"I thought SHOC were the good guys. I thought..."

"Sweetheart." The corner of his mouth quirked up in a smirk, his tone condescending. If she wasn't so exhausted, she'd kick him. "You want a good guy who'll always do the right thing? You call a council Tracker. You want a job done no matter the cost? You call SHOC. We're good if the money's right. If not..." He shrugged.

Abby licked her lips, a sliver of fear making her mouth go dry. "I can't pay you to be good."

"Yeah, well, for some reason my wolf is determined to be good for you anyway." He didn't sound happy about the situation, either. "You ready?"

No. But she didn't have a choice. She jerked her head in a brisk nod.

The scrape of metal on metal—the bar handle slamming in its casing—was followed by the clang of the panel striking the exterior wall. Before they'd even cleared the doorjamb, an alarm sounded. The high-pitched whine chased them into the stairwell and down the steps.

It spurred her to push her body harder, run faster, and match Declan's long strides step for step.

Another echoing bang reached them, the sound from above them and distant yet still too close for comfort.

As was the roar that followed. It vibrated the air around them, bouncing off the concrete walls and shaking her from inside out.

"Birch isn't a happy camper." Declan almost sounded pleased by that fact.

They finally stopped descending, and he pulled her across the near-empty garage, toward the single car that occupied the level. A sports car—low-slung and black—gleamed in the dim light.

He released her and rounded the vehicle, and she immediately reached for the door, sliding into the passenger seat and then yanking it closed. Declan slipped behind the wheel, started the engine, and threw the car into gear.

He tossed a glance her way, a smile playing on his lips. "Hold on. This is gonna get rough."

The tires squealed, echoing through the large, empty space. The car lurched forward, engine roaring. Then they were moving again. Not moving, *racing*, across the concrete parking lot. The car hit the winding exit, back bumper scraping on the ramp with a loud screech.

That was followed by a roar. Not from the car or Declan—from behind them. A beast, a shifter, and he was *pissed*.

Abby half turned in her seat and peeked out the back window in time to catch sight of someone bursting from the stairwell.

"Uh, there's a half-shifted..." She swallowed hard. She hated the surge of fear that assaulted her, but she could work past the terror. She flicked a quick glance at Declan. "Something. It's brown."

Declan changed gear. The whine of the engine altered slightly before the mechanical roar picked up again. "That's Birch. He's a grizzly."

Grizzly...Mean. Violent. Determined. Which simply freaked her out even more. "Is he gonna catch us?"

"He'll try." He snorted and then chuckled. "But we're in Ethan's baby, and we have a head start." He shook his head. "Not happening."

"But..."

"Abby." His voice was low compared to the other noises surrounding them, but it still reached out to her. It caressed her in a soft brush of invisible hands on her skin. He spared her a glance, amber eyes flashing in her direction before his gaze went back to the road. "I'm not gonna let anything happen to you."

Her cougar purred, creeping out of hiding in the back of her mind. It padded forward—curious, anxious—to be closer to Declan. And his wolf.

"You can't promise—"

His chuckle was deep and dark—threatening. She'd be afraid if every part of her didn't want to stay at his side, if every part of her didn't somehow trust him already. And wasn't that screwed up?

"No one's gonna put their paws on you." That smooth murmur reached out for her, another caress, another stroke of his voice over her skin.

They made the last turn, night sky in sight, and she could practically taste freedom.

Then she tasted her own blood as she bit her lip.

A gate, thick metal bars that'd mean more captivity if they fell into place, started to lower from the roof of the tunnel.

"Declan?" She hated the way her voice shook, the tremble in her body, and the fear that attacked her, but she couldn't suppress the sensations.

Another gear, the engine so loud she couldn't hear anything but its rumble, and the car shot forward in a last bid to escape. The gate inched closer and closer to the ground, and Abby eyed the distance between the gate and the concrete, attention not wavering for even a moment. And then...

Then they sped through the opening, the gate scraping the back half of the car, but they managed to burst free. The clear night sky embraced them, moon illuminating their path while the stars twinkled in welcome.

Free.

For that moment, anyway.

She peeked out of the back window once more, searching for anyone who still gave chase. She shouldn't have bothered, though. She should have just accepted that SHOC agents weren't ones to give up easily. The gate that'd nearly blocked their exit now retreated, their pursuers simply waiting for it to retract once more.

He'd said the others would never catch them, but...
"Can they track us? With GPS or something?"

"Nope." Declan whipped the car onto a one-way street, tires squealing in protest. The moment he finished the turn, he cut the lights. As in, the actual *headlights*.

"Don't you need those to drive?" Abby hated being scared. Like, a lot.

"Nope." He accelerated through the next turn.

Abby clung to the car's door, bracing herself for the crash to come. Because there would be a crash. Her cougar knew it, too and now, even though it wanted to rub all over Declan like he was catnip, it also wanted to get the hell away from the crazy wolf.

"Hold on." He jerked the wheel to the right, taking a hard turn that had her clinging to the door for dear life while he swung them through the bend.

Abby gripped the door handle with one hand and her seat belt with the other while she prayed. Hard. Not to a specific god—any would do. She merely wanted to get out of the mess alive. She'd take battered, bruised, and a little broken if she was still breathing when the car came to a stop.

Declan's next turn made her wonder if he had a death wish. Tires squealed and moonbeams revealed whirling clouds of smoke from burnt rubber, the acrid scent stinging her nose. The vehicle slid sideways across the asphalt. Declan just laughed, a chuckle full of crazed joy filling the car.

He changed gears again, dropping low as he pulled out

of the skid, and they shot forward, up an on-ramp and right into late-night traffic. The highway wasn't filled by cars and SUVs, but it wasn't empty either. A nice middle ground that allowed Declan to zip through the other travelers.

"You're enjoying this." She shook her head. "Like, *really* enjoying this."

"Hell yeah, baby. It's been a while since I had a good high-speed run." He jerked the wheel to the left and then right, sliding through a space that looked hardly big enough to fit her, never mind a car. But he did it, moved through the traffic like a river of water—slick, raging, unstoppable. And elated. Until he glanced at her and his smile turned into a frown. His nostrils flared, chest expanding for a moment, and then he huffed out a quick exhale. "You're scared."

"Yeah." She nodded to reiterate. "Eric and those men. Then the fight. Then the running." She skipped over the tablet part because...because her cat had lovely thoughts about Declan, but her human mind still wasn't quite sure what to make of him. "Then the kidnapping and then the re-kidnapping and then..."

And she was using "and" and "then" a lot, but damned if she could figure out how to talk like a normal person. Normal people didn't hop in sports cars with potential lunatics.

"Okay." Declan reached between them, grabbed the emergency brake, and gave it a fierce yank. They slid sideways again, the move followed by blaring honks from other drivers while they slammed on their own brakes.

The car drifted down an exit, and a flash of white filled the interior of the car for a split second. "What...?"

"Automated toll booth." They ran a red light, shooting beyond oncoming cars. "Means we'll have to ditch this one."

The smiles were completely gone, replaced with the grim, furious shifter who'd dragged her from the building.

"I'm sorry. I didn't mean to cause all this—"

"Abby." Declan reached for her, and she didn't feel the urge to flinch or cower. Not from him. Even though she'd experienced pain at the hands of SHOC members, and what she'd seen him do to the massive tiger, she didn't fear him. "No reason to apologize. I'm gonna get you safe and keep you safe. Not letting anything happen to you."

CHAPTER ELEVEN

*D*eclan whipped the car down another side street, working to get lost in the network of the small downtown roads. It was a convoluted maze of turns and one-way streets he'd memorized a long time ago.

He knew most of the team hunted them—Birch, Cole, and Ethan racing through the city while directed by Grant. The technological eye in the sky. Declan just had to get them hidden—lost in a part of town that didn't have cameras and streetlights at every corner.

Ethan had helped them escape. Would he drag his feet giving Grant any information he had about the Porsche? Probably. Ethan enjoyed annoying the hell out of the other wolf, and Declan was thankful for once for the lion's dickish behavior.

Another two turns and he followed those with a sharp third. It brought him into a tight alley, space hardly wide enough for Ethan's car. No way the SHOC van would fit down the narrow alleyway even if they caught up. Less than an inch on each side? Nah, they were gone.

Didn't mean Declan would slow down, though.

The front quarter panel scraped the brick wall to his left, and he grimaced. Ethan would be one pissed-off pussy at the damage to his car.

He whipped the wheel around, swinging them onto the next road with a loud squeal of tires. The second he joined the traffic, he brought their speed down to match the surrounding cars. A shot down the interstate for another few miles, then a handful more turns and they'd reach their destination—food, water, and a soft bed. Somewhere he could take care of Abby while he figured out how to fix this mess without them both ending up dead.

"Where...? Where are we going?" The wolf didn't like the way her voice trembled.

"We need to lie low and figure out what to do next. Get you cleaned up." He glanced at her, hating that she still wore rags that stank of the sea and were stained red with blood. "New clothes. Food. Weapons. New car."

"How far—"

"Close. About ten miles outside of Port St. James." He reached into his pocket and tugged out his cell phone. A swipe unlocked the device, and it took him no time to fire off a text.

"Texting? Seriously?" she screeched, and he winced with the high-pitched scream. "I can see my headstone now. 'Here lies Abby. Death by emoji at eighty miles an hour.' There will even be a colon and parenthesis to make a cute smiley."

Declan rolled his eyes. "I'm a master of multitasking and I'm only doing seventy-five, baby." He smirked when her growl filled the interior. "I was just contacting a friend."

Of sorts.

He flicked his attention to the rearview mirror—searching for the rest of his team—and a little of his tension eased when he didn't see them. The traffic had a nice, easy flow. Not too many cars on the highway—just enough to hide them, but still leaving them space to dart past other vehicles if he had to hit the gas. Thankfully, that room wasn't necessary. He glided across the lanes, the Porsche's ride smooth as they took the next exit.

Declan slowly rolled down a long, two-lane road past a handful of houses—his neighbors. They had no idea that the guy down the street was a werewolf who stored enough explosives in his basement to blow up the whole block. He hoped they'd never discover the truth. He liked the house. He *really* didn't want to have to blow it up.

"We're here." He turned down his driveway, manicured bushes and trimmed trees bracketing the long concrete lane. His headlights flashed over the swath of green grass that covered his front yard before settling on the ranch-style home set back from the road. It looked like everyone else's on the street—nothing special as far as the casual observer was concerned.

His neighbors didn't need to know that the walls were lined with steel and his windows were bullet resistant. They didn't need to know about the special surprises he put into place for anyone who thought it'd be a good idea to break into his home, either.

He followed the driveway around to the back of the house and rolled to a stop in front of the garage.

He shifted into park and cut the engine. "C'mon."

He climbed out and headed toward the back door, stopping only when he realized Abby hadn't moved. Trying to tamp down his annoyance, he went to the passenger door and tugged it open, lowering to a squat once he had enough room. His irritation vanished when her fear-filled eyes met his.

Scared. Hurt. Tired. It brought out some hidden caring he didn't know he possessed.

"Hey, let's go inside." He kept his voice low and tried to be as reassuring as he was capable of.

Abby's lower lip trembled, drawing his gaze. Declan wanted to nibble on that plump lip, take her mouth and kiss her so hard and deep she forgot her own name.

Instead, he reached across her to the seat belt buckle. His chest brushed hers, full breasts flush with his body. He was a piece of shit for liking it, but he did.

"We'll get you fed and clean."

Her breath fanned his cheek, and the beast howled with its sweetness. The briny tang of the sea couldn't hide her flavors when they were so close—all sex and honey with a hint of natural musk. It solidified his beast's assurance that they weren't letting anything happen to Abby. The wolf wanted to go on, to explain exactly what it desired from her, but Declan cut the beast off.

The wolf told him he was a delusional idiot if he thought he could just ignore her—and it.

Well, when the wolf was its own separate being and could talk in complete sentences, its ass could take a chance on Abby.

"C'mon." He disengaged the seat belt and retreated, letting the restraint roll back up on its own. "We don't want to be out here any longer than we have to."

"Is...Is SHOC going to find us here?"

Blue eyes met his, fear and something else battling it out across her features. He wasn't sure what was on her mind, but he could figure it out in a little while. Like, when they were in the safety of the house.

"No. This place isn't registered to me. It's hidden behind shell corporations and fake names. No one knows I own it." Or any of his other properties across the world. There was only one other person who knew where he was, and he trusted that person with his life.

Declan pushed to his feet and held out his hand, waiting for her to show a little trust in him—which she did.

Abby nodded and placed her palm on his, their fingers curling together while he helped her from the low-slung car. He wanted to keep holding her hand, but he forced himself to release her and take a step back, put a little space between them.

Otherwise he'd throw her over his shoulder and carry her off. And then she'd really have reason to be afraid.

"This way." Declan strode away. His wolf calmed a little when he heard the soft patter of her bare feet on the concrete.

He paused at the back door, just long enough to rub the thumb pad clean and press his thumb to the smooth surface. A green light flashed and the door's lock disengaged, granting them entrance to the home's mudroom. He pulled the door open and stepped back, waiting for her to enter the house before him.

Except she didn't budge. Her eyes focused on the blackness beyond them before she tipped her head back and met his stare with her cougar's eyes. The color as pale as sandy beaches caught a hint of moonlight. His own wolf inched forward, wanting a better look at the she-cat, and he didn't want to bother pushing it back. Not when fighting the animal meant taking his gaze from Abby.

He was losing his mind, allowing himself to be distracted by a *woman*, when he should focus on getting behind a secure door.

"Go inside. I can't disengage the other locks until this door is closed." Abby jerked with the harshness of his voice, but he'd be damned if he'd apologize. That didn't mean he wouldn't make sure she got the first hot shower.

She shuffled past him, and he stepped into the mud-room, tugging the door shut behind him—shutting out whatever light came from the moon. It snatched his sight, but Declan didn't need his eyes to see. He had a nose, hands, feet, and a damned good memory. He also had a trembling she-cat whose scent clouded the air with her panic.

"Abby," he murmured. "You're fine. I'm right here."

"Dark." She whimpered, and his wolf snarled, furious that she was so scared even when she was in their presence. The wolf didn't like that. At all.

Declan listened to the rasp of her breathing, the thump of her heart, and the shuffle of her feet on the tile. He didn't need to see to find her. Not when his body was drawn to her in a way that scared the shit out of him. He wanted—*needed*—Abby too much.

He reached out, arm circling her waist, and pulled her close while he sought to disengage the other security measures.

A thumbprint got them through the first door, but there was still more. He placed his palm on the plate set into the wall to the left of the door. The wolf focused and moved forward to change the temperature of his human hand until he matched his wolf form. That change was enough to trigger the next security protocol. From there it was another few tests—blood and both retinas.

"So much security."

Declan shrugged. "I don't plan on dying today. This'll keep us safe for tonight."

"Only tonight?"

Declan rubbed his thumb over her cheekbone. "Tomorrow will take care of tomorrow."

Tomorrow Declan would put a bullet in anyone who even looked at Abby, but he didn't think she'd appreciate the sentiment.

CHAPTER TWELVE

Tomorrow will take care of tomorrow. It should have comforted her, Abby supposed, but it didn't. Not when her hands still shook. Not when the pure adrenaline and terror that'd plagued her through their mad dash to safety still flowed heavily in her veins. Her knees threatened to go out from under her at any moment.

More whirring and clicking as the second door's lock disengaged and Declan withdrew. His retreat pulled a whimper from her throat, fear forcing the sound past her lips.

"Hold on to me. I'll lead you to the living room." His fingers wrapped around hers, and she clutched him with both her hands, unwilling to release him anytime soon. He didn't complain about her tight grip and merely gave her a gentle tightening in return. "Ready?"

No.

Instead, Abby whispered, "Yeah. Sure." She couldn't see him, but she could *feel* him. "I'm fine. Let's go."

Declan huffed but didn't argue with her. His boots thumped on the hard ground—tile?—and she kept pace. She shuffled along, farther and farther into the blackness before finally...

Click.

Low lighting flooded the area, bathing the home in a soft white glow and revealing their temporary sanctuary—pale walls, beige carpet, and large, plush furniture.

A tug from Declan reminded her she still clutched his hand, still clung to him for support even though she could see with ease now. She should let him go. She could walk on her own. And yet...she didn't want to release him. They were behind locked doors inside a place Declan considered safe, but she still couldn't shake her unease.

When he pulled again, she forced her fingers to uncurl and release him—let him go when all she wanted to do was pull him closer.

Abby's cougar purred. *Not* that *close.*

She remained in place while Declan flicked on other lights. More and more of the home was revealed to her—the great room, small dining area, large kitchen, and a dim hallway to Abby's left.

So *normal*-looking, but she knew Declan was anything but normal. Guns, pain, and blood were an everyday occurrence in his world. A man like him...

She shook her head and shivered, memories of Eric's attack churning in her mind. A man like Declan had been comfortable punching people out. He didn't look like the kind of guy who found happiness in the rural hills.

She shivered again—this time from cold—and rubbed her arms.

He didn't spare her a glance as he padded back across the room, heading toward an open door, and she spied a large bed. The master bedroom?

He disappeared through the doorway and still Abby remained in place, not sure what—

Declan's head poked out of the doorway. "You coming?"

She jerked and nodded. "Yeah, sorry."

"Don't apologize. Just c'mon." He vanished again.

She shuffled forward on the thick carpet. The deep pile caressed her soles, and the thumping pain in her feet lessened. What she wouldn't give for a bed just as squishy.

"Abby?" His voice was like chocolate, silk and smooth and very, very bad for her.

"Coming," she whispered. She wasn't sure why, but she always whispered in the dark. Even with so many lights on, deep shadows remained inside the house. She always kept her voice low. If she talked too loud, she'd be found, and then her parents' death would have—

She cut off that line of thinking, destroyed the path her mind wanted to travel. It'd only lead to heartache and pain, to memories that'd bury her in agony and tears.

Abby stepped into a large bedroom, with its massive king-sized bed. But then her attention immediately went to the adjoining bathroom, as she heard the shower.

Her cougar surged, anxious to scrub the sea from her skin. She tried to remind the beast that they didn't know Declan. Did the cat really think getting naked around some violent stranger was a good idea? The animal snorted, and Abby wasn't sure why she'd even bothered asking. When it came to a cat and getting clean, her feline would always vote for a shower.

Logic had no place in a battle between scrubbed skin and the stench of the sea. They'd spent too many days—and nights—stinking of the ocean when they were younger. Never again.

She padded across the room, past a large dresser and the expansive bed and further until she stood within the bathroom's doorway.

Her breath caught and eyes widened at what she found.

While the rest of the house had been a study in neutral tones and bland decorations, the bathroom was...glorious. A shower with at least a dozen showerheads, a massive jetted soaking tub, and a double vanity. Shades of silver accented with hints of bronze were threaded throughout the room, the space bright and airy without appearing feminine.

Declan leaned into the shower, his back to her, and the position drew his pants snug against his body. The dark fabric clung to his thick thighs and cupped his ass. As for his shirt...it was gone, tossed aside to leave him bare. The muscles of his back clenched and flexed as he reached into the shower, and her fingers tingled with the itch to trace every rise and fall of his body. Then she'd follow that path with her tongue and...*No*.

She could fantasize about him later. Specifically, when she was safe.

Declan withdrew from the shower and turned to face her and she really wished he had remained in place. Not two seconds ago she'd told herself that licking Declan was a bad idea, and now he'd had to show her the deep carving of his abdomen all the way to the lines at his hips.

"A. Hem." He coughed, and heat surged in her cheeks.

She wrenched her attention from those lovely lines and refocused on his face. She ignored the smile that teased his lips *and* the sensual heat in his eyes.

"You can take the first shower." He moved aside, striding to the counter and taking a seat on the gleaming granite surface.

Abby stared at him and he stared at her and she stared at him staring at her staring at *him* and...

"Privacy?" She lifted her eyebrows in question.

"Shifters aren't modest." He waved at the shower, water still pattering against the tile. "Get going."

She narrowed her eyes, attention pulled from the hot water calling her name to the annoying male who thought privacy didn't exist. "Shifters aren't modest during a run, but I'm not used to wandering around with my ass hanging out around strangers."

His lips no longer twitched, instead pulling back into a wide, sizzling smile. "That's one fine ass."

"I'm not stripping—"

The wolf moved fast. Not just fast, but *fast*. One moment he relaxed on the counter and the next less than an inch separated their bodies. He towered over her, more than six feet of muscular shifter male. His scent filled her nose.

"I worked too hard to get you here. I'm not ready to let you out of my sight yet," he murmured, his voice soft yet still somehow loud enough for her to hear over the running water.

Except when he said "yet," he made her think he meant "ever." Her cat was warming to the idea of "ever."

Abby shivered. From cold? From fear? From . . . desire?

"Declan . . ." she whispered, not sure what else she meant to say. She just . . . she liked the feel of his name on her lips. And how screwed up was that?

Very. The answer was very.

He reached for her. His large, scarred hands brushed her hair aside, tucking a few strands behind her ear before he ran a single finger down her cheek. "You're tired, hurt, and dirty. We'll start with getting you clean and move on from there." His finger traveled along her cheek to her chin, and then he brushed the pad of his finger over her lower lip. "I saved you. I need to take care of you."

"I understand." Abby nodded and forced herself to remember their situation. She wasn't his girlfriend, lover, or mate. She was a woman he'd saved and needed to keep healthy until things were resolved.

"No." He shook his head. "I don't think you do." She opened her mouth to question him, but he quickly withdrew his hand and cupped her shoulder. He nudged her toward the shower. "Get clean. I'll be here."

Those few words soothed her, calmed her in a way she couldn't explain. The night had been hectic—bloody—but she found comfort in a violent stranger. So very, very odd.

Abby stepped into the shower and sighed as the wet heat enveloped her in a welcoming embrace.

She tugged at the tattered remains of her clothes, panties practically disintegrating in her hands. A pull on her top had the fabric falling away with ease, and another yank snapped the elastic of her bra. She closed her eyes with a deep sigh and let the water's heat sink into her bones, drive away the chill that'd consumed her from the moment she'd leaped into the sea.

One more step and she was fully beneath—

A wave of dizziness had her listing to the left, and her arm shot out to catch herself before she tumbled. A combination of exhaustion, blood loss, and the disappearance of adrenaline sapped her strength.

Note to self: closing my eyes is a bad idea.

A cry escaped her lips, the sound followed by Declan's hissed "dammit," and then two large hands gripped her biceps. His hold was firm yet gentle as he supported her until she regained her balance.

"Lean against me. I won't let you fall," he murmured, and she was too tired to argue. She'd take his support for a second while she fought to banish the wooziness. Except when she gave him her weight and experienced the feel of his unwavering strength, she decided she'd take more than a second. Maybe two.

"You're gonna get all wet." Though, in one corner of her

mind, she recognized that she should be more upset with him for invading her shower. She'd get all indignant and scandalized after she had a nap.

"I think I'll survive a little water." He moved, stretching and reaching for items in the shower while remaining a steady presence at her back. "I can't say the same if you fall and hit your head." He nudged her. "Bend forward a little and wet your hair."

Abby stared at the cascade of water. "I don't think I can do that without toppling over."

Did he groan? She was sure he groaned. Maybe. But he didn't say a word, otherwise. He simply slipped one arm around her waist, his bare skin sliding along her slick flesh, and she shuddered with the contact. A tendril of awareness flooded her blood, and her cougar purred, reveling in Declan's closeness. She shoved at the beast, reminding the cat that they'd just met the wolf.

The animal reminded Abby that *she* was the one taking a shower with the near stranger. The wet nakedness was all on Abby's human shoulders. The cat was just along for the enjoyable ride.

She hated when the cat was right. Hated. It.

"I've got you." Yeah, Declan had her in several ways. "Go ahead."

She kept her mouth shut and did as he asked, fighting the vertigo when it threatened to swamp her. She lifted her arms, ruffling her hair and letting the clean water rinse away the worst of the salt water. She nearly lost her footing as she leaned into him once more, but he kept his promise and didn't let her fall.

She rested her head on his chest, sending water down his upper body, but he didn't seem to care. No, he ignored the soaking and reached for something else. The snap of a cap and then the squirt of a bottle was followed by the warm scent of sandalwood.

Declan released her waist, removing his touch for a bare moment, and then his hands were back. They sank into her hair, fingers massaging her scalp, and she moaned deep and long. His hands were gentle yet firm at the same time. When he reached the base of her skull, she dropped her head forward with a groan she felt all the way to her toes.

This time it was his breath that caught. He was the one who froze for a split second—just long enough to snare her attention. She focused on Declan, on the tenseness in his muscles and…

It wasn't just his muscles that'd grown hard. His stiff cock settled between her ass cheeks, nothing but soaked fabric separating their bodies. A jolt of unease snaked down her spine, the comfort she'd taken in his presence gone with the rise of his desire.

Abby stiffened and reached for the wall, intent on putting distance between them.

"Stop." His voice was firm but not harsh. A simple command he expected her to obey without question.

Abby was a questioning sort of girl. An accountant— auditor—had to be a person who always asked "what the hell?" "Declan, I appreciate what you've done." She ignored his snort. "But the dizziness is fading." She ignored the chuckle laced with disbelief. "I'm fine."

"Abby, here are a couple truths." One arm returned to her waist and the other hand nudged her shoulder, pushing her to stick her head back under the water. "Beautiful women make a man's dick hard. Period. Even stinking of fear, blood, and the ocean, you're a beautiful woman. You've got a body that makes men ache, *and* I'm holding you in my arms while you're all wet and naked."

She disagreed with his assessment of her beauty. She would have told him so if it weren't for the fact that the longer he talked, the rougher his voice grew. As if the wolf crept forward to override the man.

"So, yeah, you're gonna make me want, but that doesn't mean I'll take what's not freely given. I'm an asshole and a killer, but I don't hurt women."

She didn't struggle or argue when he helped her upright once more, and she *definitely* didn't whimper in disappointment when he removed his arm from around her waist. She didn't miss the feel of his callused palm on her skin *at all*. Or the heat of his palm, which felt more like a caress than firm support.

He remained a solid presence at her back as he shifted his weight and snatched something else—two somethings. In one hand he held a washcloth, a bar of soap in the other, and she grasped both. Which left him free to rest one hand on her hip while the other brushed her hair aside and bared her neck to him.

He lowered his head, lips grazing the shell of her ear while he whispered, "That doesn't mean I won't if they ask very, *very* nicely."

CHAPTER THIRTEEN

If Abby shivered or moaned *one more time*, he wasn't sure he could control himself. Not that he'd pounce on her—he hadn't been lying when he said he didn't hurt women. He wasn't an adolescent kid who'd just discovered his cock. He was a hardened killer. A mercenary. A heartless bastard.

Not someone who should even think of caressing Abby, touching her until she came and screamed his name before sliding inside her wet heat.

Nope. Not him.

Which was why he steadied her and stepped back, letting her support herself. The moment she stood firm, he put even more distance between them. He left the shower, not trusting himself so close to her any longer, and sought towels in the linen closet. He grabbed a few white fluffy bath towels and snared the robe that hung on a hook just to the closet's left. He'd still need to get clothes for her, but the sooner she covered those curves, the better.

What the fuck was wrong with him? Lusting after some stranger...

But was she really? She knew nothing about him, sure, but he'd been watching her for days. He'd read her file and kept tabs on her even when she wasn't at FosCo.

He'd...creepily stalked her. He admitted the truth. Hell, he embraced it. There was just something about Abby Carter that grabbed his attention and wouldn't let go.

The water shut off, and he imagined beads of liquid clinging to Abby's skin, sliding down her curves. God help him, he was jealous of *water*.

"Declan?" Her soft voice reached out to him and he tensed, fighting the shudder that threatened. "Can I have a towel?"

He swallowed hard and opened his eyes. Abby moved, the subtle change of her position grabbing his attention, and he met her stare in the mirror. The frosted glass shielded most of her body, but he could still see the outline of her breasts, the dip of her waist and the flare of her hips.

He was going to hell, and Abby was sending him there.

"Yeah," he rasped. Or growled. A bit of both. The fucking wolf fought him with every breath, and it was determined to be present while in Abby's company.

He snatched the towel and turned to face her, forcing himself to keep his attention above her neck. If only he didn't think her eyes were gorgeous and her lips sexy as hell.

Declan only allowed himself to get within arm's reach, and he held the towel out to her, releasing it the moment he could. Then, like a coward, he retreated to the counter.

Because he didn't hurt women.

I sure as fuck seduce them though. Can Abby be seduced?

He'd heard her moan, the hitch in her breath when she said his name...Yeah, she could be seduced. That didn't mean he should. Abby wasn't the kind of woman a man like him touched.

"I'm done. Are there any—"

This time he didn't even turn his head in her direction. He grabbed the robe and shoved it at her. "Put this on for now. I'll get you something else after I shower."

And it'd be a *cold* shower. He could let his fantasies run wild after she was safe. Then he'd think of her on her knees, his cock between those pink lips and—

"Thank you."

He rolled his shoulders and cracked his neck, moving uneasily while he tried to banish those thoughts. Now. Wasn't. The. Time.

"No problem," he grunted, and turned to face her, keeping his eyes on the shower as he took her place within the tiled area. "Just sit on the counter while I shower. I won't take long."

"I could go to the kitchen and—"

Declan froze in place. "No. You'll sit on the counter and wait." He tormented himself and glanced over his shoulder, gaze taking in her appearance in a single, sweeping look. She shouldn't look sexy in his oversized robe, but she did. "I can't keep you safe if you're not with me."

He returned his attention to the shower and focused on his next steps. Strip. Get clean. Dress so there was fucking clothing between him and Abby. Feed her. Sleep.

The wolf reminded him that he should sleep *with* her.

He shoved the animal away once more and worked on getting clean. He made sure the water was ice cold. His beast snarled at the frigid temperatures.

Then it suddenly decided frozen was okay because maybe Abby could warm them.

Horny little shit.

Declan took half as much time as Abby, efficiently ridding himself of sweat and grime before joining the little cougar. She handed him a towel, her gaze on his face and cheeks flushed pink. Then the tiniest slip of her feminine musk reached his nose, the scent of her attraction taunting his wolf.

"Like what you see, baby?" He tipped up the right side of his mouth in a smirk. Words and an expression meant to annoy her. If she was pissed, he couldn't seduce her. It was one more wall to put between them.

She pressed her lips together so tightly they formed a white slash beneath her nose and she wrenched her gaze from him to focus on the bedroom—bed—twenty feet away. He'd think she was pissed if he didn't notice the deepening of her blush and the increasing heaviness of her desire.

His cock stirred back to life and he swallowed his groan. Flirting needed to wait. "Let's get some food in you."

Declan strode past her and listened to make sure she followed. The patter of her small feet on the tile transitioned to soft padding when she moved to the carpet.

He paused beside the dresser to the right of the door just long enough to drop his towel and pull on a pair of cotton shorts. He didn't miss the small catch of her breath when the terry cloth thumped to the ground.

Shirtless, he strode through the home's main area and slowed, nudging her toward the couch.

"Go sit and rest. I'll whip up something real quick." He didn't know how to make too many things, but he could feed her.

"I thought we had to stay together." She gave a token protest, but swayed on her feet at the same time.

"I can see you from the kitchen." He nudged again. "Go."

She hesitated only a split second more before finally nodding and shuffling toward the seat. She flopped onto the worn leather and curled up into the bathrobe until all he saw was the top of Abby's head.

And those sand-hued eyes—cougar's eyes.

Declan's wolf pawed him, gently scraping his nerves to remind him that they had to feed the cougar. She'd been hurt and needed protein. Protein that only they could provide, so he needed to get his ass in gear.

He did. He turned away from Abby and strode into the kitchen. He focused on cooking—defrosting a steak in the microwave while he heated a pan so he could give it a nice sear. Shifters didn't like much more than a hint of char before they dug in, and right now he had to appeal to Abby's cougar. She needed the cat to heal her human body.

He split his attention between the stove and her unmoving form. He counted her breaths, watching as her chest rose and fell, and tried to forget what that robe hid from view.

He slipped her steak onto a plate and snared a knife and fork, quickly cutting the meat into bite-sized pieces. He snagged a bottle of water from the fridge—thankful he'd had the place stocked before the team had been dispatched to Port St. James—and went to Abby.

He placed the plate and bottle within reach on the coffee table and then knelt at her side. He took a moment to stare. Her dark lashes rested on her cheeks, the deep brown a stark contrast to her pale skin. Purple smudges marred the area beneath her eyes, proof of her exhaustion, and he hated that he had to wake her.

"Abby." He kept his voice low so he wouldn't startle her. She didn't stir. "Abby." He tried again, slightly louder. She frowned, a small crease forming between her eyebrows. He attempted to convince himself the move wasn't cute. Or sexy. *"Abby."*

Abby drew in a deep breath and released it with a low moan. Her eyelashes fluttered, gradually parting to reveal her cougar's eyes once more. Damn but he wanted her. "Declan?"

"You need to eat," he practically snarled at her, and he ignored her flinch. It wasn't her fault he had a hard time controlling his own body.

She drew in another deep breath, attention snapping from him to the plate on the nearby table. "Steak?"

He couldn't miss the yearning in her voice, and part of him was inordinately pleased that they were giving her something she wanted. Instead of answering her, he snared the plate and speared a hunk of meat. He held it carefully in front of her mouth and waited for her to take the bite.

And waited some more.

Feline eyes flicked from the meat to his face and back again, as if the cougar couldn't decide if she trusted him. *Finally,* the cat seemed to be showing some sense.

"I didn't save you to poison you, Abby." He moved closer and rubbed the steak over her lower lip. He brushed it back and forth, painting the plump bit of flesh with the meat. Her nostrils flared, and she took in a lungful of air. He knew what she scented—pure, unseasoned meat. Shifters didn't need—or want—a whole lot of seasoning. Or any seasoning, really.

Abby's tongue darted out and lapped at the bite, wiping away the pink juices that'd covered her lower lip. His cock surged with her action, hardening as if she'd licked *him* instead of a piece of beef.

When she did it again, her gaze never leaving his, he shuddered and pushed back the moan that threatened to break free. Her pupils dilated until the blackness swallowed nearly all her eye color. The musky scent of her desire tickled his nose, the aroma growing with each passing moment.

"You need to eat so you can heal." He added a growl to his voice, hoping to intimidate her at least a little. Instead, her gaze flared with a new wave of heat.

"I feel good." Dear God that sounded like a purr.

He shook his head and nudged her lips. "Open. I can't risk you not keeping up when it counts."

She didn't say anything else then. Simply parted her lips, and he placed the morsel in her mouth. She wrapped her lips around the fork tongs and slowly withdrew. The sensual slide of her lips over metal made him think of what else he could place in that perfect little mouth.

A shudder attempted to overtake him, but he pushed it back. Once again he reminded himself now wasn't the time *or* the place. Maybe once she was safe...

No.

He kept repeating that single word, making sure it echoed through his mind and slammed into his wolf with every beat of his heart. She wasn't for him.

She didn't say another word as he took care of feeding her. The quiet should have been strained, uncomfortable, or...something. But it wasn't.

He wondered if she'd hit her head and that was why she was so easygoing at the moment.

Declan placed the last bite in her mouth and then laid the empty plate and fork on the table along with a now half-empty water bottle. "Want me to cook another, or was that enough?"

"I'm full. It was delicious. Thank you." She had that sated, sleepy smile he'd seen on others in the past. The one that said she'd happily pass out once more if he let her.

Which he would. For self-preservation if nothing else.

"You're welcome." He was sure he was supposed to do something then, but Abby...

She licked her lips, and he swallowed his moan. "Thank you for everything else, too."

He hated the reminder of all the other bullshit they had to handle. "Don't thank me until you're safe."

"You mean *we're* safe."

He shot her a half grin. One he'd perfected over the years. A bit of patronizing with a dash of doubt. He'd never be safe, not truly. "Until we're safe."

She narrowed her eyes, the cougar and her human half peering at him. "Do you think you won't make it through this? That you'll..."

The scent of her worry overrode the delicious aroma of her arousal, and the wolf didn't like that *at all*.

"Sweetheart." He cupped one cheek, unable to keep his hands to himself. "You'll come out the other side of this whole. As for me, I wake up every day wondering if I'll make it past breakfast."

"But..." She shook her head. "You got me out of there, got us here like it was nothing."

"Training." He leaned over and pressed a soft kiss to her forehead before he moved away. "I've been destroying, hurting, and killing for a long time."

She snorted. "Long? You can't be that old."

Memories crept up on him, his past threatening to intrude on his present. He fought them off, but some things couldn't be banished entirely.

Declan placed the plate in the sink before he gave Abby his attention. "Baby"—he hated the way she flinched with that endearment, but it was another way for him to keep distance between them—"I was fifteen the first time I killed a man."

Abby pushed herself upright, opened her mouth and then snapped it closed. "I didn't realize SHOC recruited so young."

"They don't. I didn't join SHOC until..." His voice trailed off. Declan tilted back his head and stared at the ceiling with narrowed eyes. He tried to remember back to the first time he'd met Birch. He ran his hand along his jaw, the rough scrape of his shadow scratching his palm. "It's been about two years, now. They'd gotten word of my, uh, talents."

"You killed people," she whispered, and he didn't like the look in her eyes. Nothing good came from a woman with that sad, curious, and worried expression. Ever. "Why?"

He shook his head and got back to cleaning up after himself. Just because he'd left home at fifteen didn't mean he'd forgotten everything his mother taught him. "It was a job."

"A job? People hired you to..."

He placed the empty plate in the sink before turning to face her. He propped his hands on the counter and braced his weight on the polished stone. "People hired me to fix their problems. Permanently. Sometimes quickly and other times painfully, but it'd be done."

"And you got paid."

"Well. I got paid *well*." He didn't try to hide the pride in his voice. It'd been hard in the beginning, but he and Pike had figured things out eventually.

Abby shook her head, brow furrowed. "I don't understand. Today you rescued me."

"The wolf didn't give me a choice today, just like it didn't give me a choice when I was fifteen. It wanted, it took. A person, a life, it wants what it wants. When I worked freelance, it enjoyed the chase and the kill." He sighed and ran a hand through his short, dark locks. "I took advantage of that."

"What kind of people did you kill?" Why did she keep asking questions? Questions he wasn't sure he wanted to answer. The only positive note to her line of questioning was that it did a good job of squashing his arousal.

"The kind I was paid to kill," he drawled.

"Bad men? Good? Women? Kids?"

The wolf surged for an entirely different reason, the beast snapping and snarling at Abby's question. His eyesight flickered, colors dancing in and out of his vision while he stared at the woman huddled on the couch. His skin burned, the beast's fur attempting to burst free. His arms and hands ached, paws pushing to be freed.

"Never pups. *Never*."

"But what about their parents? Did you kill their parents?" Still Abby pushed. Still Abby taunted his wolf. He relished her voice, but not her words.

"Dammit, Abby." His gums burned, and he resisted the urge to bare his fangs at her. "I took the jobs. I took them, I eliminated the target, and I put money in my offshore accounts."

In *their* offshore accounts, but she didn't know about Pike. She wouldn't ever know about Pike as far as Declan was concerned. The less she knew about him—his life—the better.

With a shake of his head, he got back to kitchen cleanup. He'd make something for himself later. When Abby was sleeping and not badgering him with questions that made his stomach churn.

"How did you kill them?" Why couldn't she just stop pushing? *Why?*

"Does it really matter?" Because his mind didn't want to remember that part of his past.

"Yes." Of course it did. Of course it'd matter to her. Sweet, sinfully sexy Abby with a soft heart and gentle words for everyone.

He didn't turn back to her while he tried to figure out what to say. Then he wondered why he bothered. He'd given her brutal honesty up to that point. There was no reason to stop now. "It depended on what the job needed. Whether they wanted an accident or to send a message. Guns. Hands. Poison."

"Bombs?"

Declan pushed away from the counter and returned to her, his gaze on her eyes as he approached. Her eyes widened, pupils dilated, and her breath caught as she watched him move closer. Her lips parted, tongue darting out to wet them as if she prepared for his kiss, and then her natural scent teased his nose.

She didn't like him—what he did—but he knew she wanted him.

He didn't stop until his knees touched the couch and he leaned over her, one hand on the back while the other rested on the furniture's arm. He leaned down, closing the distance between their mouths until his lips nearly brushed hers. It'd be so easy to capture her lips with his own, to snatch a kiss and drug her with passion. So easy...

"I'm not a good man, Abby," he whispered, and she swallowed hard. "I killed because I'm a selfish asshole. I saved you for the same reason."

Liar. The wolf's growl consumed his mind, rolling over every other sound.

"You didn't answer my question."

"Which one?"

"Did you kill parents?" The question seemed torn from within her soul, and he hated the truth he'd have to give her. He knew her past—knew how she'd feel about his answer—and decided it was for the best. Pushing her away was a good idea.

Finally, Declan answered. "Yes."

CHAPTER FOURTEEN

Declan's stark declaration sent Abby's mind tumbling into the past. To a time when she'd been a carefree child with a sassy cougar shifter mother and a grumbling werewolf father. They'd been a study in contrasts until their last breath. Her dad snarled at anyone who got too close to his family while her mother rolled her eyes and ignored his growling. A cat and a wolf who had so much love...

Was that why she was so drawn to Declan? Because he was a ferocious wolf who threatened her in one breath and then protected her in the next?

Abby wasn't sure. She also wasn't sure if she wanted to examine her feelings for the SHOC agent any further. He'd answered her questions, stabbing her in the heart with his truth, and there was nowhere for her to run. He was the embodiment of everything she despised, and she couldn't leave him.

Shifter Operations Command wanted her—alive, at least for a little while and then who knew. Unified Humanity wanted her—probably dead.

And Declan...what did he want?

Bile churned in her stomach, the scents of smoke and burned flesh searing her nose while the memories attempted to overtake her: their small family sitting down for dinner, her father carefully helping her mother into her chair. They'd tried to hide it, but Abby had already recognized the changes in her mother's scent. Abby was going to have a little brother or sister—wolf or cougar, she hadn't cared.

Then came a knock on the front door. Her mother's smile as she rose to go answer and her father's growl because he didn't want her doing anything but sitting. When Abby tried to follow them both, her dad told her to stay put. If Mom ignored Dad she got a glare that lasted two seconds before he sighed with frustration. If Abby ignored Dad she didn't get dessert for a *week*.

So she remained in her seat and waited for them to return because there was a chocolate cake on the counter in the kitchen.

She also ignored the manners her parents drilled into her. She was *supposed* to wait for everyone to be seated before eating. She figured that since they *had* been sitting together before her parents left it was okay to eat some macaroni and cheese.

Abby had a mouthful of mac and cheese when her mother's first cry reached her. She swallowed it right before her father's roar shook the house. Her feet had just touched the floor when his yell echoed off the walls.

"Run!"

Then a deafening boom. The crackle of fire. The suffocating smoke. The darkness of the hidden closet. It'd kept her safe—protected—while destruction consumed their small house.

Then it was done and she was alone.

Unified Humanity had rid the world of two shifters whose only crime was love and creating a family.

With a bomb.

"Do you want details?" Declan's question snapped her thoughts from the past. "I can—"

"No." She shook her head to make sure he understood. "You've said enough."

More than enough.

Declan pushed away from the couch and stepped back, his intense gaze a heavy weight on her shoulders. She looked anywhere but at him. The past still intruded, the events of those first few days after her parents' deaths fighting for release. Mourning. Healing. Being sent to a godmother—a total stranger and seal shifter.

"Then I'll get you some clothes and you can rest." He turned and moved to the bedroom.

The bed in there was so large and covered in pillows and blankets, tempting her to form a squishy nest just perfect for hiding—safe and warm.

Then Declan reappeared, standing in the doorway with his amber eyes locked on her. "I laid out clothes. They'll be big, but they'll cover you. Get changed and crawl into bed. I'll be there in a minute."

"We're sharing a bed?" Was that excitement or worry churning in her gut? Maybe a bit of both.

The color of his eyes deepened, looking more like his inner wolf. "I told you I'm not letting you out of my sight."

"But…" She licked her lips, mouth dry while her tumultuous emotions continued to beat at her. She didn't feel any hint of anticipation about sharing a bed with Declan. At. All.

The cougar told her she was a big fat liar from Liarton smack-dab in the middle of the great state of Liar-isiana living on Lying Avenue.

"Remember what I said, Abby." Heat lingered in his gaze, and the spicy scent of desire drifted through the room.

He was hot as hell and he wanted her, but she *did* remember what he'd told her.

He would only take what was freely given, and even then, she'd have to ask very, *very* nicely. Abby wasn't ready to ask, so she kept her mouth shut and rose, padding toward Declan. He remained in place, amber eyes stroking her from head to toe like a physical caress, and she couldn't suppress the shudder that slid down her spine.

He didn't step aside when she reached him, not at first. He simply stared, feral eyes missing nothing. He took a deep breath, eyelids fluttering closed, and then released it just as slowly. A rumbling growl followed, but it didn't hold a hint of threat. No, it was a different kind of growl entirely.

A sexy one. One that made her nipples harder and her pussy grow heavy with a desperate ache. *Stupid wolf,* she mentally grumbled. What right did he have to be all sexy and hot and fuckable and *bad*?

Finally, Declan turned to the side to let her pass. Mostly. She had to wiggle past him, going into the room sideways, and...she sorta paused when she was halfway through. Mainly because their fronts brushed. Abby's nipples hardened further, her clit twitched, and a knee-weakening wave of desire rolled over her. And she wasn't the only one affected. Declan was just as aroused, his hard cock nudging her middle as she inched into the room.

The moment she got past him, she strode to the bed and snatched the clothes he'd left out. Clothes that still had that stiffness from being new and carried the chemical scent of its originating factory. There was something else, too. Just a hint of...Declan.

A baggy shirt and cotton pants waited for her—her bra and panties probably tossed in the bathroom garbage. Ugh, she was going to have slightly saggy, free-swinging boobs in front of God's gift to vaginas everywhere. *Gravity how I hate thee!*

She reached for the knot of her robe, fingers plucking at the tied fabric, and glanced over her shoulder at Declan. "Can I have a little privacy now?"

He snorted and crossed his arms, feet braced shoulder-width apart. Right. He wasn't leaving her. Why was she being all shy, anyway? She'd already been naked in front of him. What did it matter? Her cougar also reminded her she was a shifter. Nudity wasn't a thing to get bent out of shape about.

Then again, Abby wasn't getting bent out of shape. She was just thinking about her *actual* shape and the cellulite on her legs.

She huffed and focused on her next task. Declan's robe was big—oversized—and she kept it on while she dressed underneath. She tugged on the sweatpants. Bottom half covered, she let the robe fall from her shoulders while she reached for the shirt. She wiggled into the top, squirming as she tugged it over her head.

When she finally turned back to the big, bad, super-deadly wolf... all hints of teasing sensuality were gone.

"What happened?" Dark gray fur slipped from his pores, sliding down his arms in a river of near-black strands.

"Happened?" She frowned. "I..."

"Your back." He bit off the words, syllables muffled by the fangs now crowding his mouth.

"Oh." She grimaced. *My back.* She twisted her lips in a rueful smile. *"That."* She shook her head. "It was a long time ago."

"How long?"

Abby ran her palm down her face. "It doesn't matter."

"What happened?"

"It doesn't matter."

"Why didn't you heal properly?"

"It doesn't matter." Really, how long did it take a guy to get a clue?

"It does fucking matter!" The whole house shook with the strength of his yell, the ground trembling as the echoes filled the air. His face flushed red beneath the peppering of dark fur. His muscles tensed and veins bulged beneath his taut skin.

Okay, maybe it didn't matter to her—the cougar called her a liar—but it obviously bothered Declan. Since she really didn't feel like dealing with a feral wolf, she went to him, steps slow and careful. She moved as if she approached a natural predator—an animal rather than a shifter male. She reached for him, palm gently coming to rest on his bare chest.

Short strands of midnight fur tickled her fingertips, proof of his tenuous control of the animal inside him. "Declan," she murmured. "I'm fine."

"Who did it?" The words were a garbled mess, his inner wolf making it difficult for him to speak.

"Unified Humanity." That old pain struck her heart, but she pushed it back. "They blew up my home."

"Bombs." Hardly more than a mumble. A question and statement in one.

"Yes." She pushed the word past the strangling knot in her throat.

"Wanna see." The wolf still had control as he forced her to turn, amber eyes brighter than ever.

"Declan..."

He grunted and simply tugged on her shirt while he encouraged her to turn. He pulled it up to reveal her back. She sighed and helped, drawing it higher to show him everything. Claw-tipped fingers ghosted over her skin, the sharp tips teasing her scarred flesh while he explored her back.

He said nothing while he looked her over—traced each twisted knot with his fingertips. Then his touch disappeared, and she bit back the whimper that threatened to escape. She missed the feel of his skin on hers.

There was definitely something wrong with her. One hundred percent. She wondered if they made pills for Stockholm syndrome.

Moist, warm breath bathed her back, and Abby froze, not moving a muscle while Declan...His lips brushed her back, low and just above the edge of her sweatpants. It was the worst scar out of them all. Being confined in such a tight space while her cougar had fought to heal the damage had resulted in some ugly, twisted scar tissue.

He moved on, teasing another spot just above her hip on her left side. The kiss wasn't meant to incite passion. It was almost reverent.

The werewolf who proclaimed to be so deadly, dangerous, and unfeeling now gently touched her as if she'd shatter at any moment. Another kiss, this one to the right, a long, thick line that still gleamed shiny white even after so many years. He continued, and she closed her eyes, imagining more than six feet of violent male kneeling behind her—comforting her?

He didn't caress her. He kept his hands from her body, only his mouth learning the uneven plane of her back. Warm lips. Moist breath. The scent of the clean forest at dawn. It called to her cougar, luring it forward while lulling it into a restful calm.

His travels continued higher, not stopping until his lips finally rested at the base of her neck. She didn't have any scarring there—her cougar had been able to heal that part of her. But it was like he sensed the damage had extended beyond that twisted part of her.

Because it had.

Declan's careful handling brought tears to her eyes and she blinked them away, unwilling to break down. She hadn't cried when she'd been *shot*. She wasn't about to start now over mere memories.

Declan murmured against her unblemished skin. "I'll kill them."

Abby shook her head. "It was a long time ago. I don't even know who it was exactly. I just know it was them."

"I'm a very good hunter, sweetheart. Unified Humanity gave the order. I'll find the ones who carried it out." He still had his lips on her. As if he couldn't force himself away.

"It doesn't matter anymore."

"I can smell your pain." Now a growl traveled from Declan to her. It slithered down her spine, and she fought the oncoming tremble. "You're lying to yourself."

Abby chuckled and shook her head. "Maybe I am." She shrugged. "But we don't have time for me to burst into tears over something that happened when I was eight."

Eight years old and untouched by violence until that day.

He stood, his heat moving along her back as he changed position. He tugged her shirt back down, and then two thick arms wrapped around her. He cradled her in his strength, almost like a living, breathing wall of protection. "Why didn't your cougar heal everything properly?"

"Because after I was hurt, I hid like I'd been taught." She closed her eyes. Those stupid tears were really determined now. "I stayed curled up in a cupboard for two days. My cougar healed what it could as it could, but the position and tight quarters…"

Declan rested his cheek on top of her head. "Every time you healed, you'd twist and hurt yourself again."

Abby nodded. "And I was so weak that—"

"You were *eight*. The fact that you survived..." He sighed. "I'm going to find them."

"It doesn't—"

"It does," he snarled, but his hold remained soft and gentle. Then he withdrew, hands releasing her and arms slipping away while his warmth vanished. "Let's get you to bed."

"Yeah," she whispered, "okay." She took one step and then two, fighting her body to put distance between them. Her cougar wanted to turn and rub all over him, but...but her human mind needed space.

She crawled into bed, wiggling beneath the covers and claiming one of the pillows. On the other side, Declan did the same, settling into place with a deep sigh. Silence descended then, the sound of their breathing the only thing that broke the quiet.

Until Declan grunted and moved. In a whirl of sheets and flex of muscle Abby found herself plastered to his side. Their bodies aligned, her curves molding to his hard frame. His arms were like steel bands, hands putting her in place before he held her immobile. He pressed her ear to his chest, arm curled around her shoulders. He rubbed her shoulder, fingers dancing over her side. He traveled up and down the length of her back, shoulder to hip.

"I'm going to kill them, Abby."

Part of her wanted that. She wanted them hunted and punished for what they'd done to her life, but she didn't want that blood on her hands. "I know what you want to do, but—"

"*Will* do."

"But can you hurt them for doing the same thing you've done countless times?"

He flinched, just the tiniest twitch, before he answered. "One, I know how to count. It's not countless. Two"—he nudged her, forcing her to tip her head back and meet his stare—"never women. Never children. I told you that already. I'm not a good man, but I have limits." He lifted his free hand, callused fingertips tracing the slope of her nose, the curve of her jaw, and on to her lips. "I'll tell you something else. I haven't taken a contract in two years. Not since I joined Shifter Operations Command. I've done things I regret, but that isn't who I am anymore."

"Then who are you?"

"The wolf who isn't going to let anything—anyone—hurt you."

CHAPTER FIFTEEN

*D*eclan didn't sleep. The shit-storm had begun around eight thirty and now the clock was ticking past midnight. His mind remained alert, wolf constantly listening for intruders while his human thoughts focused on the woman in his arms—Abby.

Abby who'd been through hell—and not just what had occurred in the last few hours. Reading her file had given him bare-bones details. Seeing her back...It stabbed him with the truth and damned if it didn't *hurt*. What the fuck?

It explained her anger, though—the scent of her emotional agony that'd assaulted him with every question about his past.

He hadn't been lying when he'd assured her he didn't touch women and children. Not after what he'd seen.

Abby sighed in her sleep and rubbed her cheek on his chest. She nuzzled him, her lush body sliding against his, and he cursed the clothing that separated them. Oh, he knew it was necessary—her naked body was too damned tempting—but he hated its presence.

Damn, then she went and moaned and wiggled her hips and *like that* he was harder than nails. He rubbed his free hand over his face and pinched the bridge of his nose. She'd kill him if she kept it up. All those curves, her fresh scent and sweet little sounds.

His wolf nudged him, urging him to explore the pretty little cougar, but he shoved the animal away. They hadn't saved her to fuck her. They'd saved her... Shit, he wasn't sure why anymore. He only knew he'd been driven to shield her from harm and wouldn't let anything stand in his way.

Abby took a deep breath and released it with a soft sigh, but this time she didn't settle back into sleep. She moaned—she *really* needed to stop—and tensed.

"Declan?"

"Go back to sleep, Abby." His wolf lined each word with a growl.

She stiffened and edged away, as if she wanted to move out of his embrace. "Sorry. I didn't mean to crawl all over you. I..."

He tightened his hold, not letting her budge. She drove him crazy with her closeness, but he couldn't let her go. "Don't be sorry." He wasn't gonna tell her how much he liked having her in his arms. "Just sleep. You can rest for a while yet. We won't leave until tonight."

"How long have we been here?" she whispered, and even that aroused him.

He was such a twisted fuck. "Not too long. Not long enough."

She fell silent for a moment, but he knew it wouldn't last. He could practically hear her thinking. "What happens next?"

Declan grunted. "You're not going back to sleep, are you?" Abby shook her head, and he figured he'd have to content himself with the short time he'd held her. "Eat. Coffee. Plan our next move." Then the one after that and then the one after that. So much bullshit. He turned his gaze to her and tried to ignore her sleep-tousled hair and bedroom eyes. "You don't deserve this. Any of it."

"It's my own fault in a way." She grinned, even though she didn't have much to smile about. "Curiosity killed the cat, right? I'm too curious for my own good. I found a loose thread and pulled. When it all unraveled..."

"Curiosity isn't killing this cat. You're not gonna die." He snarled.

"You can't guarantee that."

"The fuck I can't." His pulse increased, the wolf's anger surging with the mere thought of something happening to Abby. "I didn't turn rogue just to lose you. It won't happen."

"Taking me out of there branded you a rogue?" She shuddered.

"According to SHOC—the director." He shrugged. The director was an asshole. "I'd do it again though."

"Why? I'm nobody."

He snorted. "You're Abby Carter. Survivor. Smart as hell. Hard worker. Determined. Stupid because you jumped off that pier." He pressed his lips to her temple, reminding himself that she'd lived through that dumb stunt. "*Brave* because you jumped off that pier."

"I don't feel very brave."

He shook his head. "I've met cowards." Killed more than a few. "You're not one."

"I ran."

"After you knocked one of the humans out with a calculator." He grinned. She'd been a fierce little she-cat. "Then you grabbed that tablet and bolted. You gonna tell me what's on there now? Maybe where it's hidden?"

She tensed, and he wondered if she'd trust him enough to tell him. He could guess, but he'd rather get the truth from her.

"I was auditing FosCo." She turned in his embrace, moving to her stomach and propping herself on her elbows. "I logged into one of their bank accounts and discovered they're funding Unified Humanity."

"That's why Eric Foster showed up with those other men." She nodded even though he hadn't asked a question.

"I didn't realize he got notifications when certain accounts were accessed. I don't know how he knew I was a shifter, but he did. He said it took only one phone call." A tremble shook her. "Before he got there, I downloaded every screenshot and record I could find. I figured I'd hand it over to the council. Let them see if they could piece things together and find anyone else—any other companies—that are connected to Unified Humanity."

"See?" He grinned and twined an errant lock of her hair around one finger. "I told you. Brave."

She rolled her eyes. "We'll agree to disagree."

"Uh-huh." He tucked the strands behind her ear.

"How did you know I needed help?"

Declan winced. "The team's on assignment. We were ordered to observe and see if there was any connection between FosCo and Unified Humanity."

"There is. I have the proof."

"And we have audio recordings and video of Eric's attack." He paused and figured he'd tell her the rest. "We've been watching the building for almost a week. Twenty-four hours a day."

Abby groaned and turned her head, hiding her face against his biceps. Her cheeks heated, her warmth transferring to his arm. "Oh God. You saw me..."

Declan chuckled, recalling the sway of her hips and her little shimmy. "Yeah, we did. I watched you shake your ass every night. I watched you work all day, too."

"That's a little creepy."

He just shrugged. Probably. "You should get some more sleep if you can. I'm not sure how much you'll get over the next few days. With luck, we can get your tablet and wrap this up quickly, but I doubt it."

She shook her head. "I can't sleep anymore."

Which meant he had to let her go. His wolf whined and grumbled, not wanting to release her just yet. He reminded the animal she'd probably think that was creepy, too. The animal reminded *him* that creepy or not, she'd still be in their arms.

Ignoring the beast, he lifted the blankets and rolled away from Abby before the wolf won their battle of wills. "Let's get up, then. The quicker we get this done, the quicker you can go back to your life." He didn't look at her as he strode to the bathroom. If he did, he'd pounce. "Give me a second and then the room's all yours."

"I thought you weren't going to let me out of your sight?"

Yeah, that was what he'd said. But that was before she'd slept in his arms and been all sensual and sweet as she woke.

He paused in the doorway, one foot on the cold tile. The chill chased away some of his need for her, but not nearly enough. "I'll just be gathering supplies in the living room."

It'd let him put space between them—physical, but more importantly, emotional.

He was in and out of the bathroom in moments, striding across the bedroom and out the door without a word. His wolf remained focused on Abby—the sounds of her moving around his home—while his human half moved on autopilot. He had preparations to make, supplies to gather.

Declan strode to the entertainment center and tapped

on drawers and doors. They opened on silent hinges and quiet drawer rails. Overhead lights illuminated each tray, the light glinting off his babies. Hand guns. Rifles. Knives.

He ran his fingers over the array of deadly metal, stopping when he reached a nine-millimeter handgun. He wrapped his fingers around the grip and lifted it from the tray, adjusting to the weight. He released the magazine and counted the bullets before he pushed it back into place.

The soft rustle of clothes drew his attention, and he looked to his right. Abby stood nearby, gaze trained on his hands—the gun—before she turned her stare to the others, and he couldn't miss the question in those eyes.

How many people had he killed with these guns?

"None." He didn't look at her, choosing instead to concentrate on his task. He returned the nine-millimeter to its home and moved on to the next handgun. "I haven't killed anyone with these. Practice only so I knew how they shoot, but that's it."

"How . . . ?"

Abby's voice stroked him, and his body reacted. A reminder that he needed to put space between them.

Declan smirked. "Baby," he murmured. Condescending. Cocky. Asshole. "You wanna talk about my longest shot or how hard I can make you come?"

"Neither." She licked her lips, wetting her mouth. "What's the plan today?"

"Coward." He sniggered.

And I'm an asshole.

"Are we taking all of those with us? Do we need them all?"

"Tell me something." He turned his head and met Abby's stare. She kept her mouth shut and raised her eyebrows in question. "After having guns pointed at you, getting shot, jumping off a pier to hide something in the fucking sea so it won't be found, and being picked up by SHOC. When I get your ass outta there, the rest of my team is drooling over the idea of catching you and you know we're still being hunted. Now, all that"—he whirled his finger in the air—"and you ask me if we need all these guns?"

Abby's eye flashed, cougar now staring out. "Fuck you very much."

He grinned. Damn but he liked that fire. "Well, baby, if you want it that bad—"

"Enough." She snarled at him, even going so far as to bare a fang at him. "You're having a lot of fun at my expense. It was a stupid question—I get it—but you don't have to be an asshole just because you have one."

"You're gonna be okay." Declan released a low chuckle. "If I can keep you alive." He sighed. "Speaking of... You're going to walk me through what happened—what you did—again. You're not gonna stop until I'm ready to slit your throat if I hear your voice again and then you'll say it once more."

Abby jerked back, his words piercing her as if they were bullets—sharp, hard, unavoidable. "Okay."

He huffed and ran a hand through his hair. "Sorry. Just tired." He pinched the bridge of his nose, eyes closed. "'Knowledge is Power' isn't some motivational poster. It's the truth. In my line of work, knowledge is life. I've known a lot of people who died because of ignorance. Not gonna have you be one of 'em."

CHAPTER SIXTEEN

*A*bby blindly stared out at Declan's backyard—one he'd turned into a lush oasis. Also known as a space with enough trees and foliage to make the area as private as possible without turning into a wild jungle. Because a wild jungle would result in notices from the HOA. Abby knew all about HOA notices, though hers were usually noise complaints because *someone's* cat liked snarling at seagulls at two in the morning.

And the cougar never apologized. *Never.*

New sounds within the home drew her attention. Ones that were different from the click and clack of Declan's fingers on a keyboard or the scrape of metal as he disassembled and reassembled one of his guns *again*. She'd been listening to that for what seemed like forever while he made sure they had what they needed to survive.

Knowledge was power, all right. But guns were power, too.

The slam of wood on wood—cupboard banging closed—was followed by the gurgle of running water. Then glass clicking against...stone? Declan was in the kitchen, then. She wondered how long it'd take him to hunt her down again. It'd been a while since that steak, and her stomach grumbled—empty.

With a sigh, Abby turned on the window seat and swung her legs over the edge. She straightened her back and tilted her head from side to side, then twisted at the waist and stretched her arms over her head. No tenderness or pain that would slow her down. Every hint of her wounds and exhaustion now gone after some good sleep and food.

The cougar purred, and Abby mentally stroked her inner feline, praising the she-cat for a healing job well done. It spun and flicked its tail, a hint of cockiness easing through her mind. Yeah, the cat had done good, but could it get her through what was to come?

The beast sniffed and then hissed, offended that Abby even had to ask. She ignored her inner animal and pushed to her feet, taking a moment for one last stretch before she sought out Declan with her gaze.

Declan... She practically purred his name. Muscular. Sexy. Tempting. Declan.

Declan who wasn't in sight. He'd claimed he wouldn't let her leave him, but maybe it was okay if he was doing the leaving?

She padded across the floor—away from the window seat tucked into the dining area—and toward the center of the great room. Her feet sank into soft carpet. It was a sumptuous temptation her cat had difficulty resisting. It wanted to shift and roll around on the cushioned surface, coat it in her scent so other females would know Declan was taken.

Abby thumped the cat on its nose. *No time*. Plus, he wasn't taken.

The animal disagreed. It definitely wanted to *take* Declan.

"Hungry?" Declan spoke from her right, and she drifted in that direction. He stood on the other side of the bar, empty glass resting on the counter. "You need to keep up your strength before we play the rest of this game."

"Yeah. I could eat." She nodded and headed in his direction. "But you don't have to make me anything. I can..." Amber eyes met hers, the wolf giving her a glare that had her voice trailing off. "Or not."

Declan grunted and pushed away from the counter, his movements fluid and easy. A grace she normally attributed to a cat, but he was all wolf. All dominance, aggression, and possessiveness.

Well, if he wasn't going to let her cook for herself, she could at least enjoy the view. His worn jeans—frayed at the hems and other areas whitened—hung low enough to expose the V on his hips. She let her gaze wander over his chest, caress each of those thickly carved muscles and honed body with her eyes. His stomach was flat, ridges of his abs exposed and begging for her touch—her mouth? She let her attention drift farther up his body, to his strong pecs and broad shoulders. Then to his thick biceps. Arms that had cradled her close when he'd rescued her.

He put on a show just for her. There was nothing sexier than a man—half naked and sexy as hell—in the kitchen. He opened an upper cabinet and grabbed a pan, stretching to reach the handle. The move made his jeans drop just a hint, exposing more of those muscles she wanted to lick and nibble.

Her center clenched, clit throbbing with a surge of desire, and she bit her lip to keep her whimper in check. Then...then he made it so much worse—better? He set the pan on the stove and went to the fridge, tugging on the door so it swung open. It gave her a clear view of his back, of the play of muscles while he moved, the way they slid beneath his skin. That was when he made it all worse. He leaned down to peer into the space, attention firmly on the fridge's interior.

Meanwhile, her attention was firmly on his ass. She wanted to bite and nibble him there, too. Okay, she wanted him everywhere, all of him. Oh, she wouldn't destroy herself in that way—Declan was dangerous, heartless—but that didn't mean she couldn't ogle. A lot.

"You done staring yet?" Laughter tinged his words, and she wrenched her attention from his ass. He remained bent over and peeked at her from beneath his arm. She met his teasing gaze for a split second, his twitching lips enough to make her face flush, and then shot her stare to the ground. "Or should I go ahead and strip for you?"

"I don't know what you're talking about," she mumbled.

"Liar." His chuckle turned deep and dark, like smooth chocolate that lured her forward a step before she realized she'd moved. He straightened and turned away from the fridge, nudging the door closed with his foot.

His bare foot.

Could feet be sexy?

Abby's cougar purred. Apparently.

"Come eat." He placed a carton of eggs and a bag of shredded cheese on the counter.

"You keep trying to feed me." She steeled herself for the impending encounter, prepared herself for being so close to Declan without touching him.

"Because you need to eat." He didn't give her a spare glance, just cracked an egg on the edge of the pan, a nice sizzle following the move. He tossed the empty shell in the sink and then focused on her, blue eyes intent. "We need to be ready for what's coming."

"Coming?" Her heartbeat stuttered, and fear threatened to take over.

Declan's eyes bled amber for a moment, flickering between man and wolf, and he refocused on the stove. "A team is hunting you on behalf of the director." He flipped the egg and then waved the spatula toward the corner—his computer system. "They've already hacked the traffic cams, and I have no doubt they're routing everything through facial recognition."

"I don't know what that means." Or rather, she didn't *want* to know.

He was quiet then, attention wholly on the frying pan, as if his cooking decided the fate of the world. The longer he ignored her, the more nervous she became, until she simply couldn't take it anymore.

"Declan?" He didn't make a sound, just flipped the second egg onto the plate and slid it across the counter. Declan was fast, but so was she, thanks to her cat. She reached for him, fingers wrapped around his wrist before he could fully retreat. "Declan, what does that mean?"

He stared at her hand, eyes no longer holding even a hint of his human half—the wolf was in residence. "The director wants you—what you know. Badly. Which means that team wants you even more." He turned his wrist, shifting position until he held her hand in his. And he was so gentle, so careful with her. "Bad enough to do what it takes to get it."

"Would it be wrong to give—"

"Sweetheart," he murmured, blue eyes black and staring deep into her soul. "Shifter Operations Command is a pretty name for men who do bad things. You can't imagine that the director is better than any of his agents. Regardless, Birch is feeling twitchy, and that's never a good thing. Until we know more, you're with me. Once we're holding all the cards, we'll figure out our play. For now it's just us." He pointed at the plate with his free hand. "Eat."

Abby squeezed her thighs together, core tightening and aching with a jolt of desire. He'd aroused her with a single word and a dark look, and she called herself an idiot for getting hot and bothered over the wolf because he'd told her to *eat*.

There was something very, very wrong with her. Very.

She fed herself with her free hand, the other captive in Declan's gentle grip. He traced her wrist with his thumb. So calm, so gentle. The assassin who touched her as if she'd shatter at any moment.

Maybe she would because that thought was enough of a reminder for her. Declan wasn't simply a man seducing a woman. He was a killer—cold and merciless.

She tried to withdraw from his hold, but he merely tightened his grip, keeping her captive. "You didn't tell me why."

Declan increased the pressure of his thumb on her wrist. "Your heart's racing."

"Tell me what's going on."

"Is it racing because you want me, baby?" His deep voice was a seductive caress until he got to *baby*. That was enough to drown her desire.

Abby whipped her head up, eyes snapping open, and she glared at him. "No," she snapped. "It's racing because an asshole won't let me go and won't tell me what the hell is going on."

The corner of his mouth curled up in a seductive smirk. "You keep lying to yourself if you want, but, baby"—she internally flinched—"I can smell your need. I can practically taste it on my tongue. I may be an asshole, but you like it."

She did like it, but she wasn't going to say the words aloud. "Tell me."

"You want the truth." He shook his head. "That's what you'll get."

Declan released her, and she snatched her hand from his, rubbing her wrist and trying to wash away the feel of his skin on hers.

"You need to eat because everything up to this moment has been a cakewalk and you're gonna need all the strength you can get just to survive what's coming."

CHAPTER SEVENTEEN

*T*he beast scraped Declan from the inside out, determined to gain its freedom so it could soothe the damage he'd done. But he didn't want the wolf smoothing things over. He—they—needed the distance. The thing inside him, his feral half, had one too many long-term ideas about Abby. It didn't care that Declan wasn't a long-term guy. He was the go-to guy if a woman needed an itch scratched and didn't care if he'd blown up a yacht five minutes before he walked through her door.

Abby would care. A lot.

"What do you mean? What's coming?"

Sweet naive Abby with her pale sparkling blue eyes and golden hair. God, he wanted to taste her. Wanted to take her and keep her safe from all the bullshit that was about to go down.

"Gimme this." He pulled her plate away and placed it in the sink. "We can go over to the desk."

He pretended his dick wasn't rock hard and he rounded the counter. Not looking at her, he strode to the computer station, intent on getting the dangerous explanation done and over with before he did something stupid. Like bend her over the couch and...

And she wasn't following. He paused and turned back to her. "Abby?"

Her face flushed red, all pink and sexy, and his cock throbbed. Hell, it'd been hard from the moment he'd first heard her wake. He needed to get rid of her and get into some other woman's bed. Soon. Before the wolf convinced him to take her.

Abby's attention drifted down his body, and he had to admit he was fucking pleased that she liked what she saw. She licked those plump lips, her breathing speeding up while the delicious scent of her arousal filled the air.

"Still don't want me, baby?" He smirked because it pissed her off. Called her *baby* for the same reason. It was fun, ruffling her fur and being the recipient of fiery glares.

"No," she snapped, but her darkening blush told him she lied. Eh, he'd let her keep lying to herself. It'd make his life easier when it was time to walk away. If she kept giving him those "fuck me" looks, he was bound to have her. The only question was whether it'd be hard and fast or gentle and slow.

"All right, then." He returned to his path, not stopping until he got to his desk. Entering his password took less than two seconds and then they were in his system.

"These guys"—he waved his hand toward the left screen—"are the team hunting you. Decent enough. Not as seasoned as my own, but they do what they're told for the 'greater good' or some shit." He flicked her a glance and caught her confused expression. "They joined SHOC voluntarily."

"You didn't?"

He had to open his fucking mouth, didn't he?

"Let's say that I was *encouraged* to put my skills to use in an alternative capacity."

Abby grinned and he sure as hell wasn't pleased about it. "Really? Kill the wrong guy?"

Declan shrugged. "*Didn't* kill the guy."

At least, that was what'd originally put him on the council's radar. Then he'd gotten out of the game and Birch showed up and... Two years of bullshit he didn't like thinking about.

"Most teams are made up of men who've found that SHOC is a nice alternative."

"To what?"

"Death," he drawled. "We do the dirty work that needs to be done. SHOC has an accord with the council that gives us diplomatic immunity when it comes to freelance work." He shrugged. "We can't turn into serial killers or start slaughtering humans left and right, but we don't have to keep looking over our shoulders when we take on a little action on the side."

She swallowed hard, and he could practically read her thoughts. She wanted to know about his past—whom he'd killed—but on the other hand, she didn't. "And that team?"

"Like I said, they're puppies. Their team is made up of ex-Trackers turned agents who were born and bred to appease their superiors. That used to be the council." He glared at the screen displaying the team moving around their safe house. "They just want to please the director. No matter the cost."

"I'm a shifter," she said. "Isn't SHOC supposed to help and protect...?"

Declan pitied her. He really did.

"Sweetheart," he murmured, liking the way the endearment rolled off his tongue a little too much. He reached for her hand, and when she didn't pull away, he tugged her all the way onto his lap—one arm around her waist and the other still holding that delicate hand. He liked having her close, touching her and holding her. He'd hate himself for it later, hate himself for staining her with the darkness that clung to his skin. For now he'd enjoy her nearness.

"We're not dealing with the council here. The SHOC director is a lot like the rest of my team—dirty and not giving a damn about anything but completing a job."

Her lower lip trembled, and he felt like the asshole who told a bunch of kids that Santa wasn't real. "But we could call the council, right? They could..."

"When it comes to intense shit like this? I don't trust anyone."

"Not even your team?"

Declan's wolf sneered at him, the animal's general "you're an idiot" attitude more than clear. "I would trust my team," he allowed slowly. "But I won't call them in for this. Not when it means going against SHOC. I don't want them to be branded rogue for something I did alone."

He leaned forward and tapped a few keys, then grabbed his mouse, sliding the cursor from screen to screen.

Declan clicked another corner of the screen, bringing it into focus. "The team tasked with retrieving you are into traffic cams and some of the big-boy security systems for the buildings surrounding your home."

Abby jolted, and he stroked her back, palm sliding up and down her spine. "They'd know if we were coming."

"Yes." No sense in lying. He gestured at a different set of images. "On this side is Eric Foster—FosCo—and by extension, Unified Humanity. His guys tapped in, too, but their tech is slower. As soon as we pass a traffic cam, we'll end up with SHOC on us before UH gets their thumbs out of their asses."

"You hacked into UH *and* SHOC? How?"

Declan snorted. "Baby"—he hated the way she flinched, but it was for the best. She was sweetness and light and he...wasn't—"I didn't live this long by being stupid. My eyes are everywhere."

He pulled up footage from the previous night, the recordings he'd pieced together to make a mini-movie of her dash to freedom. It showed Abby racing away from FosCo right until she reached the edge of the pier. He paused the recording there—an ethereal image of her standing on the precipice and prepared to jump.

"I *don't* have eyes in the ocean. Where did you hide the tablet?"

Abby hesitated, lower lip caught between her teeth and indecision plain on her face.

He squeezed her hip. "I can't protect you if you don't give me a little trust."

Abby sighed, and her shoulders slumped. "Can you pull up a map of the coast? There's a little island—Palm Island."

"You hid the tablet on an island?" He raised a single brow. "You *swam* to an island, hid the tablet, and then swam to shore? That's some stamina."

Stamina he wouldn't mind enjoying. How long could they fuck before she got tired?

"*After* I got shot."

"Yeah, I remember." Hated that he remembered, but he did. "So we'll have to steal a boat." He brought up the map she'd requested and scanned the coastal marinas. "How long will it take you to find the tablet once we hit the island?"

"Not long. I know exactly where I left it."

"Five minutes? Fifteen? I need numbers, ba—" He snapped his mouth closed and tried again. "I can't plan without numbers."

"Five, then." She jerked her head in a stiff nod. "I can get it in five."

"Good. The less time we're exposed, the lower the risk."

"I don't want you hurt because of me, Declan. You can hand me over to the director."

"No, I really can't." Because fuck all, it would be a lot easier to wash his hands of everything. Except...except something deep twisted at the mere idea of letting her get more than ten feet from him.

She didn't say anything for a moment, and he waited, tensed and ready to snap at her if she started in with that "hand me over" bullshit again.

"Okay," she whispered. "We'll avoid SHOC and UH, but what about your own team? Where are they?"

Declan shook his head, hating the answer. "I have no idea, but we'll worry about that later."

For now they were going over the plan. And once this shit was sorted, he was gone. She'd go back to her number-crunching life and he'd...force himself to be anywhere but with her.

CHAPTER EIGHTEEN

COLE

*C*ole figured he should probably listen to Director Quade's bitching. *Should*, but wasn't. It was one of those "same shit, different day" things. It all boiled down to the same message: the team fucked up, so they'd better fix it, dammit. They might.

And then they might not.

It depended on whether he—*they*—felt like it. Right then Cole was trying to juggle six balls of C-4 while sitting in a chair balanced on two legs. His record was five.

"One girl. How fucking hard is it to hold on to one fucking girl?" The head of SHOC snarled—his inner snake baring its poisonous fangs. Yeah, the director of Shifter Operations Command was a snake. Literally.

Waves of the man's fury darted through the room. The asshole who was *supposed* to have gone to the southern field office had decided to head on over and supervise Abby's retrieval instead. Lucky them.

"Apparently," Cole drawled, and slowly turned his attention to the raging bear, focus split between the C-4 and the director, "very."

The snake shifter's gaze seared him, but Cole couldn't find an ounce of fear. His tiger obeyed orders by choice, not some knee-knocking terror. Right now it wanted to *choose* to lift his tail and spray the asshole with piss for shits and giggles.

"You." The director pointed and glared at Cole.

Cole lifted one corner of his mouth in a smirk. "Me."

"You knew about this." He stomped closer to Cole. "He's your partner, and you——"

The nearer Director Quade drew, the more agitated his tiger became. The striped cat rose within Cole's mind with a low, rumbling snarl. He caught each tumbling ball of C-4 in his hands, one after another until he held all six.

"*I* have a name." He adjusted his weight, and the other two legs of the chair *thump*ed to the ground. "*I* am part of a team." He placed the balls on the table that separated him from the director. "*I* don't like your fucking tone."

Quade leaned across the table, midnight eyes boring into his own. The bastard's snake was on the rise, and Cole let his own beast edge closer.

"You joined SHOC and agreed to do as ordered." The deadly black mamba curled his lip. "You were *ordered* to secure the prisoner and turn her over so she could be interrogated."

"Interrogated?" Ethan came into the room, the lion's walk smooth and slow, as if he were relaxed, but Cole knew better. The lion shifter hated Quade just as much as anyone. "I was under the impression you had a few questions for her. A couple of finer points to discuss before you patted her on the head and sent her on her way."

The director spun. "What I do with a prisoner——"

"Aw, she's a prisoner?" Grant whined around a mouthful of sandwich. His boots thumped heavily on the thin carpet. "When did that happen?"

"After your communications *mysteriously*"—the director's heavy glare landed on Grant—"went down."

"I know, right?" Grant's eyes were wide. "What's up with that?" He shook his head and took another bite of his sub. "Funny how shit randomly breaks. Know what I mean?"

Cole snorted and rolled his eyes.

"You, Mr. Shaw"—the director's midnight eyes narrowed on Grant—"were hired—"

"Drafted," Cole coughed, but the director ignored him.

"For a specific purpose." Quade continued as if Cole hadn't interrupted. "If you cannot meet the requirements of your job, you will find yourself in a council prison."

Ethan strolled deeper into the room, eyes on his cell phone until he came to a stop at Cole's side. He tucked his phone away and crossed his arms over his chest. "Then the council will find its newest prisoner missing within twenty-four hours of him walking through the front door." The lion tipped his head to the side. "Or did you forget who I am?"

Ethan wasn't just a pretty boy with pretty cars. He was a ghost—in and out of any situation before anyone registered his presence.

Grant joined them as well, hopping onto the table, legs swinging.

"I want her." The snake followed the words with a long hiss.

Cole tipped his head to the side. "How's it feel to want?"

"You will locate and secure her." The threat was obvious in Director Quade's voice.

"Or what?" Cole growled. His tiger didn't take threats

well. "Why do you have such a hard-on for her?" He crossed his arms over his chest and matched Ethan's stance. "She's cute, sure, but what about her had you hauling ass and stumbling into the middle of our op?"

"She might have information on Unified Humanity. She could be an excellent source."

"I think he saw a video of Abby shaking her ass and wants to tap that," Grant murmured not so quietly.

Cole reached over and whacked the wolf in the head. "Shut the fuck up."

"I'd tap that." The wolf shrugged and then shook his shoulders. "She did that little shimmy when—"

"I will drop you where you stand if you keep talking." He pointed a claw-tipped finger at Grant.

Grant just took another bite of his sandwich and spoke around the mouthful. "I'm sitting."

Cole ignored the wolf. Declan could kick Grant's ass for being disrespectful of Abby when they finally found the fucker. Instead, he spoke to Ethan. "Ethan, tell me something. You've been with SHOC for a while, right?"

"Going on ten years," Ethan said, and then grinned wide, exposing his elongated fangs. "They said I was a troubled teen. I like to think of myself as a prodigy."

"You jacking cars is a thing of beauty. And your driving? *God damn.*" Cole nodded, and he could practically see the steam coming out of the director's ears. "But when was the last time the director of Shifter Operations Command entered the field to apprehend an everyday shifter?"

Ethan grunted. "Never."

"Huh. Makes you wonder what his game is."

"This is insubordination." The director truly did hiss then. "Abby Carter is—"

"A nobody accountant who was in the wrong place at

the wrong time." Birch strolled in, limbs loose and relaxed. At least that was how he appeared to the casual observer— to the people who didn't know the grizzly better. The team alpha didn't stop until he stood between the team and the director. "Nothing more. Nothing less."

"An accountant that your weapons specialist decided to kidnap for no reason?" Quade's voice was deceptively calm. Cole saw the menace in his eyes.

"You saw her ass. He *definitely* had a reason," Grant said, and Cole resisted the urge to whack the werewolf again.

The director was quiet for a moment and then two. "I expect all of you to stand aside for the secondary team. If you impede this search, I will see all of you in a council prison."

Quade didn't say anything after that. He spun on his heel and stomped from the room, leaving the stench of fury in his wake.

But Cole wondered if he caught the slightest touch of fear. His tiger liked to think so, but Cole wasn't sure. Now he understood why Birch was twitchy about the director's behavior. Quade had been too enraged, too determined to have Abby.

The moment Quade disappeared, their tight cluster relaxed. Ethan retreated to lean against the wall. The lion hated leaving his back vulnerable. Birch took his normal position at the front of the room—facing their band of psychotic mongrels. Cole flopped into his seat and tipped his chair back until he balanced on two legs once more.

Quiet reigned for a little while, each of them focused on their own bullshit, and finally Cole decided to get the conversation going. "Anyone wanna address the missing werewolf in the room?"

Ethan grunted, gaze on his cell phone. The lion was

obsessed with some crop-growing, money-sucking game. Grant echoed the sound, his mouth full.

And Birch...He got a text message. A low *ding* shot through the room and drew their attention. Birch didn't give his cell phone number out, which meant he sure as hell didn't get text messages. Except, apparently, he did.

"Ooh, Birch has a girlfriend..." Grant singsonged, then chuckled.

Cole just shook his head. "Birch is gonna rip your head off your neck if you make fun of his girlfriend."

"Children. You're all fucking children." Birch rolled his eyes and tapped on his phone's screen.

"Yo, Grant." Ethan looked up from his game. "How come you didn't know Birch had a girl? You can't find Declan or his kitty. Now you didn't know about Birch's piece on the side. What the fuck good are you?"

"Asshole." Grant put his sandwich aside, which meant the wolf was *pissed*. "I wasn't the one who let Declan wander off with my untagged car."

Cole grinned. It was always fun to watch the puppy and kitty go at it, and he had a front-row seat.

Until Birch sighed and stomped between the two men. "Can we *not*?" The team alpha pushed against Ethan's chest and then Grant's. "We got shit to do. Like find Declan."

"Grant tried. He failed," Cole called out, all helpful and shit.

Birch's phone *ding*ed again, but the bear's dark gaze didn't turn to the device. It settled heavily on Cole. "Fortunately, I have my own resources."

CHAPTER NINETEEN

Watching Declan pack supplies, his mood darkening with his every movement, Abby decided their plan was bad. Perhaps the worst plan ever known to plandom.

A *better* plan was to remain in Declan's hidey-hole and come up with a new one. One that didn't involve leaving said hidey-hole.

Ever.

Not because she wanted to be locked up with Declan—that'd just be a bonus—but because she was pretty done with risking her life.

"Abby?" His voice wasn't loud, but she felt it all the way to her toes. It danced along her nerves and plucked each one, making her even more aware of Declan as a man—as a prospective *something*.

The cougar thought that *something* might start with the letter "m" and possibly end with "ate." The cat didn't care about his past.

"You ready?" His steps were silent, but she could almost *feel* him moving, sense when he drew closer. Then he stood in front of her, six feet of muscular male dressed in black from head to toe. Dark. Foreboding. Dangerous. Deadly. She had to remember he was very, very deadly.

"Yeah. Sorry I didn't answer right away. I'm ready."

"Something wrong?" He stepped closer, his large presence overwhelming her. He drew even nearer and lifted his hands, cupping her cheeks in his scarred palms. Amber eyes stared into hers, searching her gaze for something. What?

"I'd tell you we can wait," he murmured.

"But we can't." Abby pulled away and turned her attention to finishing her preparations. She snatched the jacket he'd given her and kept her gaze down while she tugged on the black coat. "It's fine." She straightened the fabric, smoothing out the wrinkles. She did anything to avoid looking at him. Anything to avoid getting caught by his intense gaze once more. "I'm ready. Let's go."

Declan tilted his head to the side, eyes narrowed, and she forced herself to remain immobile. She wasn't going to squirm beneath his gaze. She wasn't going to give him any other hint of emotion.

He grunted and stepped back. "All right, then." He turned and strode back the way he'd come, his long strides putting space between them, and she did her best to keep up. "Let's do this."

Declan didn't stop until he'd reached the home's exit, two duffels bracketing the hallway while a gun rested on a nearby end table. When she joined him, she reached for one of the bags only to have him wrap his hand around her wrist—stopping her.

"I'm carrying these. The gun's for you." He tipped his chin toward the weapon.

"I don't know what I'm doing with guns."

"This"—he picked up the gun, snapped the magazine into place, and wracked the slide—"has a grip safety. If you're holding it and pull the trigger, it'll fire." His lips twitched. "Try not to hit me."

She gave him a tight-lipped smile and drawled, "Aw, you've ruined my fun already."

Declan snorted and grabbed the two bags in one hand. "Uh-huh. Just focus on shooting back at anyone who shoots at us." He glanced at her over his shoulder. "Can you do that?"

"I'm an accountant, Declan. You want me to count the number of bullets in a magazine, I will. You want me to count them as *you* shoot at people, I'll do that, too. The actual shooting and killing..." She swallowed hard and pressed a hand—her *empty* hand—to her stomach and prayed she wouldn't lose her lunch everywhere. Memories flashed; images of broken bodies and bright red blood filled her mind. So much blood. "That's not something I can handle."

He took a deep breath and tipped his head back, releasing it slowly. "If we don't get that tablet and turn it over to the SHOC director, you'll be running for the rest of your life. You'll be hunted to the four corners of the Earth, Abby. Is that how you want to live?"

She wasn't going to cry—she wasn't. The only way to avoid crying was to laugh. Even if the laughter was fake.

"Declan?"

"Yes?" He released a long, heavy sigh.

"The Earth is round."

Utter. Silence. It was as if even the house held its breath and fell quiet after her attempt at a joke. It wasn't a very funny joke in all honesty, but it should have broken some of the tension. Even a tiny bit.

But Declan remained in place, hands on his hips and face turned up to the ceiling for another dozen heartbeats before he gave her his attention once more. "Abby?"

She nibbled her lower lip for a minute and then realized

it betrayed her nervousness so she stopped. Of course, that was before she remembered he could scent her unease, but it wasn't like she could tell the cat to stop smelling up the joint.

"Yeah?"

"You're not funny." The words were flat, but the corner of his mouth had the tiniest hint of a curl.

"You think I'm hilarious," she countered, and she had no idea where the urge to tease came from. Possibly because if she wasn't laughing, she'd be crying, and wasn't that just another reason to cry?

"I think—" A low tone, the beeping soft, interrupted him, and Declan glanced at his watch. He tapped a small button and lowered his wrist, any hints of his smile gone in that instant.

"It's time." She said the words even though they both knew what would happen next.

"It's time." He nodded. "Don't shoot me, don't shoot yourself, and don't get shot."

"It sounds so easy." She fake chuckled.

He didn't respond. It was now or never, and never wasn't an option.

The door slid aside, letting the cool night air into the home. The air and something else. Something small and metal that bounced off the door's steel frame. It *ping*ed— *several* things *ping*ed—one after another and another, and it took Abby a moment to register what was happening.

And then she did. The bad guys who were supposed to shoot at them as they were *chased* through the streets decided to cut out the chasing aspect.

They were right outside, and they'd skipped straight to the shooting.

CHAPTER TWENTY

*F*uck him sideways with a barbed-wire-wrapped baseball
bat. Shit was hitting the fan *now*. Not later.

Another bullet slammed into the door's frame, then rico-
cheted and embedded itself in the drywall-covered concrete
of the home's entryway. That was followed by another and
another, the attackers doing their best to hit him and Abby.

Declan's wolf howled and barked, its fury palpable. The
beast pushed and shoved at Declan's mind, demanding to be
released. It wanted to hunt, kill, the ones who dared attack. Not
because it was worried about its own ass. No, the beast was furious about the threat the attackers posed to Abby.

Unacceptable.

The stink of gunpowder filled the air, his animal picking
out the scent. He drew in a deep breath, sorted through the
wispy smoke and dust, and tried to identify their attackers.

The beast helped, adding its abilities to his human nose,
and then the truth hit him.

"It's UH," he snarled, fangs pushing free of his gums
with a renewed wave of rage and fury.

"Unified Humanity?" Abby's voice trembled, and he
spared her a glance. He didn't spy any wounds, which
meant the shaking came from fear, not pain.

"Yes." Declan grabbed the nearest bag and withdrew several guns, laying them out carefully on the floor. He checked the magazines and chambered a bullet in each one.

"How did they find us? I thought you said no one knows about this house."

Yeah, he knew what he'd said, and he was going to make sure he left one of the fuckers out there alive long enough to get the truth out of him. Then he'd put a bullet right between the asshole's eyes.

"I did. They don't."

"So how—"

Declan took a deep breath and swallowed the snarl that threatened to break free. It wasn't Abby's fault. "I don't know, but I will. Just as soon as I get my paws on one of them."

He holstered his weapons, sliding them into place with practiced ease, but they were all backup to his preferred method—claws. He formed tight fists with his hands and then relaxed the fierce grip. Fingertips blackened, the wolf's claws in place while the beast also altered their shape. Bones cracked and muscles stretched, rearranging so they'd become the perfect hand-to-hand killing machines.

Fur slid over skin, dark gray with shots of silver. The transition was so fast the sting of the change didn't register before it was complete. Now his two-legged form would fully blend with the night, black clothes and the animal's hues making him disappear in the shadows.

His shoulders broadened, the fabric of his shirt stretching to accommodate the increased breadth. That was followed by a bump of strength to the rest of his body, the beast adding its power. It was anxious to have their attackers' blood on its paws and flowing down its throat.

The wolf hungered for death, for destruction, for the

cries of his prey and the sound of their begging in his ears. Their fear already teased his nose, the delicate hints of terror drifting to him on the gentle winds that passed through the open door. They attacked, but were afraid.

They should be.

Another wave of fear assaulted him, the stench greater than the others, more concentrated and piercing and... coated in a blanket of near-panicked feline.

The beast happily took joy in the terror of others, but not Abby. Never Abby.

Small changes complete, Declan turned his focus to her. She cowered on the opposite side of the doorway, back pressed to the wall and the nine-millimeter handgun clutched between her breasts. She was shaking with terror.

He wanted to go to her, reassure her, but that would have to come after this was done. He waited for a lull in the shooting and whispered to her, "Abby." Once he had her undivided attention, he issued orders. He was asking a lot of her, but there wasn't anyone else around. "I'm going out there."

She shook her head, her hair whipping through the air with her speed. He countered that with a sharp nod. "Yes, I am. And you're going to lay cover fire." He tipped his head toward the gun in her arms. "You don't have to aim. Just make sure you don't hit me."

"No." She mouthed the word, any sound lost to the renewed flurry of shots.

"Yes. Nonnegotiable. You're going to lay cover." He cracked his neck and rolled his shoulders, loosening up before he got to what he did best—killing. "I'm going to slip outside. I'll let you know when it's safe to come out."

"What if they catch you and force you to yell for me and then—"

Declan's lips twitched, and he managed to swallow the laugh threatening to break free. "Not happening."

"They could—"

"Sweetheart," he murmured, liking the way some of her fear bled away just a little too much. "There's no killing me. I've been hunted, battled, and bled almost dry and I'm still here. They're nothing."

Her lower lip trembled. "Is that like the old 'I had to walk to school in the snow uphill both ways' thing?"

"No." He shook his head. He had to give it to her. Scared out of her mind and she still tried for a joke. "It's the 'when I was fifteen I killed my alpha' thing."

Not exactly the way he'd wanted to reveal all that—fuck it, he hadn't wanted to talk about it at all—but the shit was there.

He tipped his head toward their attackers. "Empty the magazine and then hide in here. I'll be back in a few minutes."

Her face paled, eyes widening. Fuck, he hated seeing her scared. "A few..."

"Shoot, Abby." He growled the words, adding a curl to his lip to expose a single fang. The threat was clear, the push one that she needed no matter how much he disliked the action.

She straightened away from the wall and rose to her knees. She changed her hold on the weapon, carefully wrapping her hands around the grip before she gave him a firm nod. "Okay."

Declan grunted. "Good girl."

He focused on the exterior, his wolf's vision making it easy to pick out the location of their attackers. They hid within the brush, trees acting like cover for them. They didn't realize the cover was for *him*. Each bush and tree was positioned exactly as he desired so that attack—retribution—was easy.

"Go." He bit off the word and she reacted, peeking around the edge of the door and squeezing the trigger.

Pop. Pop. Pop. He counted each of her bullets, timing his actions based on how many she had left. Even with an extended magazine, he had only sixteen rounds—fifteen in the mag and one in the chamber—to get the job done.

The first was easy, a duck and then roll followed by a leap that put him behind attacker one. A snap of his neck and Declan slowly lowered the body to the ground.

Second required a little climbing, a shimmy up a tree—each movement precise and perfectly balanced so he didn't upset the massive pine. That man ended up with a broken neck as well, a sharp twist doing the job.

Pop. Pop.

Abby still shot into the dark, and Declan moved to the next target. He swung to the ground and landed in a low crouch. He crept through the blackness, his beast allowing him to see and sense the ones who meant Abby harm. Sure, they probably wanted to kill him, too, but he wasn't concerned about himself. Whatever happened, he'd live. He was too evil to die since the devil would just kick his ass back when he appeared in hell.

A soft crackle, the spit of a radio, came from his right, and he changed course. Low whispers drew him forward, two men arguing over something. It didn't matter. Only their deaths mattered.

He moved until he stood no less than three feet from the two men, a whispered exchange joining the sounds of Abby's shots.

Declan took advantage of their distraction. He darted forward, his movements quick and fluid. His wolf howled in excitement, the beast already prepared to revel in what was to come. He reached for the man on his left, half-shifted fingers curled and nails ready to pierce flesh. His claws sank deep into his opponent's throat.

With his right, he grasped the back of the male's neck and held him captive for a moment. Only long enough to finish killing his friend. Then he snapped the second man's neck with a quick wrench.

Two more down, four total.

Not enough.

He tipped his head back and scented the breeze, the animal searching beyond the scents of death that surrounded him. The wolf identified two others. It'd been a six-man team sent after them.

He ducked through the brush, tasting the air and following the low sounds that came from the shadows. The rustle and snap of twigs and leaves acted like a beacon for his wolf.

He remained silent, letting Abby's shots mask his movements and taking advantage of the men's inattention. They worried about getting shot. Declan worried about how long it'd take him to kill the last two. He wasn't sure how UH had found him, but if those idiots had figured out his location, SHOC wasn't far behind. If they were behind at all. Were they just waiting to see if UH would do the job for them?

The snap of a branch cut through a lull in the fight and he turned left, heading back toward the entrance to the bunker. To his left and then a hint right. Clouds parted to reveal the moon, and he spied his quarry. He wasn't carrying a handgun like the others. No, he had a rifle, one braced and ready to be fired—at Abby.

One hand went to the barrel, and Declan yanked the gun

out of the man's grip while his other hand...He reached around his neck, sank his claws in deep, and jerked, filling his palm with flesh and blood once more.

Which left him with one target—one last human intent on getting to Abby.

Declan focused on the sounds surrounding him, the ones that slipped through his body and reverberated in his bones. Except he didn't have to be careful or cautious. Not when Abby's shots came one after another, hardly a pause in between. Not when her piercing scream accompanied the sounds. Another weapon fired just as quickly, the source of the shots moving through the forest.

"Declan!" Pure panic that was more than just fear or terror. It delved into his soul and nearly wrenched him inside out with the unending need to be with Abby.

He didn't think about himself or the dangers he faced by revealing his position. He broke into a dead run, dodging and ducking trees and branches, leaping over low bushes and sliding across the leaf-strewn ground. He didn't slow and his steps didn't falter when he burst past the tree line. In fact, he doubled his speed, the scene before him spurring his wolf to move faster, run harder.

A human male stood above Abby, dressed in black and with weapons strapped to his body. Declan didn't care about what he wore, only about what he held.

A gun.

Pointed at Abby.

And then it fired.

CHAPTER TWENTY-ONE

*B*eing shot *sucked*. It sucked more than being chased by a killer whale, and Abby actually *had* been chased by a killer whale, followed by a polar bear and *then* a bull moose once. That had been a bad day.

Plus, she hadn't even been allowed to hurt the guy who'd shot her, dammit. The least Declan could have done was leave the guy breathing long enough for her to shoot him back. Or kick him in the balls. Or even better, *both*.

Both sounded good.

"You'll have to get over it. He's already dead." A tug and tear of cloth followed Declan's words, and she turned her attention to the partially shifted wolf doing his best to do . . . something.

"Huh?"

"You can't shoot him or kick him in the balls." He paused and shrugged. "Well, you could, but he wouldn't feel anything."

"What are we talking about?" She frowned and squinted, trying to follow the conversation, but things weren't going that well. Stuff looked very fuzzy.

"Abby, focus on me, okay?" Another tear of cloth and he jiggled her leg.

"I am focusing— *Holy fuck what are you doing?*"

Now she remembered. Before she'd gone off with her violent thoughts, she'd been shot. It seemed Declan's method of fixing her was to cut her fucking leg off.

"I'm not cutting your leg off," he growled, the deep rumbling more calming than threatening. Even his amber-hued glare soothed her ragged nerves. "I'm making sure you don't die."

"Dying would be bad," she murmured. "This hurts really bad. More than the other time I got shot."

Hurt didn't describe the burning sensation, the fire in her blood, and the scrape of nails inside her skull. She'd bitch about her cat attacking her, but the feline was in just as bad a shape as her human side.

"Well, yeah. Poison bullets will do that," he drawled.

"I don't like that you're not more upset about this." And no, she couldn't keep the grumbling growl out of her voice.

"Sweetheart." A single finger beneath her chin lifted her head. When had it fallen forward? "I wish I could bring them all back so I could kill them again. Slowly. Painfully. They hurt you, and my wolf is fucking pissed that I can't return the favor." His eyes were all wolf—no hint of his human mind lurking in the background. "I'm very, *very* upset."

"That's nice." She liked that he cared. Liked it more than she should since as hot as Declan might be, he wasn't for her. No matter how loud the she-cat yowled.

"Yeah," he drawled. "Nice."

He pushed to his feet and she just sat there, staring up at six feet of hunky werewolf. So much power, so much dominance. She wanted to lick him all over.

"Baby, you can do whatever you want to me once I get you patched up and safe."

Ugh. *Baby*. And apparently, she'd said that aloud. Nice. "I don't want to do anything to you."

Liar.

"Liar." Declan echoed her thoughts. He had to be some kind of voodoo magician to read her mind that way. He sighed and shook his head. "Let's go."

"Go where?"

He ran a hand down his face and sifted his fingers through his hair. "You need medical attention."

He tipped his head toward her leg, and she turned her attention there as well.

"Huh. There's a hole in my leg." She looked to the large werewolf. "Did we know there's a hole in my leg?"

"Yes, we did."

"Oh." When had that happened? She glanced at her surroundings. Oh. Right. Dead people. Guns. *Pop*. "Are we going to fix it?"

"Does it hurt?" Declan answered her question with a question.

"No." She shook her head, and he groaned.

"The poison is making it hard for your cat to do its job, and shock is settling in. We need to get you out of here. Lift your arms. I'm going to pick you up and you need to hold on."

"I don't think—"

Declan didn't let her think. He only let her feel. As in, feel his arm sliding beneath her legs while the other went around her back. Then there was the feel of being lifted. And the feel of his tightening grip. And the feel of his fingers very, very close to the *hole in her leg*.

A scream rocketed up her throat, threatening to break free and dive right past her lips, but her cougar snarled at her to be quiet. Abby would show the cougar being fucking quiet, the little she-bitch.

But she understood the point the animal tried to make, which was why she didn't scream. Instead, she turned her head and sank her teeth into Declan's shoulder. Fabric filled her mouth, his scent filled her nose, and his taste crept past the cloth to dance over her taste buds.

Declan grunted but didn't say a word. He simply turned and strode off into the dark with her cradled in his arms. Each jarring step sent a jolt of pain along her spine, but it disappeared as quickly as it arrived.

Shock was a beautiful, beautiful thing.

"It's not beautiful," he growled.

"Makes it not hurt," she mumbled, and leaned her head against his shoulder.

"Hurting reminds you that you're alive."

Abby snorted. "I don't need the reminder."

She'd never forget that she lived while others had died.

"Who died?"

Okay, she *didn't* like that shock made her say all her thoughts out loud. "No one."

Everyone.

"Abby—"

"How come I didn't go into shock the first time I got shot? Would have made the swim easier." By, like, a lot.

Declan shrugged in answer. "Who died?"

Abby shrugged. If it worked for him, it could work for her. She didn't want to answer his question. "What kind of poison is in me?"

"We're coming back to who died." His glare came to rest on her shoulders, heavy and determined.

They'd never get back to it if she had her way. "I can't go to the hospital."

He snorted. "I didn't survive this long by making stupid decisions."

"That house was stupid." She closed her eyes and groaned, burying her face against his shoulder. "I'm sorry. That was mean."

"I don't know how they found us, but I will find out before this is over. I'm also going to get a whole new set of fucking safe houses after I blow up the current ones." The growl in his voice told her he wasn't joking. "And it isn't mean if it's the truth." Something soft and sweet brushed her temple. Declan's lips? Nah. "The answer to your question—we're going to see a dead man."

For some reason that tickled her. It made her smile and giggle. She released his shoulder and waved at the darkness behind them. "There's a dead man back there."

"Six."

"Six what?"

"There are *six dead men* back there."

"Oh." She stared at his profile, the strong length of his nose and the small bump. She kept her eyes on the carved edge of his strong jaw. She also observed the tension in his muscles when he clenched his teeth. "You killed six?"

He shrugged. "More like five and a half. You got a few shots into the sixth. He would have bled out. I just nudged things along."

Abby's stomach lurched and she swallowed hard, fighting to keep her nausea at bay. "I killed..."

"Would have killed, but didn't." His steps slowed, and he nudged her forehead with his chin. "Hey." She tipped her head back and met his intent stare. "None of that blood back there is on your hands. It's all me, understand? This is my world and those stains are on my soul, not yours."

Her chin wobbled and tears stung her eyes, tears wholly unrelated to the hole in her leg and tied to the one in her heart.

"You hear me?" His yellow eyes were intent, the moon's dim glow reflecting off the beast's gaze.

"I ..." she whispered, and he glared at her, the wolf's anger prodding at her while he waited for her agreement. "I hear you."

Declan grunted. "Good."

He returned to his trudge through the woods, his pace even and measured as he traveled the randomly winding path.

"Declan? Where are we going?"

"Can you just go back to quietly dying for a little while?" he snapped at her, and she met his annoyed stare with a glare of her own.

"Well, excuse me for breathing, asshole."

He continued stomping through the underbrush until they came to a long stretch of barren road. Lights shined in the distance, a low glow that acted like a beacon—luring them onward.

Curiosity got the better of her and she spoke. "Is that where we're going?"

"That's where we're stealing a car."

"A nice car?" She raised her eyebrows. "Like a luxury car or something?"

"Want to ride in stolen class, baby?"

She didn't even flinch at the endearment anymore. Her heart simply turned in on itself, shrinking smaller and smaller each time. "No. It's just ... If someone has an older car that needs to be fixed up, then maybe that's all they can afford. If the person has a super-expensive, fancy ride, they might have better insurance or more disposable income."

"A thief with a conscience?"

"Stop laughing at me and let's steal a car already," she snapped.

He chuckled. "Yes, ma'am."

Declan carried her closer and closer to the distant light. His breathing remained even, and there was no hint that he grew tired. Soon they reached the source of the lights and he lowered her to the ground in a shadowed corner of the parking lot.

"You good?"

Abby nodded even though she was very, very not good. The shock had worn off and the pain returned, the pounding of her heart a physical throb in her thigh.

"Good. Stay put. I'll be right back with a *fancy* car."

"And the owner doesn't have kids," she rushed out. "Or anyone ill in their family." She nibbled her lower lip. "And they can't be ill either because—"

Rough fingers came to rest against her lips. "I'll get a car from someone who will be mildly annoyed by the inconvenience but it won't cause a major disruption in their lives, okay?"

Abby nodded once more, lips sliding over his scratchy skin.

"Good. Give me five minutes."

Five minutes to steal a car. She wondered how long it'd be before they met with the man who was supposed to be dead. Then she wondered if maybe Declan had been shot and he was caught in the grasp of shock and poison, too. Maybe he thought they were going to see a zombie?

No. She mentally shook her head. She hadn't scented his blood—only her own. She was the one off her rocker.

Headlights nearly blinded her, wrenching her from her thoughts, and she focused on the world around her once more. The world that included a vehicle slowly approaching. One with Declan behind the wheel.

And—once he had her settled in the passenger seat—

a deep breath told her it wasn't owned by a parent, the owner didn't have an ill relative, *and* the owner was in good health.

Once she was done sorting through the scents in the small space, she turned a wide smile on Declan. That wide smile even remained in place for a little while.

At least until he spoke. "I even checked his insurance card. We can total it and he'll be fine."

CHAPTER TWENTY-TWO

Stealing a car from a gas station wasn't the smartest move, but it was the quickest way to get them from *point A* to *Point Kicking in Pike's Door*. One quick car ride later and they'd traveled from Declan's safe house to the center of Port St. James.

He cradled Abby in his arms, her breasts pressed to his chest, and he pretended not to notice how good it felt to hold her close.

The wolf noticed. The wolf liked it—*a lot*—even if she was a feline and their pups might spit up the occasional hairball.

Fuck that. There wouldn't be hairballs because there wouldn't be pups.

The wolf wanted to know how it felt to be delusional.

Declan nudged the wolf back and returned his attention to caring for Abby. He'd only been half joking when he'd mentioned totaling the car, but he'd settled for abandoning it a few blocks from Pike's place. Shitty part of town filled with shady people who wouldn't report anything to the cops. Or at least wouldn't make a call until they'd stolen what they wanted from the vehicle.

They wouldn't mention a man all in black carrying a

giggling woman down the street, either. And how Abby managed to laugh with a bullet embedded in her thigh he would never know. It did beat tears, though. Man, he couldn't take a woman's tears.

Declan strode up Pike's crumbling sidewalk—cracked, coated in black mold, and overtaken by weeds. He didn't slow his approach when he reached the two low stairs that led to Pike's poor excuse for a front porch. He skipped both, placed his right foot on the edge of the concrete slab and his left... well, it came up and he drove the heel of his boot into the steel-coated panel, just to the right of the knob, and the door jolted inward with a resounding *crack*.

Declan stepped back and ducked, waiting for what was to come next. Two low *pop*s and *thud*s immediately followed, bullets striking the doorframe where he'd stood only moments before.

"Anybody dead?" Pike called out, and Declan rolled his eyes.

"If I were dead, could I tell you?" he drawled, and stepped into sight, ducking once more when the other man took another shot. "Dammit, Pike."

Abby decided it was a good time to laugh and released a tinkling series of chuckles. "He shot at you."

Declan turned his attention to the woman in his arms, her glazed eyes and flushed face pointed in his direction. "Yes, he did, but it's not funny."

She snuggled close, rubbing her cheek on his chest, and released a soft sigh. "Okay."

Damn she wasn't doing good. Her quick agreement and the sensuous way she lay against him made him wonder just what kind of shit was in that bullet.

"Declan?" That familiar deep rasp came from within the run-down house.

"Who else has the balls to break down your fucking door, asshole?" he snarled, and stepped into the dark home. "Turn on a fucking light."

Pike just snorted and hit a switch, a soft *snick* preceding a flare of brightness. A gold glow fell across the space, illuminating Pike's living room.

"Cleaner than I expected," Declan murmured.

No pizza boxes or take-out containers. Then he turned his attention to the other man. Declan expected to see long hair, scruffy bristles on Pike's face, and his ever-present bottle of beer in hand. Even if shifters had a helluva time getting drunk, it didn't mean Pike didn't try. Hard.

Except this version of Pike was clean-cut, freshly shaved, and clutching a soda instead of alcohol.

"What happened to you?"

Pike lifted a single brow. "What happened to you?" He waved a hand toward Abby. "And who's that?"

Right. He wasn't there to check in on Pike. He had a different—more important—purpose.

"I've been shot at a lot, and this..." He tipped his head toward the woman in his arms.

"I'm Abby." She breathed deep and huffed out the breath, her breathing growing more difficult the longer that bullet stayed inside her. "I actually got shot. Twice."

Fur, shades of gray that ranged from near black to the lightest brush, slid forward to replace Pike's skin, while his eyes flashed bright amber, and Declan wondered if he'd end up fighting someone else instead of helping Abby.

Except as quickly as the man's beast had rushed forward, it withdrew, retreating into Pike's human shape. "Sorry." He cracked his neck. "I'm good."

"He's not a fish." The softly whispered words drifted through the room. "He should be a fish."

Pike's anger over Abby's injury vanished, replaced by a dark glare. One she didn't see because she'd closed her eyes, more of her weight resting against him.

"I'm tired, Declan."

He ignored Pike and focused on Abby, pressing his lips to the crown of her head. He drew in her scent—not because he needed her flavors to fill him more than he needed air. No, he needed to know how far the poison traveled, how firm a hold it had on her body.

Too hard. Too much.

"I know, sweetheart. Let's get you patched up, and then you can sleep."

"But not in the water? Don't wanna sleep in the water."

"Not in the water." He had no idea where she'd come up with that, but he'd promise her the world to keep her happy.

"Because that's where fish sleep."

"And Pike's not a fish." He refused to look at Pike, but there was no way he could suppress the smile that leaped to his lips.

A rolling growl slid through the room, Pike's annoyance a physical thing within the space. Declan opened his mouth, ready to counter the growl with a snarl, but Abby beat him to it in her own way.

"Shhh, Mr. Not-Fishy. Good puppies don't growl." She even lifted her hand and petted the air as if a dog were within reach.

"Declan..." Pike's annoyance slammed into him, but Declan didn't have the strength to censure Abby. Not when her face paled even more and her breathing transitioned from slow and easy to rapid and uneven.

"Need a room and your kit, Pike. She's got a poisoned bullet in her thigh that needs to come out."

Pike glared at him, then her, and then Declan once more. "I'm not a fucking hospital."

"Like I could take a damned cougar to a hospital?" Declan strode deeper into the room. "Tell me where I'm going or I'll lay her on the first bed I find." He let his wolf come forward. "Then I'll tear you—and this place—apart until I find what I need."

Pike rolled his eyes. "When'd you become such a bitch over a woman?"

"About twenty-four hours ago." Really, four days ago. The first time he'd watched her shake her ass.

Pike shook his head. "This way."

He led Declan down a nearby hall, the narrow space dark and crowded. Nice area to draw opponents and pick 'em off easy with—he lifted his attention and located the hole in the ceiling at the end of the hall—a sniper rifle. Dead before they knew Pike was near.

Pike nudged open a door. "Put her there. I'll get the supplies."

Declan strode into the room and lowered her to the narrow bed. "Abby?" He gently called her name and gave her shoulder a soft shake. "Abby, I'm going to have to cut your pants off."

"Have a headache, Declan. Maybe later," she mumbled, and patted his hand.

He just chuckled and shook his head. "Abby..."

"I have to wash my hair."

"Abby," he murmured.

"I'm not in the mood to get jiggy with it." She glared at him, the cougar staring out through Abby's eyes. "Can't you find porn like a normal guy?"

A snort came from behind him, and he glanced over his shoulder. Pike stood in the doorway, bag in hand

and smirk on his lips. "Yeah, Dec, can't you watch porn?"

"Shut up, asshole, and give me the bag." He curled his lip—exposing a fang—and held out his hand. The moment the handle rested on his palm, he drew it close and laid it beside her. "And, Abby, I don't wanna fuck"—right that second—"I need to get that bullet out."

"Later though?" Glassy eyes met his, her smile so soft and sweet and tempting as hell.

"Later." His wolf howled, fucking thrilled with the idea. Horny asshole.

The beast still wasn't disagreeing.

"Okay." She turned her head and nuzzled the pillow, giving a little wiggle before she sighed and relaxed into the mattress. "Wake me when it's over."

Pike snorted. "She serious?"

Declan clenched his hand into a tight fist and resisted the urge to punch the man in the face for laughing at Abby. *Shit*. He had it bad.

"Pike?" He was determined to remain calm until he got through this shit with Abby. Then he'd gut Pike like he *was* a fish and Declan was a bear in fucking salmon-spawning season. "Shut up and come hold her down."

Pike grunted and strolled forward, moving slow as molasses. If Declan didn't need the other wolf so much, he'd kill him.

Pike knelt on the other side of the bed and leaned forward, arms hovering above Abby's unconscious body. "Chest and knees?"

"Yeah." Guilt churned in Declan's gut. He hated what was about to happen, but it had to be done. "Hopefully I won't have to search long."

"Mind telling me why you aren't taking her to one

of your Shit Dick docs? Or why Team Fuckhole isn't here?"

Yes, Declan was going to tear Pike into tiny pieces when this was through. "It's SHOC—"

"Not Shit Dick."

"And my team will tear a hole in your ass—"

"So big and all that bullshit." Pike snorted. "You're still so easy to rile up. Didn't answer my question, though."

"We caught her. I took her." Declan shrugged. He left out the part about rescuing her from Unified Humanity first.

"Why?" Pike raised his eyebrows, and he shrugged again.

"Seemed like the thing to do at the time."

Declan decided the conversation was done and reached for Abby's pants. Instead of pulling them from her body, he simply enlarged the hole around her wound. He wasn't about to let Pike get too good of a look at what belonged to *him*. He still wasn't addressing the "belonged to him" portion of his thoughts, either.

"You ready?" He shot Pike a questioning look and waited for his nod. "Then hold her still and pray she stays out."

The first cut into her skin told him God wasn't answering their prayers. In fact, God gave him a big old "fuck off" in the shape of feline claws, pointed fangs, and long hisses that made his blood run cold.

CHAPTER TWENTY-THREE

*C*onsciousness returned slowly, Abby's mind easing awake in gradual increments. An ache encompassed her from head to toe, and the throbbing pain attempted to lure her back to sleep. But for some reason, she couldn't. There was a reason she had to open her eyes. Right?

Abby furrowed her brow, mind muddling through her body's aches on a hunt for why she couldn't just stay on the comfortable bed and hide from reality.

Reality... The word was no more than a whisper. There was a reason she still lived—a reason she hadn't died and was instead saved by a...

She furrowed her brow and murmured, "Saved by a fish?"

A low, masculine chuckle came from her left, and the gentle caress of a large hand soon followed. "Not a fish. Wolf."

Declan. She sighed in relief and something else. Something that felt like pleasure, but she'd never say that aloud. Fingers sifted through her hair, brushing strands away from her face. She turned her head and nuzzled his palm, breathing in his natural, woodsy scent. A scent that soothed the restless animal inside her.

More than restless—near panicked. The beast alternated between snarls at Abby and purrs directed at Declan with bouts of weak chuffing in between. The cat had been frightened—more than frightened—by her injury.

Injury?

"I was..." With those two words, Declan pulled away from her, his touch retreating, and she whined. *She*—Abby—not the cougar. Her body cried out for him. Even weakened by her wound, she wanted Declan close—touching her, surrounding her. "No." She lifted her arms—or tried to. Fabric held her captive, her body so weak she could hardly toss off a sheet. "Don't go."

She didn't care if she sounded needy, like a child desperate for comfort. His scent, his presence, soothed whatever invisible rough edges continued to cut into her body and soul.

"Easy," he soothed, palm returning, fingers rubbing small circles on her skin. "I'm right here."

Abby purred—*purred*—and nuzzled him. She rubbed her cheek on his rough palm and fought against the sheet until she could half roll toward him. An ache bloomed in her thigh, but it was nothing compared to the pain she'd experienced shortly after being...

"I was shot." She breathed deep and released the air with a soft sigh. "You killed everyone?" She kept her eyes closed, but raised her brows with the question. Declan grunted, and she took that as his agreement. "Then you stole a car?"

He snorted. "An expensive car that didn't belong to a single parent or a person who had someone ill in their life. You were also happy that they had good insurance."

She quirked her lip in a half smile at his annoyance. It sounded like her. Even shot, she worried about others. "It's fuzzy after that."

She ceased nuzzling Declan but kept her cheek rested on his hand. But just because she stopped moving didn't mean he did. His thumb traced circles on her cheekbone, the touch gentle and sweet, even though she knew how quickly his hands could kill.

"I'm surprised you remember that much." His words were soft. "More surprised that you're awake."

"Take a licking and keep on swimming." Old wounds, old emotional pain and agony, pushed forward with that memory. "'Cause if you're not the winner, you might be dinner."

He stiffened. *"What?"*

Abby pried one eye open and considered that a victory. She'd worry about the other one in a minute. Specifically, after she'd stopped Declan from wolfing out. She got one arm free and reached for him. Weakness dragged her down, and the farthest she got was his forearm. She'd aimed for his face, but any amount of skin would work.

"Shhh . . . It's a herd joke."

"A *what* joke?" She felt—rather than heard—his growl. It vibrated through him, encompassing his body, and soon the tremble filled her as well.

"Seal shifter herd. Did SHOC do any research on me?"

He slowly nodded. "Yeah, but—"

She shrugged. "The alpha didn't have the patience to deal with a cougar in his seal herd, but if I was going to be part of the herd, I'd be *part of the herd*."

"What the hell does that mean?"

He seemed to get angrier with her every word, and the more upset he got, the more fur appeared. Dark gray fur slid free of his pores, gradually overtaking his cheeks before heading south and stretching across his shoulders.

She quirked her lips in a teasing smile. "You're sexy when you're all mad. Did you know that?"

"Abby," he snapped at her, but she didn't have the energy to be annoyed. Or afraid. She should probably fear a large wolf shifter that'd managed to kill so many men so quickly, but she didn't. Maybe tomorrow.

"Wild animals don't care if you're a shifter. Swims took us into predator territory more than once."

"I'll kill him."

"It's over." She shuddered, a hint of that old fear surging inside her. "It's over." She whispered the words to herself more than to Declan.

"Is it?" So soft, so caring. Surprising considering his past.

"Yeah." She kept her voice low. "I left and I've never been back." She had no reason to return. No family, no friends...nothing.

"Did you find a pride? Isn't that what cats do?"

"Lions do that. The rest of us are pretty solitary."

"So you've been alone."

"I've been me." She shrugged. "I've been happy."

"Liar."

She chuckled. "Maybe. But I don't have to evade killer whales."

"Just SHOC and UH," he drawled.

"But not whales." She wiggled in place and tugged on the sheets shielding her body. She got her other arm free, and the room's cool air slipped beneath the soft fabric. That was about the time she realized—"I'm naked."

"Yeah." Declan's attention pulled from her and he focused on the wall, a hint of pink staining his cheeks.

"And you're blushing?"

That earned her a glare. "You were shot and covered in blood."

Oh, right. Shot. Now she remembered. She'd let him divert her for a little while, but reality intruded once again. "Where are we? And the fish? It's dead, right? I think I remember that."

Declan shook his head. "Not a fish, a wolf. His name is Pike, and he's alive."

"That's a shitty name for a wolf."

He sighed and pinched the bridge of his nose with his free hand. "Your filter still hasn't returned." He shook his head. "He's only pretending to be dead, and his name is what he wants it to be."

"Is he on the run from the mob? Is it like witness protection?"

"Abby." He growled low. He probably wouldn't make the sound if he knew she didn't find it the least bit threatening. He'd just saved her life. He wasn't going to kill her now.

"If it's not the mob, what is it?"

"Complicated." That growl continued, his expression grim.

"Try me."

Declan ran his palm over his face and released a heavy sigh. "If I don't, will you stop asking?"

She shook her head. "No."

"It's an old story, and you need to rest." The pressure on her cheek lessened—Declan pulling away—and her cougar whined with the impending loss.

She placed her hand over his and...and did something she hadn't done for a very long time. She begged. Heartfelt, bone-deep, soul-touching begged. "Please don't leave me."

Declan's breath caught, and he froze, his blue eyes bleeding amber before turning blue once more. "I'm just going outside—"

"Please," she rasped. The last time he'd left her… "Just…talk to me. Tell me something, anything. I don't…"

I don't want to be alone.

"You don't understand how dangerous you are, do you?" He went from caressing her cheek to tracing her lower lip.

"I'm not," she whispered, the words barely audible.

"Oh, you are." He gave her a rueful grin. "You make me do things I shouldn't. Make me feel."

"There's nothing wrong with feelings." Except when she didn't want to face them. Except when she took her heartache and pain and shoved it so deep it could no longer touch her.

"Sweetheart." The startling blue of his eyes remained in place, his human half in full control. "My feelings died the day I discovered my alpha with…"

CHAPTER TWENTY-FOUR

*D*eclan had been relieved when Abby opened her eyes five hours after he'd dug the poisoned bullet out of her body. Now he wished she'd go back to sleep. If only to avoid the conversation he'd found himself dragged into.

"I discovered my alpha with..." The words were there, suppressed for so long. But releasing them meant experiencing the agony and betrayal all over again. It meant feeling claws ripping through his flesh once more.

He should keep the memories all bottled up. Should tuck them away like he'd promised and never let them see the light of day. But this was Abby, and she had him doing everything he shouldn't do. She gave him impossible thoughts and pointless dreams that didn't seem quite so pointless anymore. Maybe starting at the end was the problem. Maybe he had to go back—closer to the beginning.

"When I turned two, it became obvious I was an alpha pup." He grinned, earlier memories driving out some of the darkness that lingered. "I began organizing raiding parties for cookies and, if we got caught, jail breaks."

"You terrorized your parents."

"I terrorized every parent in the *pack*." He paused, small

smile still in place. "And when Jacob was old enough, it was the two of us causing trouble."

"Jacob?"

"My brother. He's two years younger. Not quite as strong, but smart as hell."

Annoying and bothersome with a penchant for shooting at brothers who kick down their doors.

Declan kept his hand in place, thumb brushing Abby's lower lip. He used the touch to anchor him in the present while he let his mind drift to the past.

"When I turned twelve, I started training with the alpha. I was the oldest alpha pup, and he named me as the next in line. I felt so important. Being the alpha." He shook his head. "It's supposed to be about caring for the pack. *Everything* he does is for the betterment of everyone. When he takes the oath and forms that bond with his wolves, he's driven by instinct to protect and never harm without cause."

"But?"

There was a "but" in every story. More than one in Declan's.

He released a rueful chuckle, lips quirked in a half smile. "But after three years in training I discovered that what's written in books—the stories passed from elders to pups—isn't always true for everyone."

Delicate fingers slipped through his hair, and he realized she'd changed position. She'd eased closer, pulled that sheet taut across her plump breasts, and stroked him as if he were a child in need of comfort. He didn't need comfort. He hadn't then, and he didn't now.

But maybe she needed to give it, which was why he remained still and let her brush his hair aside, sift her fingers through his strands, and caress the side of his neck.

She needed it, not him.

Right.

"I trained six days a week with the alpha. I went to school during the day, and then I went to the pack house for training—Saturday through Thursday with only Friday night to myself." He snorted, remembering the alpha's order to go out and have a little fun. *Good alphas can't lead without letting the animal have a little fun.*

His stomach clenched as he recalled how the alpha liked to have a "little fun." He breathed deep and pushed away the nausea that bubbled inside him. He had to get through the telling. She needed to understand the kind of man she touched, the kind of man she spent time with.

"I broke the rules. A girl stood me up and I was pissed, so I went to the pack house to work out. I thought I'd see if any of the guards wanted to spar to burn off my anger." He could still hear the screams. The begging and pleading.

She cupped the back of his skull and pulled, but he remained in place. "No, I need—"

"You can explain it next to me just as well as you can kneeling beside the bed. Now, c'mere."

She was right. More than being right, he simply wanted her touch. He wanted more of her and—if his wolf got its way—all of her. Even if he didn't deserve one of her smiles. He'd always taken what he wanted. He'd take her.

"Move over." The wolf filled those two words, beast rejoicing at their impending closeness.

Abby wiggled and shifted, moving until she balanced on the edge of the mattress. Before he could talk himself out of it, he crawled in beside her. But that wasn't all. He pulled her close, naked curves flush with the hard planes of his side. He wore nothing but a pair of worn jeans, which meant he could rejoice in the feel of her warmth meshing with his chest.

She rested her cheek on his chest, her warm, moist breath fanning his heated skin, and he breathed deep, drawing in her natural flavors. She was more than a naked body. More than a pain in the ass. More than ... simply more than anything—anyone—he'd ever known.

Scared the shit outta him.

Pleased the fuck outta him, too.

Declan let his hands wander, fingers ghosting over silken flesh, and he allowed himself to *feel* her body. It'd been different when she'd needed care. Now he wouldn't hate himself for exploring her.

"Tell me." It was a soft whisper, moist air caressing his chest. She lifted her hand and laid it over his heart, her soft palm covering the most broken part of him. "Tell me."

Two words. If only it were that easy.

He closed his eyes and let his touch wander, let himself trace her spine and revel in the feel of her hair sliding through his fingers. "That pack was fucked. Top down, it was fucked up." He sighed, his mind leading him back to that time. "I just never saw it because I was an alpha pup. Weaker wolves ..." He shook his head and swallowed hard. His throat wasn't clogging up. It wasn't. His eyes sure as hell weren't burning, either. "They suffered and I had no idea."

"But you did something about it." Her words were filled with unbreakable conviction. Not a hint of doubt.

"How do you know I did anything? I'm not some kind of hero who—"

She lifted her head and pressed a single finger to his lips. "We'll agree to disagree on this one."

Declan rolled his eyes and grunted, not speaking again until she was back in place. Her presence was the only thing keeping him sane while he told the screwed-up story.

"I didn't knock on the front door—just walked right on in as if I lived at the pack house already. The alpha told me to treat it like home, and I did."

He fought for air, his throat threatening to snap closed and never open again. His throat felt tight. Maybe he was getting sick. Shifters didn't catch diseases, but there was a first time for everything.

"I heard…" Declan cleared his throat. "I heard her whining before I even made it up the porch steps. I knew." He licked his lips. "I knew what that cry meant. I knew the sounds wolves made when they were scared—hurt." Could Abby hear him anymore? He could hardly hear himself talk. "I heard her, and I leaped up those steps. I rushed through that door and hunted her through the massive place."

Opulence. Marble. Hardwood floors. More than a pack needed, but the alpha had always wanted to flaunt his status.

"I found her." Declan's cheeks were wet. He'd have to tell Pike that his fucking roof leaked because he sure as hell wasn't crying. "I found her with the alpha. She hadn't stood me up. I found the strongest wolf in our pack—the alpha—*abusing* my girlfriend."

He couldn't say the words. Not the real ones.

"I died that day, Abby. Alphas are meant to…" Fuck if he was crying over this bullshit. Pike's roof leak was bad. "She was broken, bloody. He took that spark out of her eyes."

"What did you take?"

He'd never said the words. Hell, he'd never told anyone about this. He shifted their positions—Abby on her back while he lay on his side next to her. He met her stare, gaze intent.

"I took his life." Four words. He couldn't look at her while he explained the rest. Not while the wounds from that time were so fresh. "I didn't have a plan. I simply acted. The alpha tried to talk. Maybe. But I wasn't listening. He hadn't listened to her. I wouldn't listen to him. I don't even remember half of what I did."

Which was a lie. He remembered it all. Painfully. Clearly. Eternally.

"When I was done, I left that room—the pack—and never looked back." He forced himself to look at her, to meet her stare even though the wolf wanted to tuck tail and run. "Do you understand now? I don't have a heart. I don't do feelings. That part of me died all those years ago, and smiles or laughter aren't gonna bring it back."

"I don't believe that."

He snorted. "Why?"

She tucked his hair behind his ear, fingers stroking his jaw. "You protected your girlfriend. You protected me."

"I've killed people for money," he snapped. "Don't paint me with a brush coated in sunshine, Abby. I'm heartless, I don't have a conscience, and I'll happily put a bullet through someone's head for the right price."

She shook her head and lifted her other arm, her hands wreaking havoc on his senses. "You may be a killer, but that's not all you are, Declan."

"What am I? Tell me since you seem to know so much about me."

"You're mine."

CHAPTER TWENTY-FIVE

*A*bby tried not to be hurt by his snort or the derisive twist of his lips. She tried not to let his impending denial jab her in the heart. Because it was coming. She could see the shift of emotions in his features, the change in his eyes. He'd deny her, and maybe that was for the best.

His first killing...after what the girl had been through...was justified. More than justified in her opinion. But the deaths since then. They tore at her, grabbed her arms and pulled her in two.

"Yours? You think—"

"Why'd you join SHOC? For the money?" She pushed on, not letting him respond. "The prestige?"

That mocking smile widened. "I didn't have a choice, remember? Besides, it's a tax write-off. My little bit of charity work to offset my freelance income."

"You're trying to push me away."

"You pushed yourself away," he countered. "You asked me if I killed parents. Asked if I left orphans scattered around the world. I did. I do. That hasn't changed." He chuckled and shook his head, but she kept her hands in place, fingers caressing his skin and his soft hair. "That'll never change. I freelance when I'm not busy with SHOC.

Sometimes I manage to sneak in a job or two while we're on a mission."

She *had* pulled away from him. She'd built up a nice brick wall between them, but her cougar...her cougar wanted it gone. The animal saw the heart of Declan's beast and judged him as worthy. Worthy of what, she wasn't sure and wasn't ready to know. Not...not yet.

"How do you pick them?" She stroked his jaw, rough scrape of his scruff replaced by his wolf's soft fur.

"Huh?"

"How do you pick your jobs? How do you decide who you'll kill and who you won't? Do you accept every assignment tossed your way?"

"What does it matter?" He shot the words at her, harsh and fast.

"Tell me." She pleaded with him with her eyes, silently begging him to answer. In her heart, she knew what he'd say, but she needed the words. "Disgruntled housewives? Angry business partners? Scorned lovers? Who do you choose? How do you choose?"

With each question, his breathing increased, his lungs heaving. He collapsed forward, forehead resting on hers, his eyes closed. She shut hers as well, simply *being* with him in that moment.

Abby wrapped her arms around him, crossing them behind his neck and holding him tightly. He wouldn't escape her, not until he lanced the wound and let it out.

"Tell me." Her lips gently brushed his as she released the words.

"Evil. I go after evil." A drop of wetness fell to her cheek, a single bead that hit her skin and slid down her face. A tear—Declan's tear. "I attack and destroy it until nothing is left. That means that sometimes kids suffer. Sometimes they lose parents they might have loved in their own way, but those people..." He shuddered, and she tightened her hold. "They needed killing."

His lashes brushed her eyelids as he opened his eyes, and she did the same, meeting his intent blue stare. "Do you understand now?"

So many questions in his gaze. So many emotions that flickered through eyes the color of the sky. This wasn't the wolf's pain, but the man's, and she understood.

"Yes," she whispered, and arched her back, straining upward until her lips caressed his. Just a hint of a touch, a barely there stroke that she felt all the way to her core.

"Abby," he murmured against her mouth, and a new tension overcame his body. "We can't. You were just—"

"Kiss me, Declan. Just kiss me." She'd start with a simple kiss.

She sensed his indecision, a struggle inside that made him tremble. A tiny, nearly imperceptible shake, but one she felt nonetheless. She practically shouted in triumph, but swallowed the yell. Instead, she stretched her neck and pulled on his once again, bringing their mouths back together.

He slipped his tongue into her mouth, delving deep and exploring her with a single sweep. Their tongues twined, strokes and caresses mimicking what they desired most.

And they both desired.

Her pussy ached, growing hot and slick with every beat of her heart. He surrounded her and filled her, his scent and taste enveloping her in an arousing cloud of need.

Declan's cock hardened against her hip. His thick length settled snuggly to her curves. His warmth passed through the layers of fabric separating them, the sheet and his boxer briefs shielding the proof of his desire. He rocked his hips and she shifted hers, giving him a hint of friction, and he moaned into her mouth.

Abby wanted to give him pleasure, to give him everything. She wanted that thick hardness between her thighs, sliding against her moist slit and then sinking deep inside her. She wanted his passion. She wanted it all.

Her thighs parted slightly as her body silently pleaded for more. She ran her hands over Declan's back, stroking his skin, touching every part of him she could reach. But it wasn't enough. It'd never be enough.

Abby pulled away from his mouth, separating their lips just long enough to...

"Declan." She breathed his name against his lips, forming the word before delving into their kiss once more.

What they'd shared before had been heated passion, but this went so much deeper. This was simply *more*.

She tugged on him. Craving more contact, she ignored the twinge in her leg. "Declan, please."

"Abby," he rasped, and she met his now-amber eyes. "We can't. I want..." He shuddered, a ripple of gray dancing over his shoulders. "But I'm not that big of an asshole."

Abby slipped her hand between them, smoothed it down the flat planes of his stomach and didn't stop until she reached the proof of his desire.

"Fuck." He shuddered so hard the bed shook and his length twitched against her palm.

"Please," she murmured against his lips. "Just this. I need..." So bad, so much, she thought she'd lose her mind.

"You're gonna kill me." The words were rough, almost angry, but his touch was gentle and slow.

Careful.

The sheet was pulled aside, and suddenly Declan was above her. His hands explored her body, his legs twined with hers, and she gave him the same treatment. She traced every inch she could reach, learned the rises and falls of his carved body—the way it fit perfectly against hers.

Their mouths continued their erotic dance while they studied each other with their hands.

Still it wasn't enough. Her nipples pebbled to hard points and her core was slick and prepared for his possession—but it wasn't enough to push her over the edge.

She reached into his boxer briefs, inching beneath the taut fabric until her fingers brushed what she sought. She wrapped her fingers around his thickness and gave him the gentlest of squeezes. This moment was for her, a chance to simply feel evidence of his desire for her. And then...

Then she tightened her hold ever so slightly, a squeeze that drew a deep moan from Declan. From there, she stroked his thick length, gliding up and down. He groaned and growled, his hips flexing with her every movement.

At the same time, his hands drifted on, one large palm sliding down her stomach and farther south to cup her mound. He pressed, putting pressure against her folds, and she cried out for him. "Declan!"

She arched her back and rolled her hips, searching for more.

"Right here," he murmured against her shoulder, lips drifting over her skin.

She shuddered, her body moving in time with his. They both rocked their hips in a matching rhythm while they took—and gave—pleasure.

Declan slid a finger between her folds, sliding easily through her wetness until he teased her very center.

"Yes." She hissed the word.

"Abby," he rasped, the word both a question and a plea. She knew his thoughts since she had no doubt they mirrored her own.

What are you doing to me?

Please don't stop.

She didn't. He didn't. They made love—*fucked*—and yet didn't.

Whatever they did, whatever anyone wanted to call it, it still made her pant and moan with the growing ecstasy.

He circled her clit, and she let herself be swept away with the sensations. She imagined it was his mouth on her pussy, his cock sliding in and out of her sheath. Her mind drew out the fantasy, an image of her straddling Declan, his hardness stretching her core. She'd ride him, cry for him, beg him . . . come for him.

"Declan . . ." A shudder overtook her, one that didn't end when it reached her toes. No, it retraced its path, dancing along her veins and easing back up her legs. The pleasure plucked her nerves, bringing them to life with each flex and twist of muscle. She mewled and whined, needing more, but already it felt like too much.

Too much but not enough and still too much and . . . And her body was being torn apart by the bliss, pulled in a thousand directions while Declan tortured her.

And she tortured him.

She gave as good as she got, drawing and pushing them both to the precipice. It was near, just out of reach, but soon she'd jump and embrace that ultimate joy. She'd . . .

"Declan . . ." Her muscles tensed, body curling upward with the overwhelming wave of deliciousness.

"Here," he growled low, beast not man. "Give it to me."

A scream. Long and loud. It came from her very soul, the source of life and love and everything that made her Abby. Her pussy clenched around Declan's finger. And Declan...Declan stiffened and released his own sounds, a wolf's howl while he came. A wet warmth bathed her hand, proof he'd reached the pinnacle along with her.

Part of her didn't want the orgasm to end. It was too delicious, too perfect. She wanted to hold on to it—him— forever.

That single thought was followed by her cougar's purr, the cat thrilled with the idea of...keeping Declan.

Keeping Declan?

No.

But...

He...

"Abby." Two syllables. Just two syllables left his mouth, but there were so many other words hidden in his voice, hidden within his tone, in the way he said her name and the hitch in his speech. She knew what he meant because she knew *him*.

And it scared her. Down to her toes, down to her *soul*, the idea scared her.

"Perfect," he murmured, and nuzzled her neck, his damp, warm breath bathing her skin. "So perfect."

"Declan." She released his softening length and withdrew her hand. "I—"

He groaned and growled, rolling away from her in a blur of movement. She nearly whined at the loss of his touch. He returned almost as quickly as he'd left, now nude and beneath the covers at her side. The jeans were turned into a makeshift cloth to wipe away their passion before they were tossed away.

Then it was just them. In the dark together, and yet she somehow felt a little alone.

Until he pulled her into his arms. Until the deadly assassin tugged her close and gave her a gentle kiss on the forehead.

"Sleep."

CHAPTER TWENTY-SIX

*T*his time he'd kill Pike for real. He'd disembowel the asshole and leave him for the vultures.

The pounding—Pike banging on the bedroom door—came again. It'd already woken Declan, and if it pulled Abby from sleep...

Dead.

He slid from beneath Abby, stomped to the door, and wrenched it open. He didn't care about his nudity. Let the man see his dick swinging. It was what the ass got for interrupting.

Pike stood just on the other side, fist raised as if he was about to bang once more.

He glared at the other man and dropped his voice to a low growl. "Don't you fucking dare."

Pike smirked, his glance taking in Declan before flicking over his shoulder and focusing on Abby. Declan followed the other man's line of sight and spied Abby, all right. *All* of Abby.

"Nice," Pike murmured, and it was too much for Declan's wolf to tolerate. Another male looking at her? Wanting her when Declan hadn't claimed her? Not happening.

His hand transformed to wolf-like paw in an instant. He

grabbed the male's throat and pushed him back, not stopping until the other wolf struck the hallway wall with a deep *thud*.

He leaned in close, crowded Pike until hardly any space separated their bodies. His gums stung for a split second, and then he had the wolf's fangs at his disposal—long, pale, and deadly.

"You don't look at her. You understand?" Declan whispered the words, growl in his voice but still low so he wouldn't wake Abby. "You don't even think about her."

"Dec…" Pike tried to speak, but Declan tightened his hold.

"She's mine, Pike. You think of her like a brother would. You *don't* look at her like you wanna fuck her. Do you get that?" Something else stirred in Declan's blood, that midnight darkness that craved death, the bits and pieces of evil that still plagued him. It told him to finish Pike—eliminate the threat—permanently. It didn't care about their connection—their history.

Pike opened his mouth and wheezed.

"Just nod. You don't need to speak to nod."

The wolf nodded, a barely perceptible jerk of his chin.

"Declan?" Soft. Sleepy. Feminine. His. Then came the delicate patter of her feet as she left the bed and drew nearer.

Declan cracked his neck and rolled his shoulders, wolf disappearing in a rush of fur and claws.

"What's wrong? Why are you…naked?" Her husky voice rolled over him in a soothing caress, calming the animal further.

In some ways, anyway. There was a specific part of him that perked up and wanted nothing to do with calm.

Wolf gone, he released Pike and turned to face Abby.

"Pike was knocking and I didn't want him to wake you. You need more sleep. Go on back to bed." He padded forward until he filled the doorway, blocking her from Pike's view. No one got to see her like that, all sleep tussled and covered in nothing but a sheet. The white swath of fabric caressed her curves, hinting at what the cloth hid from others.

"I'll be there in a minute." Less if he just flat-out killed Pike. Which was an option if Declan could close the door. He didn't think breaking a neck in front of her would put her in the mood, and he *needed* her in the mood.

"But..." Drowsy blue eyes blinked up at him, golden tendrils of her hair falling across her face, and he tucked the strands behind her ear. "But don't we need to..."

Declan put a crooked finger beneath her chin and encouraged her to tip her head back a little more. He lowered his mouth and brushed her lips with his. It was supposed to end there, but she had to go and sigh. He tugged her closer, ready to steal a little more. He'd just—

"Ahem." A low cough followed.

Declan pulled his lips from hers and released a growl, long and low. "Mother. Fucker." He set Abby away from him and spun, facing Pike once more. "I'm gonna kill you."

The rustle of cloth told him Abby moved, repositioned herself to his right, and he eased in that direction. He didn't want Pike's last sight to be of her. Then she had to be a pain in his ass and move left.

He glanced over his shoulder at her, and his anger surged. She didn't have that sleepy, sexy look anymore. "Who's this?"

Declan sighed and ran a hand down his face. Snippets of the night, pre-orgasm, flickered through his mind. "This is Pike. You were out of it when we got here. This is his place, and he"—he shot Pike a glare that'd kill a weaker man—"is gonna leave us the fuck alone now."

"He..." Abby squinted, her gaze bouncing between them. "The dead man?"

"Yes." He kept his narrow-eyed stare on Pike.

"He looks alive." She pointed at Pike. "And a lot like you. Like you two could be..."

"Brothers," Pike purred, and Declan clenched his fist. He hadn't hauled his brother's ass around for the last fifteen years just to send his fist through the wolf's head. "Didn't Declan tell you?"

Abby's attention settled on Declan. "I thought you said his name was Jacob?"

Declan ignored Pike and turned to face Abby. "It's complicated."

"Not that complicated," Pike grumbled. "A guy fakes his own death and you act like—"

"You wouldn't have *had* to fake your own death if you'd fucking listen and stay out of shit you know nothing about, but *nooo*, you just have to—"

"Kiss my ass, Declan. You wouldn't have made it out of the last contract if I hadn't—"

"Are you fucking *kidding me*?"

"I came to tell you that Team Fuckhole is having coffee in the kitchen." Pike's attention flicked to Declan's dick and back to his face. "Put your cock away before you come out."

"You called them?" Declan snarled. "What the fuck?"

Pike shook his head and snorted. "You think they didn't know you'd end up here? They're assholes, not idiots."

"They're not taking her." He'd go through them all if they tried.

"Like I said, not idiots." With that, he turned and left,

striding down the hall as if Declan hadn't threatened to kill him, which meant that now he was alone. With Abby. Who was *naked* under that sheet.

His wolf liked the way his thoughts were headed and gave an approving chuff, wanting to cover her in his scent. But looking at her, the wide eyes, parted lips, and shock written all over her features . . . Nah, naked time wasn't in the immediate future.

"We need to get dressed," he said, and backed her into the room once again. The moment he had space, he nudged the door shut, putting that barrier between them and a bunch of bullshit he wasn't ready to deal with quite yet. "There are some clothes here. They'll be big, but at least you'll be covered."

And not prancing around in a sheet. Sun shone through the window, rays dancing over her body and revealing even more of her. The brightness made the fabric nearly invisible—the dark pink of her nipples, the dip of her waist, and those curls at the juncture of her thighs.

The rustle of fabric, a small hand on his arm . . . He'd killed men last night without a thought—he was a tough asshole—but apparently he was nothing when it came to Abby.

"Pike is your brother, Jacob, and he faked his own death?" When she said it that way, it did sound a little odd, but he didn't have time to explain. "And when he said Team Fuckhole, did he mean your SHOC team?"

"Yes to both. Put this stuff on and meet me in the kitchen."

"But will they . . . ?" She pressed a hand to her throat.

"It looks like the team is going to help deal with this." He gave her one last hard kiss. Just in case Ethan knew what'd happened to his sports car and managed to land a punch. Hurt like hell to kiss with a busted lip. "Get dressed. I'll see you in the kitchen."

Declan smacked her ass, flat of his palm curving to rub away any sting, and he couldn't help but smile at her squeak and growled "Declan."

Yeah, he smiled then, but as soon as he stepped into the kitchen and faced his team, it turned into a glare. "You assholes are gonna be fucking polite and fucking apologetic, or I'll fucking kill your fucking asses right now."

"That's a whole lot of fucking." Birch raised a single brow.

Of course Pike couldn't keep his mouth shut and snorted. "'Cause he didn't get any fucking last night."

"You piece of shit." He snarled the words and leaped. Not because he spoke the truth, but because Declan needed to work off some of his sexual frustration and Pike was closest.

CHAPTER TWENTY-SEVEN

When Abby walked into the room five minutes later no one noticed her standing just inside the long hallway, beneath the arch that separated the great room from the bedrooms. They were all too focused on Pike—Jacob, though she wasn't sure if the others knew of the brother/death fakeage going on there—and Declan rolling around on the ground. They traded punches and bites, claws occasionally flashing.

Pike delivered a hard punch with a fast right, nailing Declan's cheek, and Declan returned it with a head butt. The crunch told her he'd broken Pike's nose. She winced. That had to hurt.

Then thoughts of hurting vanished. She'd been such an idiot—so intent on following the growls and snarls—she hadn't realized what she'd be rushing *into*.

Like, a great room filled with men who she assumed were Declan's SHOC team. And her arrival? That wince? It had drawn attention.

Not from all of them. Three remained focused on the brothers trading blows, but one of them ... *He* sat at a dining table, his chair kicked back as he balanced his weight on two chair legs. His feet rested on the table's smooth top, and he had his hands linked behind his head.

A hat shielded half his face from view, but she didn't need to see all of him to *know* his gaze was on her. Dark. Intent. Heavy. A tremor slid down her spine, and she swallowed hard and took a step back into the shadows. She wished the dark would swallow her whole and hide her from his view, but it didn't.

His eyes flared brightly, a gold that remained focused on her, his stare unwavering. Cold. She shivered. Like ice—barren and emotionless. He didn't flinch when Pike and Declan crashed into the wall, sending pictures tumbling from their nails.

Everyone was at ease. *He* was not.

Everyone cheered and laughed. *He* did not.

Everyone ignored Abby. *He. Did. Not.*

Abby took a step back, and he let his weight bring the chair back to four feet.

Another step. Would any of the doors in the house hold back...? She wasn't sure exactly *what* kind of animal he was on the inside. Not a wolf—the eye color wasn't right. A big cat, then. Lion? No, the jawline and coloring didn't match one of those felines. Tiger?

Her heart raced, and adrenaline flooded her veins. She didn't know—didn't *need* to know—his species. Danger surrounded him in an invisible cloak, and her pulse doubled.

Yeah. Tiger. A tiger who was all about *her*.

The tiger rose from his chair and took a step, pausing only to speak to one of the other shifters for a split second before he was intent on her again. Intent. Determined.

"Declan?" Her voice—her whole body—trembled, but she remained stuck in place. Terror gripped her tighter and tighter as the stranger neared.

That quickly, the fight between Pike and Declan ended

and she faced two broad backs pressed shoulder to shoulder—twin wolf growls directed away from her.

"Back the fuck off, Cole." It was Declan's voice, but the growl that followed was unfamiliar, a rumbling roll so like Declan's yet not.

It was Pike. Pike threatening a tiger on her behalf—defending her just like Declan said he would.

"Aw, c'mon, Dec," the tiger mumbled, and Abby pressed up to her tiptoes to peek over the brothers' shoulders. The tiger—Cole—stood halfway between his seat and their small trio, but instead of staring at her like she was dinner…he suddenly looked anywhere *but* at her. "Just gonna talk to her a little."

Gone was the feral intensity, and in its place was over six feet of slightly embarrassed badass. The "badass" was assumed since he was one of Declan's team members, but the pink tinge to his cheeks was unmistakable.

"No, you're not," Declan countered. "Your ass is staying over there and your mouth is staying shut." She'd seen him coldly angry, deadly, but this was different. Harsher. Wilder, which made him even more dangerous. "No one's talking to her. No one's even *looking* at her. As far as the team is concerned, she doesn't exist."

Declan stepped forward, his skin now sporting more than a little gray fur and his fingers turned claw. She didn't have time to think or question what she did next. She simply went into action.

With that single step, she had enough room to slip between the brothers and move in front of the furious wolf. She blocked his path and eased closer, resting her cheek on his chest while she wrapped her arms around his waist.

"Declan. Stop." Hardly more than a whisper, but it was enough. Her presence, her voice, halted his approach. The tension remained, his body prepared to launch at Cole, but he didn't shove her aside and go after the tiger. He simply stayed in place, let her hold him captive while his beast drove him to take on the other shifter.

"Well, damn. She's like a dick whisperer or something. Stopped his cock with one word." Ethan's voice was filled with awe, his words low, but it did the job.

It broke the rising tension, popped the growing bubble of violence and deflated it with a handful of words. Declan shuddered, his muscles relaxing. His shoulders curled forward while he slipped his arms around her as well.

"Abby." His voice still held the wolf.

"I'm right here. I'm fine. I was just..." *Scared. Terrified. Petrified.* Any one of those would work. The sudden scrutiny, the intense stare... "Surprised. I was just surprised for a minute."

Declan snorted, and Pike chuckled, but Pike had to take it a step further and comment. "Your girl's not a good liar."

"Aw, man..." Grant—werewolf, if she remembered Declan's description correctly—stomped into view, whining like a five-year-old. "You already called dibs? Figures," he grumbled. "I'm stuck behind the computer and that asshole gets the girl."

Abby turned just in time to see Ethan chuck something across the room at Grant.

Grant jumped up and caught it with his mouth, then chewed. He looked toward Abby, wide grin on his lips while he chomped his food, and gave her a wink.

"Grant, you're a wolf, not a fucking dog." Yet another man eased into sight.

Grant shrugged. "I'm a man, I'm hungry, and that was food." Grant jerked his chin toward their small group and spoke to Pike. "Puppy, what else ya got? Dinner rolls ain't gonna cut it if we've got to go balls to the wall tonight."

"You guys aren't doing anything." Declan's growl was back, and she shushed him, rubbing his arm gently. "That's not working twice, Abby," he drawled. "I'm determined, not preparing to take Cole down."

It was worth a shot.

"Take *me* down?" Cole chuckled. "You're deluded if you think your scrawny, flea-bitten ass can do anything other than bark at my cat."

Declan tensed and pushed against her. "Motherfu—"

Declan wasn't "scorched earth" angry, but he *was* "annoyed seal pup who'd had his first cod snatched by his older brother" angry. And that was something Abby was qualified to handle.

"*Hey!*" she yelled. Tried to. Mostly raised her voice a little bit because in all honesty, every single shifter in the house towered over her. Declan pushed against her, his superior strength forcing her feet to slide over the carpet. Abby shoved back, but he just kept on coming. "I mean it. Stop."

Declan wasn't listening, and when she glanced over her shoulder, she spied Cole bouncing on his toes and shaking his arms, like a boxer loosening up for a fight.

"That isn't helping." She grunted and pushed against him a little harder.

"Twenty on Cole," Grant called out.

"I'll take that bet, but you're just throwing away money. Declan's got sexual frustration on his side," Ethan added.

"Forty that Declan is the first to end up with a broken bone." Even Pike joined in.

The only one who hadn't hopped into the betting game was the last stranger. He simply roared. That was it. He opened his mouth, drew in a heaving breath, and released a roar so loud it shook the house down to its foundation.

That had to be Birch, the team alpha.

The deafening sound continued, Birch's face flushed with the strength it took to silence the men with a single bellow.

Fur sprouted along his cheekbones, eyes bleeding black while his mouth cracked and reshaped to mimic his inner animal's maw. Birch bowed his back, mouth to the ceiling, and the last echoes of his roar escaped him with a final push of air from his lungs.

And then it was over...

Silence. Utter silence.

It wasn't Birch's volume or his roar—she'd grown up with wild polar bears always on the hunt for the herd— that surprised Abby. It was the reaction of the men. All of them—even Pike, and he wasn't a member of SHOC—fell quiet. More than quiet.

Her attention drifted from one agent to another, eyes touching each one and finding them all holding a similar pose—head bent, eyes down. Not so much in a show of submissiveness, but like rowdy children who'd been caught doing something they shouldn't.

Grant went so far as to kick the carpet as if he was scuffing the dirt. "Sorry, Birch."

"Sorry." Then Ethan.

Cole simply grunted, while Declan huffed. She figured that was probably the most Birch would get out of those two.

Pike snorted as if he didn't care and padded toward the kitchen. "Whatever. I'm hungry."

Yeah, he acted like he didn't care, but she saw him pause beside Birch, murmur a word or two, and then the bear slammed his hand on the wolf's shoulder.

"You got any steaks?" Grant jogged after Pike.

"You've got paws; go chase something down." Pike sounded annoyed and yet not, as if it was an old argument, a normal routine the wolves went through.

"We're going to eat and then we're going to plan," Birch stated, soft, unassuming. No growls or snarls, a simple statement that somehow got everyone moving and working toward their goals.

Food.

Then they'd hunt . . . for information.

CHAPTER TWENTY-EIGHT

COLE

Cole didn't do jealousy. If he wanted what someone else had, well, he'd take it. Or buy it.

Except staring at Abby snuggled in Declan's arms and seeing that possessive glint in his teammate's eyes...he wasn't sure the taking would be easy. As for buying... Abby wasn't the kind of chick to tuck a few hundred dollar bills in her bra and crawl onto his lap. She was sweetness and light with sharp claws and a backbone of steel.

Which made him want her even more. Dammit.

He tore his attention from the couple and refocused on whatever the hell Birch was bitching about *now*. The team plus Pike and Abby sat around Pike's scarred dining room table, arguing over who went where and did what. He hadn't exactly been paying attention. Staring at Abby's blushing cheeks was more fun than listening to growls.

"Someone remind me when I can blow shit up?" He tipped his chair back and twined his fingers behind his head. "Or at least shoot someone? I know guns are Declan's game, but I'm getting desperate for a little blood."

Birch glared at him, Ethan snickered, and Grant ignored him in favor of a steak he'd gotten *somewhere*. Declan's attention was all on Abby, and then she had to go and *giggle*. Pike's focus remained on the map spread across the table.

Cole narrowed his eyes, staring at the little puppy while he studied the map. The kid hadn't joined SHOC with his brother, Declan—at Declan's insistence—so he wasn't sure why the puppy was included in the planning session.

But he was. He stood over the city's plans, fingers tracing the shoreline.

Sure, Cole could understand why the director made Birch twitchy. He simply wondered why Pike *didn't* have the grizzly shifter on edge. Because Pike sent his tiger's senses tingling, and the cat remained uneasy the longer Pike stared at that map.

Cole turned his attention to Birch. He ignored the bear's grumbles and caught his team alpha's eyes. He flicked his focus to Pike and back to Birch, then lifted his eyebrows in question.

The grizzly pressed his lips together and shook his head, remaining silent.

Ethan snorted and leaned close. "Subtle."

He elbowed the lion. "Fuck off."

"Focus, assholes." Birch's voice cut through their joking. He didn't yell, but shouting wasn't necessary. They knew their jobs—when to settle in and when to dare Grant to shotgun a case of beer.

Birch snatched the map from Pike and leaned over the large diagram. He pointed at a small island just off the coast. "The tablet we need is hidden here on Palm Island, right, Abby?"

Abby's face paled, and she nodded like a bobblehead toy. Aw, poor kitty was afraid of the bear.

Sure, Declan tried to calm her, but Cole's tiger assured him they could do a better job. She seemed fine getting up close and personal with a psychopath. He and Abby would get along well. He simply had to get rid of Declan first. Cole's tiger purred at the idea, saliva flooding his mouth, and he kicked the cat's ass to the back of his mind.

They were brothers—not by blood, but by choice.

Fuck. He needed to get laid. He had to be able to find a nice little piece who looked all sweet and innocent like Abby. *Had to.*

Birch tapped on another area of the map. "This is the accounting firm—Ogilve, Piers, and Patterson."

"You mean O.P.P.," Ethan murmured.

"Yeah, you know me." Declan tipped his chin toward Ethan.

Grant snickered. "It'd be wrong to whip up a mix tape for the mission that began with 'O.P.P.' by Naughty by Nature, right?"

"Yes." Birch's voice was flat, face expressionless.

"Awesome." Grant snapped and then made finger guns at their team alpha. "I'll work on that once you're done ordering us to break into O.P.P. and download their servers."

Birch ignored Grant and got back to plans.

Cole decided to ignore Birch in favor of staring at Abby on the down low. Oh, he listened—mostly—so he knew he'd have to gear up and haul out around ten, but he left the other details to Grant and Ethan. Ethan did the driving and Grant handled the tech. He was only muscle and guns for this little trip.

"Everyone know what the hell they're doing?" Birch's voice rose, snaring Cole's attention once more.

"Your decision is final. You're not letting me take part in this op?" Pike's voice dropped to a low growl, the words rumbling through the room.

"Pike..." Declan matched his younger brother's growl, but the pup kept talking as if he didn't hear the wolf.

Pike stood and squared off against Birch. "Declan came to me for help. You can't—"

Well, maybe Cole would get a chance to work off his excess energy before they had to leave. There was a lot his tiger would tolerate. Like the Energizer Bunny, he'd keep going and going and going...until someone fucked with what belonged to him.

Cole didn't have a family—he had the four men around the table.

"Puppy." He rolled to his feet, his movement smooth courtesy of his cat. He placed his palms on the worn table-top and leaned forward. "You need to think real hard before you finish that thought, 'cause it sounds like you're giving my team alpha an order. But you know better than to do that, don't you?"

Amber eyes met Cole's, Pike's wolf riding the edge of the other man's control. He was a big wolf—rivaling Declan in size and strength—but Cole had the man in height and pure bulk. He didn't want to get into a fight with Pike, but he would. The team could give Birch shit, but no one else. Not unless they wanted to meet Cole's claws up close and personal.

Pike clenched his teeth, jaw flexing, and a vein throbbed in his temple, but he remained silent.

"Puppy?" Cole quirked a brow. "You weren't demanding anything from Birch, were you?"

"Pike," Declan snapped.

"No." Pike ripped his gaze from Cole and turned his stare to the map.

"All right, then." Cole eased back into his seat. The moment he relaxed into the chair, conversation returned, the others murmuring, plotting, and planning.

It didn't take long for Birch to finish issuing orders and end their little meeting. They had their assignments. Now it was a matter of execute and regroup. Each member of the team peeled away. They all had their own prep rituals—including Cole.

Which was how he ended up outside, sitting on the edge of Pike's back porch, and...listening in on Pike's phone call. A call that included statements like, "on my way" and "Palm Island."

Cole strode after the pup, his anger rising hot and fast as he realized Pike was telling *someone* about their plans. Only to have a large presence block his path.

A wave of strength—dominance—crashed over him just as a single order sank into his mind. "Stay."

CHAPTER TWENTY-NINE

*A*bby wouldn't look at him. *Hadn't* looked at him from the moment they climbed into the car. It'd been just north of forty-eight hours since Declan had wrenched Abby from SHOC custody, and hopefully the ordeal would be over soon.

The three of them—him, Birch, and Abby—had left Pike's tasked with retrieving the tablet.

Declan talked to Birch and Birch talked back.

Birch talked to Abby and Abby murmured back.

But when Declan tried to hold a damn conversation with her, he got half-stuttered answers and her flat-out refusal to even look his way.

Abby was hiding something. Declan knew it just like he knew how to assemble a Glock blindfolded while parajumping. He knew it just like he knew how to kill a man with one finger. And he knew it like he knew the curves of her body and the moans she made just before she came.

What he *didn't* know was what she was lying *about*. But he would soon. She couldn't keep up her game of pretend forever.

Cole, Ethan, and Grant were off breaking into Ogilve, Piers, and Patterson in search of any additional data on

FosCo, along with information on the accounting firm's other clients. Clients that might have deep, long-standing ties to Unified Humanity as well.

Pike hadn't been included in their plans. He was a "civilian" despite his past association with SHOC.

Which left Declan with Birch at his back and Abby… lying to him.

Birch piloted the small boat they'd "borrowed." A quick little thing that would get them from the shore to Pine Island and back again. They didn't need fancy, just fast.

Abby sat near the bow, clinging to the side of the craft. The vessel sped across the black waters, wind tugging at her blond hair. He wanted to be back at Pike's, wrapped around her, his face buried in that hair. Instead they were on a damned boat and hunting for a tablet that hopefully held proof of FosCo's activities and a ticket to safety for Abby.

Declan eased forward, carefully making his way to Abby, and he slid onto the bench seat behind her. Even with the sticky, briny scent of the sea surrounding them, he could still capture her natural smell. Crisp air. Dew-touched trees. Sweet like flowers. And so fucking sexy. His cock was hard just thinking about her, smelling her, and when he let his mind wander toward imagining her naked…

He dropped his head forward and leaned into Abby, resting his forehead on her shoulder. He managed to swallow his groan—barely. She tilted her head to the side, rubbing her cheek on his skull.

Because she was driven to by her cat? Or was it a feline apology for lying?

Probably a little of both.

He turned his head so his lips brushed her ear. "Abby," he murmured. "Wanna tell me why you're—"

But she cut him off. Not letting him finish the question. "We're close. Birch should slow down."

Declan sighed. "When we beach, you're going to tell me why you're lying."

She blinked at him, eyes wide, guileless. He could practically read her mind. *I don't know what you're talking about.*

"I . . ." She grimaced, a hint of guilt fluttering across her features. "We're not beaching. He should stop about twenty feet from the south end."

"He—"

"Go tell him before he gets too close and can't stop before he comes up against the rocks." Abby nudged him with her shoulder, and he gave her a glare. One that would have frightened the average person. Apparently making her come ruined his ability to intimidate her.

Declan half turned and held his hand out to Birch, hand flat and palm facing his team alpha. Then he brought it to his forehead, palm down as if he saluted Birch when he was telling the bear to keep an eye out.

The engine dropped to a low idle, momentum and the current carrying the vessel forward. The small waves rocked the boat, and his wolf's hearing picked up the low whoosh of water lapping at the island's shore.

"We're here," Abby whispered, and Declan formed a fist, silently instructing Birch to cut the engine entirely.

Once silence surrounded them, Birch moved close. Even with the boat swaying, the bear shifter looked damned intimidating when he crossed his arms over his chest. "Someone wanna tell me why we're stopping so far out?"

Declan turned his attention to the woman who'd dragged their asses to some nothing of an island. "Abby?"

She kept quiet and turned her gaze to the bottom of

the boat, but that didn't mean she was motionless. Nah, he couldn't get that lucky. Because as he and Birch watched, she snared the hem of her shirt and pulled it upward.

Declan reached for her, snatching the fabric and tugging it back down. "What are you doing?"

She scrunched her nose. "Can I tell you later?"

He leaned closer and drew in a deep breath. The sting of unease with a hint of worry and fear burned his nose. His wolf wanted to sneeze and banish the scent. Declan simply wanted to know what the fuck was going on. "No. You can tell me now."

Abby grimaced.

"Abby..." He added a little growl, his beast finally realizing all was not well.

"Um..." She nibbled her lower lip.

At least until Birch's feral growl vibrated the air around them. "Tell us."

"It's in an underwater cave."

Declan couldn't help it; he roared. "It's—" He cut off the rest of his question, remembering they were trying to be quiet. "This isn't something you could have revealed before we left the coast? We would have stolen a diver's boat."

Abby propped her hands on her hips, one cocked slightly to the side when she shifted her weight. "It's only mostly underwater. I don't exactly swim out here with climbing gear. I go in from the bottom."

"You're not going—" Declan started.

"She is." The bear cut him off. "She's got this. She goes down, she gets it, she comes back, and we're out. We're spending more time arguing than it'd take her to go and return."

Declan dropped his head forward and took a deep breath, fighting the urge to throw Birch overboard and then tie up

Abby so she couldn't do something stupid like jump off the boat.

Unfortunately, the idea came too late. Because Abby... jumped off the boat.

He spun in place, eyes searching the darkness, and found a pile of clothes where she should have been standing. He rushed to the side and peered over, glaring at the trail of bubbles that popped to the surface of the water. A shimmer of golden fur shined through the darkness, the moon's light caressing her partially shifted form, and then she was gone. Swallowed by the midnight waters.

"Dammit, Abby." He snarled and growled, the wolf pissed at what she'd done and even more furious that she wasn't standing in front of him so he could wring her damn neck.

"Birch." He shook his head. "If she gets hurt..."

The bear sighed and tipped his head back. "God save me from lovesick males."

Declan rolled his eyes. "God should save you from pissed-off wolves."

Because he sure as hell wasn't lovesick. Cocksick, maybe. But not lovesick.

"Look." Birch pointed at Declan. "Everyone pulls their weight on this team, and they do what they're best at." He pointed at the water. "This is what she's best at."

"She's not part of the fucking team." He snarled the words, voice low but filled with every ounce of fury his wolf could gather. "She's a civilian. She's here because the director is gunning for her and I won't turn her over to that sadistic fuck. Civilians don't do shit in the field. It's why Pike's not here or with the rest of the team."

"That's it? That's all she is? A civilian who has something that will appease the director and give us more intel on Unified Humanity. Nothing else? She's got no other connection to you?" Birch lifted a single brow, smirk on his lips, and Declan wanted to claw it right off the smug prick's face.

Was that all she was? No, but making her more meant she'd be at risk. It meant that tying her life to his could see her roped into an op. If one half of a couple was in, they were both in.

And Declan didn't want her anywhere near danger.

"Yeah, she's just a civilian," he rasped.

"Then when she gets back, we'll park her with the team and treat her as a civvy." The dick sounded so damned cocky.

"Fine," Declan growled. "But no one lays a paw on her. No one."

Because if they did, he'd rip it off.

Birch just shrugged and turned his attention to the water. They *both* turned their attention to the dark, churning water, stares unwavering as they waited. Twenty feet down, then another twenty up just to get inside. Then she'd retrace her path. Birch had said it wouldn't take her too long, but...

But she hadn't returned. Not in five minutes and not in ten.

His body vibrated with his wolf's growing frustration and anger, the animal debating between lashing out at Birch and diving into the water himself. A flurry of bubbles, a blossoming of red, and a scent that caused his hair to stand on end made the decision.

"Human," he hissed, and mixed in with the human's blood now surfacing was the scent of..."*Abby*."

CHAPTER THIRTY

*C*ontrary to popular belief, tasting human blood didn't suddenly turn Abby into a flesh-craving beast intent on murdering all of humanity. Oh, her beast wanted to do some murdering, but not for consumption—for being pissed off. The cat hissed and snarled in the back of her mind, tail whipping and claws flexing and contracting—as if her nails were thirsty for blood as well.

And it wasn't just *any* human she wanted, either. She wanted the asshole with the tranq gun. The one who'd shot her just as she exited the cave mouth. The drug had been fast acting, dragging at her the moment the needle pierced flesh. She'd tried to resist her attackers, had even gotten her fangs and claws into one of the men, but soon lost the underwater battle.

She'd been tossed into this fully tiled room, complete with drains set into the floor. It was empty save a shiny metal table and her—shackled to a chair, wearing nothing but a bra and panties. Now she waited to see who'd walk through the door. So far no one had appeared, but she doubted they'd leave her alone forever. Not when they knew who—*what*—she was.

That was something she recalled during her partially unconscious travels. There'd been hands—rough when they hauled her around. Then voices—snickering, derisive, and taunting.

A familiar one amid them all. Dark, angry, vicious... Eric Foster. Mr. Foster hadn't been pleased about Abby's escape *or* what she'd had in her hands when she'd fled.

Which meant she was with Unified Humanity and hadn't been taken by another SHOC team. The human blood had been a clue, and this man's statement locked her guess into place.

"Can't we make her shift and skin her? She killed Roger."

Abby had mentally smiled at that one. Roger was dead because she'd torn off a good chunk of his hand and then more than a little of his throat. *She* hadn't killed him per se, but she'd nudged his life closer to its end. A lot closer. She hadn't cared for the "skin her" part of the guy's statement, though. She liked her skin exactly where it was—on her.

But back to the tiled room and the chains and the cold. Couldn't they keep her warm and kill her? Did they have to make her freeze before they got to whatever they planned on doing to her?

Abby snorted. There was something wrong with her when her first thoughts—after being kidnapped—were to complain about the temperature. Not her impending... whatever the humans planned.

It was Declan's fault. Declan's and SHOC's, and she'd blame cougars for being solitary and prideless, too. If she'd had a pride, they would have helped keep her safe. Her cougar joined in on spreading the anger around, though it did feel she was being unfair when it came to blaming cougars and their naturally solitary nature.

Traitor.

Ugh. Maybe she was losing her mind. That was as good an explanation as any. Her thoughts ran in scattered directions, mind grabbing on to one thread only to have it snap so she'd pick up another. It meant she bounced from wet to Declan to cold to Declan to ...

No, her thoughts weren't scattered, not really. Her mind simply kept going back to the man—wolf—who'd gotten her into this mess. She missed that argumentative, dominating, gorgeous wolf. She wouldn't mind him kidnapping her—again.

If he could find her. She'd been hauled through the ocean, spirited away in a boat, then driven through the city in an SUV. Too many scents would overwhelm the trail.

Well, she'd get her own happy ass out of the clusterfuck she'd stumbled into. Raised voices came from outside the room, deep tenors intermixed with lighthearted laughs. She recognized one voice—that laugh. It was the asshole who'd wanted to skin her.

He drew closer by the second. Maybe she'd get lucky and the group of idiots would keep on walking and ... They paused just outside the door, booming voices echoing through the solid sheet of metal that separated them.

"What are we bothering with her for? Just let me kill her and be done with it. Foster got what he wanted." One voice. It seemed familiar, but she couldn't place it.

"It's not your job to make that decision. Foster wants to know what else she has in that head of hers. Why do you think he wants you interrogating her? He said you like playing rough." Roger's friend chuckled. Did sadistic, heartless bastards like the people in UH even have friends?

"I like what I like." That familiar-ish voice again, and it

was followed by a handful of beeps, as if he typed something on a keypad.

He was coming in—panic sent her heart rate soaring. She closed her eyes and dropped her head forward, feigning unconsciousness. Maybe if they thought she was out of it, they'd leave her alone. Perfect plan. Prey in the wild played dead and it worked for their stupid natural predators.

She was desperate prey. They were stupid, asshole, should-be-dead predators.

Abby forced her body to relax and concentrated on unclenching her muscles. She slowed her breathing and begged her cougar to stay in the background. Busting out fur and fangs while out of it wouldn't exactly sell her "I'm still passed out" plan.

The door screeched as it slid open, metal on metal.

"I like getting dirty." Two heavy *thud*s, one step and then another. "I like doing what I'm told." That voice pricked at her ears, the cougar's curiosity surging, and she mentally whacked the cat on the nose. Her curiosity was going to get them both killed. The little shit.

"But what I *don't* like is an audience." The masculine voice came out hard and flat, and even Abby recognized the order in his tone. No negotiation. The man wanted to be alone—with her.

So not good.

"Aw, c'mon. I heard they can take a lot before they die on you. I've never played with a shifter. Just lemme go one round." The whiny jerk. She didn't want to know what he meant about one "round," and she never wanted to find out.

"Goodbye, George." Metal scraped metal once more, the squeal and grind sending a jagged shiver down her spine. Like nails on chalkboard, a horror-movie bad guy dragging a knife along a house window, or the big bad wolf huffing and puffing at someone's front door.

Rubber squeaked on the tile, and then came the slow, rhythmic *thud* of those boots on the hard surface as he approached. Methodical. Unhurried. Heavy with foreboding. This guy wasn't in a rush. Abby wasn't going anywhere and he knew it. Each step was a taunt, a foreshadowing of what was to come. Would he hit her just as slowly? Would he take his time while he cut her? Wasn't that what UH did? She'd heard stories, whispers from the older seals in the herd.

Would he—

A wave of warmth eased around her, her captor now circling her and surrounding her with his scent. It teased her nose, a hint of something known yet not. She parted her lips just enough for her to draw in the man's scent. The cougar lent a hand, tasting his flavors and trying to put a name to the aroma. The seawater still filled her nose, masking most of the scents. All but one—fear. She mentally shook her head. As if a member of UH would be afraid of a shifter in chains—*tight* chains.

"I know you're awake." That husky voice came, his breath ghosting over her cheek, and a hint of his scruff brushed her skin. His lips feathered over her ear.

Close—so dangerously close. The cat urged her to turn her head and take a chunk out of the human.

But she didn't. She remained in place, feigning sleep, while she hoped he'd give up and leave her alone. Leave her be just long enough for Declan and SHOC to find her. Because he would. Maybe not because he cared for her— all they'd shared was passion—but at least because UH had the tablet and they'd want it back.

Abby's animal grumbled and huffed, scraped at her

mind when she thought of Declan as nothing more than a bed buddy. He was more than that, and the cat couldn't understand why Abby's human half hadn't accepted that truth yet.

If she didn't let hope grow in her heart, there was no way she could suffer the pain of disappointment.

The man ran his nose along her jaw, the warm tip sliding toward her chin and not stopping until he'd continued to her other ear. "You smell good. Even covered in sea water. Is that why he likes you? Is that why he betrayed SHOC?"

She wasn't going to react to his words. She wasn't. Unified Humanity wouldn't learn anything from her.

Not. Happening.

"The longer you pretend, the more it'll hurt, you know." His voice changed, a hint of a smile filling his words, as if he hoped she'd continue her charade so he could hurt her.

Abby clung to her relaxed state, determined to hold out against this man. But then...then a palm landed on her knee, fingers curling around the outside of her right leg. That hand traveled north along her thigh—slow, methodical, and easing closer and closer to the juncture of her thighs.

Her cougar whined and snarled, demanding she stop the coming attack. It wanted to fight. It wanted to claw and bite and bathe in the blood of their enemy.

"Open your eyes, kitty." Fingertips teased ever upward. "And maybe I'll stop. Or did the wolf not do it for you? Do you want a real man? You're pretty enough for a furry." A little farther, his first knuckle catching on the stretchy lace. "Open your eyes."

That last order did it. Not because he injured her, but because his lips brushed hers, a soft caress that made her stomach lurch and her body move without thought. She jerked her head away from him, leaning back as much as she could while she opened her eyes.

And froze.

"Pike?"

Pike. Jacob. Werewolf. Her tormentor?

"What...?" Movement slowly returned to Abby, and she shook her head. "What are you doing?"

The man she'd met was gone. The man who'd stood shoulder to shoulder with Declan—to defend her—had vanished. *That* Pike wasn't in front of her. She didn't know who this was.

Malice sparkled in his blue eyes, a hint of anticipation and joy joining the emotion. He enjoyed this—taunting her, scaring her.

"Hello, pretty, pretty pussy," he murmured, and curled his fingers into the curve of her ass. He didn't break skin, merely squeezed until the pain of his hold suffused her. "Nice of you to wake up."

"What are you doing?" She repeated her question, mind unable to form any other words. That same question repeated on an unending loop, and she wanted—*needed*—an answer.

Pike didn't give her one. He released her and straightened, pulling his arm back as he rose, and then *crack*. The back of his hand collided with her temple and her head whipped right, forced aside by the strength of his slap. Skin split, the searing pain jolting through her body, and blood flowed from the wound. It slithered down her body, covering her arm.

This was why grates were set into the tile floor.

"You speak when spoken to."

Her cougar snarled and pushed forward, but she shoved it into a mental cage. She couldn't shift and attack. Maybe later, but not then. They had to be careful, smart. Didn't the she-cat remember getting cornered by a polar bear? They'd lived because they didn't panic and lash out. Abby needed *that* version of her cougar.

With the cougar's assistance, the wound on her head burned as skin sought to stitch—

"Nu-uh." Pike gripped her face, fingertips digging into the slash on her head. "Your kitty doesn't get to heal you. Not yet. I want to see you bleed for a little while."

The cat snarled and bared its fangs but ceased its attempt to fix the damage. For now.

"Much better." He smiled wide, pristine, white, *human-shaped* teeth revealed with the evil grin. "Good kitty."

He even went so far as to pat her head as if she were a pet.

"Now"—he leaned down and rested his hands on his knees—"you're going to sit there like a good little pet and tell me everything you know and everything you revealed to others."

No, she really wouldn't, and not only because she didn't know much. Because she would never betray her kind. Not to Unified Humanity. Not ever. Not like *him*.

Instead of saying the words aloud, she simply gave him two hard shakes of her head, the denial firm and unmistakable.

Pike straightened, took a step back, and then began a lazy stroll around her. "I just can't decide what to do with you. There are so many options. On one hand Foster ordered me to get you talking. On the other"—he clicked his tongue—"I just wanna play."

Another tremble, goose bumps rising on her skin. She didn't want to play with Pike. At all. Unfortunately, she didn't get a choice.

"Does that sound good to you, sweetheart?" A smirk,

one she wanted to claw off his face. "That wolfie not giving you what you need?" Pike reached down and grabbed his crotch, shaking his hand slightly. "You want a real man?"

Abby sneered, lifting her lip to bare her still human canine. "Maybe if you bring me one." She glared at him, her taunting stare sliding down his body from head to toe before she met his eyes once more. "Because all I see right now is a piece of shit." She pulled at her bindings, straining to reach him. "A weak, *insignificant* piece of shit not worthy to lick my boots."

If she'd been wearing any.

His eyes flared, a flash of amber for the barest of moments. There was something else in his eyes, too. Pain?

He leaned down, bracing his hands on the arms of the metal chair. "That's a lot of big talk for someone who's staring death in the face. Keep pulling on those chains, baby. Isn't that what he calls you?" He lowered his voice. "Keep pulling on them—try to break free. It'll give me an excuse to hurt you even more."

"Should I beg for my life and promise you my undying love, *Pike*?"

"Little bitch." He spat the words in her face, saliva splattering against her heated skin. "Don't know when to shut up, do you?"

"What the hell are you doing? You're working for UH? *Really?*" Another shake. "I never thought I'd see the day when a shif—"

His next movement was fast, a blur of his hand rising and then a shot of pain to...her ear? What the hell?

"Speak when spoken to." The words were a growl, and she lifted her head to meet his intense stare.

"Fuck. You." *Probably* not the best response, but the only one that came to mind.

Pike chuckled and backed away, shaking his head. "You're trying to get me to end it too soon. You don't want to give me a chance to enjoy myself."

Honestly, she'd been reacting on instinct rather than with some sort of grand plan in mind, but she wouldn't tell him that.

His lips curled into a dark smile, a smirk she swore she'd seen before...on Declan? "Are all shifters this stupid?"

No. *No.* Just...no. Tons of guys smirked. It was a thing with men. They thought they were all sexy when they quirked their lips even though half the men who tried the expression just looked like they were constipated.

Pike's smirk wasn't familiar in any way. It sure as hell didn't remind her of Declan.

She stared at the man in front of her, eyeing his nose, the angle of his jaw, and those blue eyes. *Stop it.* She wasn't following that line of thought.

"Of course we're not all dumb. I think it's just cougars." She pulled her lips back into a wide, feral smile. "And wolves."

Pike narrowed his eyes, and she felt his cold glare all the way to the marrow of her bones. "What did you tell SHOC about what you learned at FosCo?" Abby shook her head, and he lowered to her height once again. "Come on, sweetheart. Just tell me what I want to know and this won't have to hurt so much."

She snorted. "I don't know anything. How about you tell me why you're doing this, instead?"

He ignored her question. "You don't know anything? Hmmm...That's why you with one of their SHOC teams? Why you were working at FosCo? Because you don't know anything?" He poked out his lower lip, eyebrows furrowed.

"Poor baby, just happened to be in the wrong place at the wrong time, is that it?"

He tapped her cheek. "One more try, sweetheart. Tell me what you—and now the others—know, or things are going to get real."

"I don't know what you're talking about."

"I don't want to hurt you more than I have to." Another expression covered his features, one that pushed the truth to the forefront of her mind.

She didn't know why Pike had betrayed the shifters in this way, but it wasn't *only* shifters that he'd betrayed. "Why? Is it because you don't like getting blood on your hands? Or is it only 'furry' blood? Maybe you have a thing about torturing women." She captured his stare with hers, making sure her gaze didn't waver while she delivered her final guess. "Or maybe it's because you don't like betraying your *brother*."

CHAPTER THIRTY-ONE

*D*eclan now understood why zoo animals paced. They were hungry for their captors, anxious to break free and destroy whoever had them locked in a tiny cage. He wanted to be free to run and hunt, but instead he'd remained locked behind reinforced bars for the last two hours.

He hadn't stopped growling from the moment Birch restrained him. Oh, there was no arguing that the rope and chains had been necessary, but logic wasn't high on Declan's list of "shit to think about." At the top was worry about Abby, then escaping, then hunting Abby while killing anyone who stood in his way.

A new sound filtered through the walls of his prison in Pike's basement. Two of the walls were concrete, made of bricks and mortar—the house's foundation. He moved to the closest wall and rested his ear against the hard surface. His wolf was already pushed forward, straining to help Declan sort through the sounds.

Rolling tires over rocks and glass. Big tires, heavy vehicle, moving slowly through the darkness. The grating of metal on metal followed by the softest squeak of the transport's springs. Something—someone—heavy exited the vehicle.

The deep *thud* of someone's approach. No, more than one. Three large men—his team. He knew the sounds of their walks as well as they knew his. The vibrations slid through him, the feel of their boots on the walkway and then the front porch shaking his bones. Then came the squeak of the front door opening. Dirt rained down from the basement's ceiling, dust loosened as they strode through the small home's entryway.

The team was there. They'd support him in his fight with Birch. They would let him free to find Abby—to destroy whoever had taken her. They *had* to because...because he didn't have Pike to depend on. The damn wolf hadn't been home when Birch had dragged him into the house, and he still hadn't returned. Gone. Vanished. Like so many times before. The fucking kid...Declan sighed and shook his head. That fucking kid. Pike had bitched because Birch wouldn't let him participate in the op and then made like a rabbit—running and hiding.

Declan's wolf snarled, furious about Pike's abandonment, but he did his best to soothe the near-feral beast. He could be angry with Pike later. His focus had to be on Abby.

Declan pushed away from the wall and tipped his head to the side, closing his eyes as he listened for the activities above. Low murmurs, too low for him to hear. The clinks and thuds of the men removing their gear and the bouncing springs of a protesting mattress. It seemed they were dropping everything on the same bed. Good. He'd need it all when he escaped.

When. Not if. *When*.

Everyone in his way would...die. If Birch, Cole, Grant, or Ethan attempted to keep him locked away, he couldn't guarantee their safety. Right now he couldn't think beyond the blood in those churning waters, the humans who'd had their hands on his mate.

Mate.

It couldn't be...He wasn't the type of male who...He wasn't mate material, and yet his wolf howled, a hint of sadness and joy in the sound. It was overjoyed he'd finally recognized the truth—Abby belonged to them—but aching to have her at their side once more.

Now he understood the drive to steal her, to keep her safe, to touch her when he should have stayed away. She deserved more—better—than him, but her fate was sealed, and the truth expanded to fill his body. It changed from a hesitant guess to an unbreakable certainty.

Abby was *his*. And his SHOC team was keeping them apart.

Declan brought more of the animal forward, encouraged it to gift him with increased strength and larger size. His shoulders broadened, fur sliding free. His arms thickened while his fingers gradually took on the shape of paws. The animal's fury coursed through his veins, adrenaline and blood thirst pushing him to break free.

Run.

Hunt.

Find.

Not yet, he said to the wolf. He needed to know what SHOC had learned before he broke free. Did they know where she was?

"What the hell, Birch?" Ethan didn't have a ton of respect when annoyed. "We're in deep and then you're breaking into the com with some order to—"

A low murmur cut Ethan off. Declan couldn't hear the words, but he knew that tone—the timbre of that rumble. Birch spoke. The team listened.

"What?" Ethan.

"Aw, shit." Grant.

"Where is he now?" Cole's voice was flat, no-nonsense. Evaluate, plan, and execute.

Birch answered once more, the bear's voice too low...

"I looked at that before we left. Pike's cage won't hold him for long." The tiger spoke the truth. Declan had already taken the time to inspect the bars, the brackets, and bolts that secured the cage. Could it keep him captive? For a little while. He was too motivated, too determined to get free.

"Ideas, then?" Birch murmured, his voice followed by the scrape of chairs on worn linoleum in the kitchen. "You guys get the data?"

A smack of plastic on Formica. A USB on the tabletop?

"Pulled the whole server before your interruption had security on our ass." Ethan still sounded damned pissed about the disruption, too.

"Casualties?" The bear asked the question as if it didn't matter to him. Life or death, he simply had to make a report. But the team knew the truth, the team knew Birch had his own demons.

"Bumps and bruises, but I didn't kill anyone." Cole snorted. "Wouldn't have been fair. They were practically puppies." The tiger grunted. "Didn't even have guns. Just bullshit pepper spray. No fun in it." He could imagine Cole's shrug.

"Grant, you'll work on digging through the data you guys grabbed. Look to see if there are any FosCo holdings tied to Unified Humanity. Actually, I need to know about anything that's tied to UH on that USB drive."

"You think that's who took her?" Grant's dark rasp held more than a hint of the man's animal.

"Yeah." Birch sounded grim, frustrated. "I have headquarters researching known UH locations and any activity surrounding them. Initial eval is that they'll have stayed close, but there aren't any records of UH or FosCo holdings in this or surrounding towns." He sighed. "A whole lot of fucking nothing so far."

Declan didn't know anything about FosCo's real estate, but something tickled the back of his mind. Something that'd happened years ago near here and...and it danced just out of reach.

"Did we get the tablet at least?" Cole again. "Not for nothing, but if we've got what we came for, we can walk away. No one needs to know that Declan lost it. We can tell the other team that she's gone and give the director the tablet. Just sweep this shit under the rug and move the fuck on."

Declan hadn't wanted to kill his team, but Cole would die. The idea that he'd leave Abby...His wolf growled and followed it up with a howl, fury over Cole's indifference straining his control over the beast.

"No. No tablet. We need to get her—and the tablet—in our hands. At minimum, the tablet." Declan didn't like Birch quantifying who—what—was more important.

"So, what do we do?" Grant spoke up. He was a good wolf but liked having clear direction. It annoyed Declan to no end. Being an alpha meant doing what he wanted when he wanted, but packs needed betas, and their team was a pack of sorts.

"Research. Go through the data."

And while they did that, he'd do some work of his own.

Maybe what he was about to do was stupid as hell and he should just sit around with his thumb up his ass while his team did the rest.

Except he wasn't that guy.

Declan was the guy who silently worked at the boards in the far corner, the ones that once removed, would give him access to the small bedroom above. It'd taken time, time he hadn't wanted to waste, but it was worth it in the end.

He got into the bedroom with hardly a sound, nothing more than a low creak coming from one of the older boards as he pulled himself up through the hole he'd created. He scanned the space and grinned at what he found—weapons and gear galore.

Standing in the center of the room, gaze moving across the space, that niggling thought in the back of his mind pushed forward once more.

One town over, big house on a big piece of land. Tall fences that shielded the home from neighbors...He could picture it as it'd been all those years ago. But it hadn't been registered to FosCo then. Or Unified Humanity. He squeezed his eyes shut, trying to remember who'd owned the property, but the name wouldn't come to him. Dammit.

He refocused on the room. There was the predictable neat pile from Cole, the random mess from Ethan, and Grant's area was a little in between. Guns were cared for. Clothes? Not so much.

Declan remained silent while he crossed the room and tugged on a tactical vest. Then came the weapons, guns and blades strapped to his body until he figured he was as ready as he was going to be. Guns, mags, knives, a grenade or two, and a com unit settled into place.

The memory still teased him as he prepared to escape, and with each passing second, certainty grew. Liv at headquarters was a badass techno bitch. She hadn't found anything yet, and Grant was just starting his search. He could sit around and wait. Or he could do what his gut was screaming at him to do.

Rumors had led him to a building years ago, and he'd purged it of Unified Humanity to atone for the sins in his past. He had a funny feeling they'd refilled it with their crazed kind. He knew how he'd get there—a man never forgot how to steal a car. He knew exactly how many he could kill with what he wore. The wolf would take care of the rest.

He padded to the window and ran his gaze over the frame, searching for any security measure his brother might have put into place. Nothing obvious, but who knew. For now he'd go quiet rather than shatter the glass.

Declan placed his hands on the bottom edge of the window and held his breath as he tugged, lifting the panel and letting in the night air. A tendril of relief suffused his blood, and he sighed, thankful Pike was a big enough idiot to leave his home without any kind of alarm.

Then the alarm went off and Declan cursed his brother for being all prepared and shit. He threw the window up and dove through the opening, rolling as he hit the ground. He kept the tumble going until he gained his feet, and then he ran. He bolted into a ground-eating pace, leaving his team behind while he let the wolf free to do as it desired.

Hunt.

CHAPTER THIRTY-TWO

*D*eclan skirted the ragged lawn, sticking to the perimeter, staying in the shadows while he sought an entrance to the dilapidated house. If he recalled the layout correctly, a bolt-hole would get him into the winding corridors beneath the home, bypassing the guards inside. Sure, he'd have to kill the guys up top eventually, but remaining undetected for a little while would let him find Abby quicker. Then he'd fight their way out.

His beast growled, shaking Declan. It didn't like thinking about Abby being in such danger. Declan didn't either, but he had to take solace in the fact that he'd avenge his mate for every hint of pain they caused.

His mate. Each time he thought of her—said her name in his mind or whispered it beneath his breath—the certainty strengthened. He'd always sought something—something to fill the hungry beast inside him and fill the bottomless hole in his heart. It had come in the form of a cougar shifter named Abby.

Declan continued his path, steps nearly silent as he moved through the welcoming dark. He soon reached the backyard, the area just as run-down as the front half of the house. It appeared to be a forgotten place—a building filled with people who didn't care about the home.

Declan cared about it—it and what it held. Because at that moment the wind shifted and a ghost of feminine scent teased his nose. A sweetly seductive aroma his wolf knew without a doubt.

"Abby." He breathed out her name, his lips tingling as he spoke. As if she gave him a gentle kiss when he said her name aloud.

The wind changed once more, and with the subtle shift came something else, something that had the wolf leaping forward without thought, old reflexes snapping into place as if he'd never left his previous life.

The crunch of a blade of grass. Just one. Some would dismiss the soft sound, but those were the same people who'd die beneath his claws.

In one smooth move, he whipped the gun strapped to his left thigh from its holster, the glide of metal on its custom casing silent. Without diverting his attention from the house, he pointed the weapon at the intruder, arm steady and aim perfect.

No other sounds came from his left, the darkness broken only by the random echoes from inside the home.

"Easy way to get yourself killed," Declan murmured low.

"You don't have my silencer, and the muzzle flash would betray your position." Cole didn't sound the slightest bit concerned, no hint of sour fear coming from the tiger, nor a tremble in his voice. Then again, Cole was like him— tired, old, jaded.

Until Declan had met Abby and now... things were different. Good different or bad different? He wasn't sure. It depended on whether he lived through the next half hour.

"Don't think I can take down a handful of humans?" Declan snickered.

Cole grunted. "Got a plan, or are we just winging it?"

If Cole was willing to help, Declan had to toss the original plan aside. "Are the others here?"

"Heads up."

He lifted his right hand and caught the device the tiger tossed while he kept his gun trained on the male. Sure, he listened to what Cole had to say, but until he knew more, he'd keep the man at a distance.

He sure as fuck wasn't going back into some damned cage.

Declan slipped in the earpiece and turned it on. "Declan in."

"Team on deck." Birch was all business, but Declan sensed a hint of fury. "No records. Entry?"

The whole fucking team is here. There are no fucking records on file. How the fuck are we getting in there, Declan?

Birch said a lot when he was barely speaking.

"There's a storm cellar."

A low click filled his ear, a notice that someone else on the team was about to speak. "There's a ten-digit keypad," Ethan said, but Declan knew that already. "Code?"

"Known," Declan murmured. "Self-programmed."

It'd been his last task before he'd left the carnage behind. Just in case he'd needed to return, he'd wanted easy access with his personal backdoor code.

"Repeat visit?" Grant sounded surprised, but no one else said a word.

They all had secrets from the past. Declan wasn't about to have a heart-to-heart while Abby remained in the hands of Unified Humanity.

"Who's on point?" Cole asked from his left, voice filling both ears.

Declan hated giving up control, but his wolf was too close to losing it. The beast could think of nothing but its mate. Fuck battle tactics and strategy. He'd defer to his team alpha for this one. "Birch?"

Birch sounded more normal when he spoke. "Grant's up. Cole on our six. Low, tight…"

"First." They finished the order as a group.

Keep their asses low, keep a tight formation, and shoot the assholes before they got their own off.

Grant peeled away from the fence, sticking to the shadows of the few trees in the backyard. The trees were half dead and sad with drooping branches, but the gloom kept their movements hidden.

Then there was Birch, and Declan slipped into formation behind the team alpha. Ethan followed, and Cole joined them at the back. Five men in a line, ready to risk their lives for…

"She's my mate. They've touched her. They die."

The whole team froze in place—not even breathing. Finally, Birch spoke. "They die. Move out."

They moved as they'd been trained—as one. Their steps matched, their strides identical so they could walk in each other's path. Someone coming across their boot prints wouldn't know that five men attacked. They'd assume there was only one.

Until reports flooded the security station. Then it'd be too late.

They reached the deep shadow of the back of the house, the moon gifting them with cover, and they dropped into low squats. Declan's wolf's sight let him peer through the midnight black, to lay eyes on his teammates.

Each male was dressed all in black, a gun in one hand and the other in the shape of a claw. Two halves making up a whole, two parts of each man working together to save Abby.

"Code?" Grant grabbed his attention.

Declan recited the numbers from memory, the digits seared into his head for eternity. The date of his last kill—the last bullet he'd shot for money.

Grant pressed the keypad, and soon the whir of the lock disengaging sounded. They remained in place a beat longer, waiting for any alarm or sound from inside. Then they were in motion once more, through the door and trooping down a bright hall.

Declan's wolf sorted through the plethora of scents, the hints of gunpowder, sweat, and the rotten flavor of hatred.

"I scent at least twenty. One female," Declan said. No one had to question the identity of the female. Abby's terror consumed the air, filling the space with her fear, but there was another scent he recognized from yesterday. "Foster."

"One known male—friendly." Birch's words made Declan jolt. A *known* male? A friendly? "Move out." Birch gave an order, and they all complied, training overtaking Declan's curiosity.

They dealt with the first duo they came across quickly and quietly. They'd take their time, eliminate enemies as they went. They *would not* turn the op into a bloodbath.

How many times had Declan heard those instructions in the past? Too many to count. Though this time Birch hadn't drummed the words into their heads before they breached the cellar doors. So when he heard Abby's scream, he didn't feel *too* bad about breaking formation and launching into a dead run. His boots pounded on the white linoleum, the rapid, heavy thuds announcing his presence to one and all.

He didn't care, because Abby screamed. Again. His adrenaline, the beast, pushed him onward.

Curses echoed down the hall in his wake, the team damning him for busting out of line, but he couldn't find a single fuck to give about their anger. Not when a human man was in his path. Punch with his claw. A strike to the nose with the butt of his gun. Finally, a slash that sank through flesh and scraped his carotid artery.

More humans. More deaths. He hadn't come across Foster yet. He should have killed him when he had the chance.

With every fallen body, he drew closer to Abby, the stench of her pure terror growing with each step closer. The sounds of fighting, his team's struggles, reached him, and he was suddenly torn. He could run on and kill everyone in his path, mow every human down until he reached Abby. Or he could help protect his team. He'd abandoned them, broken formation for his own selfish needs, and...

Birch stopped mid-fight to meet Declan's gaze. "Go!" he roared.

Declan bolted, breaking into a ground-eating run. He hunted Abby, he hunted his *mate*, and all else could fuck off as far as he was concerned.

He turned another corner and then another, spying a set of stairs at the end of the hall. The second his feet touched the top step, he jumped, using his beast's agility to get from one floor to the next with a single leap. He went down one level and then two and then...

He stopped.

Blood. All Abby's, though there was another scent that teased his beast... No, he needed to focus on his mate. The amount of terror and the existence of the blood confused him, the past attempting to overlay the present and cloud his thoughts. He wasn't with his old pack, and he didn't smell his girlfriend's blood. He wasn't rescuing his girlfriend. He was in a UH compound, and Abby needed him.

The farther he traveled down the hall, the more concentrated the scent became.

Declan turned yet another corner, still hunting, and then there was her voice. Furious. Pained. Taunting. It came from his immediate right, a solid metal door that didn't appear to be anything special. But it was. It was the single item that stood between him and Abby.

He didn't hesitate to attack. He went at the door, a boot to the handle, which he followed up with a hard slam of his shoulder. The door wrenched from its hinges, the grinding scrape of metal piercing the air with a complaining screech as it was torn from its tracks. That was when he saw Abby—his mate—secured to a chair in the middle of the room. Half naked. Cold. Scared. Hurt. Bruises and shallow scrapes marred her body—they didn't worry him—but where had the blood come from?

A low growl—familiar? *No*—drew his gaze to the only other person in the room. To the man stained with Abby's blood.

Something new filled him. Hotter. Stronger. Fiercer.

And wholly focused on killing...his brother.

CHAPTER THIRTY-THREE

*A*bby had known he would come. She'd only hoped Pike wouldn't be in the room when he did. Because looking at her and Pike, there was no disputing the truth—the wolf had hurt her.

She still couldn't figure out why Pike didn't just pass along his own knowledge to Unified Humanity. Pike wasn't in SHOC, but he knew the answers to his questions just as well as she did. Which meant there had to be something else.

Something they'd never know if Declan killed Pike.

"Declan." Pike's voice was flat, unemotional. "Nice of you to come."

"*You*," Declan rasped, and Abby's heart ached for him.

She saw the emotions in his eyes, the way his shoulders trembled and the curve of his stomach as he lurched. His brother's betrayal speared him deep, digging into his soul, and she wanted nothing more than to go to him. She ached to pull him into her arms and pretend none of this had ever happened.

Pike smirked. "Me."

The twist of his lips was cocky bravado, but Abby spotted the fear as well. Her world, her entire life, depended on the details in the world around her. Whether it was listening for a polar bear or catching sight of another's emotional pain, her life depended on her abilities.

"Declan," she whispered. She'd lost her voice at some point. Now she could only scream, and even that nearly brought her to tears. "Declan." She tried again, tugging against her bindings. The jangle of her chains and last whispered plea got his attention. "Declan."

Those wolf eyes landed on her, his narrow-eyed stare taking in her appearance once more. She needed him to push past the pain of betrayal and think clearly. If he let his beast take too much control, the wolf would—

Pike destroyed her attempt at distracting Declan. In truth, it didn't take much—a simple shift of his weight from one foot to the other. The connection she had to Declan snapped like a dried twig.

That was the moment Declan went after his brother. He tossed aside his gun and leaped, transitioning as he flew. The wolf's maw appeared, and his other hand shifted into a claw. Fangs grew, long and sharp, descending from his gums. His shoulders broadened, and arms thickened. That increase in size continued down his body, legs stretching his pants to their limits.

Dark gray fur—nearly black—covered him from snout to tail, and his eyes glowed an eerie amber. A yellow that wasn't *quite* that of a natural wolf. It betrayed his status as something *more*, something *better*. To her anyway.

And his size . . . A natural wolf stood two and a half feet at the shoulders, but Declan easily hit nearly four feet, and the rest of him was just as large. The snout, the teeth, the paws and thick muscles that hid beneath his midnight fur.

Bigger than any wolf she'd ever seen.

Declan landed on Pike with a snarl, and the other wolf

grunted when his back struck the hard tile. But while Declan embraced his beast, Pike...didn't.

He took Declan's punches, one after another after another. He didn't retaliate, only defended, blocking Declan
when he would have captured Pike's throat between his
jaws.

They rolled, exchanging the dominant position, while
Declan continued to beat on Pike—beat on his *brother*.

"Declan!" The shout was hardly more than a wheeze,
her voice abandoning her. Neither wolf gave her a glance.
She turned inward, sought her cougar, and beckoned her
forward. They couldn't get out of this, end the battle and escape, if they remained bound.

Her cougar released a soft whine. It didn't want to come
out. It didn't want to experience pain. It'd had enough over
the last couple of days.

Abby talked to the cat. *And we can't mate him if he loses
his mind after he kills his brother.*

The cat purred at the word "mate." Purred and rubbed
and changed her tune when she realized Abby was giving in
to the inevitable. Declan was hers—theirs—and their future
could be over before it began if they didn't figure this mess
out. Like Declan, Abby began to shift.

The bindings would still take some work, but there were
differences between human-shaped Abby and cat-shaped
Abby. Differences that allowed first one wrist and then the
other to jerk free of her chains while Pike was distracted.

She glanced at Declan and Pike, at Pike's limp body
and Declan's continued shift. It wouldn't be long before her
mate was done. Then Pike would be *done*.

Her legs shifted next, making it easy to pull out of
the cuffs that bound her. And the moment she had unre-
stricted movement, the cat withdrew, returning human feet

and leaving only delicate claws at the tips of her fingers.
The cat knew human was needed, but they didn't want to be
unarmed.

As if Declan would ever hurt her.

But Pike would. Pike *had.*

Declan's shift was nearly complete, his exhaustion plain.
He shouldn't have taken this long to change. Or he was simply giving Pike plenty of time to match him.

She tried to call Declan's name, but she had no voice.

Five feet separated her from the two men. Then four.
Then three. With that next step, Declan's shift completed,
his wolf fully in control and aching for blood. There was a
hunger for death in his eyes, one that would be sated only
by eliminating Pike.

She couldn't let that happen. Not when questions remained. Questions that could be answered only by the unconscious shifter.

Which was why, when she should have stayed out of the
way, Abby fell forward. She stumbled one step and then another until her bare knees hit tile and her chest fell across
Pike's. She was a battered blanket of protection. Now Declan would either recognize her presence or kill her, but it
would give Pike a chance. It would give *Declan* a chance.
He already carried too many kills on his conscience. She
wouldn't let him add this death, too—no matter how pissed
she was at Pike herself.

Hot fangs pressed tight to her neck, saliva dripping, and
hot breath fanned the side of her face. She was captured, her
neck vulnerable and in the place of Pike's. Her life was in
his jaws. He tightened his bite, fangs digging in to her skin
but not yet piercing her flesh.

Until he froze.

The wolf above her growled. It was a pure threat, the

beast's frustration voiced aloud. He could be as angry as he liked. It wouldn't change her actions. Standing between the brothers—saving Pike—seemed so *right*. Pike might be sentenced to death for his actions, but he wouldn't die at Declan's claws. It would kill her mate. Kill him.

Abby swallowed hard and licked her chapped lips, working to bring a little moisture to her mouth so she could attempt to talk once more. "Declan, stop." She winced with the effort and the rough scrape of her throat, but she pushed on. "You have to stop." His renewed growl told her he didn't agree. "Please." That growl increased in volume, and she shuddered. "Please, Declan. Please stop."

A single tear escaped her eye, trailing down her cheek and sliding through blood until it fell to the tile.

Declan whined, the wolf shuddering, and then released a whimper while he shifted his weight from foot to foot. Indecision. Worry. Finally the wolf opened his jaws. He retreated slowly, carefully, until her neck was no longer held immobile by his deadly fangs.

He moved away yet stayed close the entire time. He let her ease off Pike, and she stayed on her knees, unable to even consider pushing to her feet.

At least that'd been her plan until a new wave of threats piled into the room. One after another they rushed into the space, fangs bared, claws flexed, and guns searching for a target.

The rest of Declan's team.

CHAPTER THIRTY-FOUR

If they shot Declan, she'd kill them. Kill them all. She wasn't sure how, but it'd happen. It would take time, planning, money if she had to hire someone like Declan, but by the end they'd all be buried six feet under.

"Abby, wanna tell me what I'm looking at?" Birch's gaze flicked through the room. There was so much blood, it was hard to discern hers from Pike's from Declan's.

She opened her mouth, ready to say *something*, but Declan chose that moment to move. Not toward Birch, but her. He darted across the slick tile floor until he stood in front of her. Legs braced, muscles stiff, ruff standing on end, and teeth bared—he acted as a physical shield between her and his team. A shield? Or a possessive claiming?

Regardless, Birch squeezed the trigger, and a bullet slammed into the tile where Declan once stood.

"What the hell?" She managed to shout the words, her cougar having healed enough of her vocal cords to make speech possible. At least for that one yell. She wheezed the moment her bellow left her mouth, a new wave of pain squeezing her throat.

Three other guns pointed in their direction. At Declan.

She swallowed hard once more and begged her cat for help, pleaded with her to heal her voice instead of her cuts and bruises. The feline whined, torn between listening and preparing their body for a fight. If it came to that.

Her throat tingled, followed by a healing burn and a scratchy itch as flesh knitted back together. She coughed and wheezed, then cleared her throat.

"Easy," she said in an attempt to calm the beast. "I'm right here. I'm alive. I'm okay."

The wolf snorted, and the team echoed the scoff, which only served to draw Declan's fury once more.

"Don't listen to them, Declan." She kept her voice soft and low. "They don't matter." Abby's fingers brushed fur, and she sank them into his bloody ruff. "You saved me and protected me. They just want to help."

Cole changed position, the tiniest shift of his weight from one foot to the other, and destroyed the minute progress she'd made.

"*Cole*, keep your ass still." The cougar even went so far as to add a growl to her voice. Sure, the tiger could tear her to shreds without breaking into a sweat, but the idea of losing Declan trumped any pain the other man could inflict.

Another growl from Declan, more soft shushes from Abby. "Easy, Declan."

She moved the tiniest bit closer, knees scooching across the uneven tile while she closed the distance between them. His attention remained locked on the males in front of them while she crawled nearer and nearer. So close her bare stomach brushed his side.

"I'm right here," she whispered, and leaned forward, giving him some of her weight, proving that she lived and breathed because of him. "I'm right here. You got to me. You protected me. I'm okay."

She sifted her fingers through his matted fur once more, sliding her arm around his rib cage and finally resting her head between his shoulders. She listened to his heartbeat, the pulse steady despite his obvious fury. The heart of a killer. One who stared at danger and didn't feel an ounce of fear.

But he was ready to fight—to die—for her, wasn't he?

"I'm okay." She breathed deep and exhaled slowly, sending her breath swirling around them. He needed to creep past the aromas of the blood and find hers. "I'm okay and you're going to take me home."

His growl renewed, bursting through the room like a shot. Her cougar purred, the animal able to translate his rumble. It was pure possessiveness and a soul-deep determination to keep her at his side.

"Your home, Declan. We're going together. We're going to let your team deal with Pike, huh?" The growl changed, anger creeping into the rolling rumble. "The team will handle him. They won't let him go. Shhh..." She rubbed her cheek on his back. "He'll be punished, but right now I need you, huh?"

He narrowed his eyes, attention stroking what little of her he could see, and she could pinpoint the moment he was reminded she wore very little. Possessiveness filled his wolf's gaze once more, and the growl returned, directed at the conscious males in the room.

"They don't want me, Declan," she rushed to assure him, keeping her volume low.

Grant had to talk. "Well, I mean, I'd—"

The sound of flesh striking flesh was quickly followed by a grunt, and she hoped one of the other men had hit Grant to shut him up.

"Birch, how do we get out of here?" Abby stroked the

spot behind Declan's ear, carefully petting him—even if he wasn't a dog—to calm him once more.

"Helo's inbound. Less than five, and that's about how long it'll take to get to the surface." The bear spoke, but when she glanced at him, she realized his attention was on the unconscious Pike behind them, not on her and Declan.

"Birch?" She waited until his eyes met hers. "He hurt me, but I don't think he's..." She couldn't figure out how to put it into words. "There's something off. Just...talk to him before you do anything, okay?"

Birch grunted, and she figured that was the most she'd get as far as agreements went. He brought a hand to his ear, attention split between her and Declan and whatever voice came over the com. "Let's go. They're dropping in for a landing, and I want to get to work on this place."

"Okay." She stroked Declan once again, touch gentle. "You ready, wolf?" She combed his fur with her fingers. "We're going to walk out of here. No one is going to try to take me or hurt me, huh?"

He kept up his growl but with a tiny change, a shift of the tone that told her he grumbled out of habit instead of true unease and anger.

"We'll give escort." Birch broke in once more. "Grant takes point, and for the love of fuck, Grant, keep your trap shut."

Declan huffed in annoyance, but she felt his muscles relax, some of the greatest tension bleeding away.

"Okay, we're ready." As Abby pushed to her feet, she swayed, her legs wobbly. But she could work through the lingering pain and exhaustion. If she didn't, there was no telling what Declan would do—to the others and to Pike.

She kept one hand buried in his ruff, fingers fisting the strands, and she used that grip as both a restraint and support. She didn't want him diving after anyone, but she wasn't sure she could stand on her own either.

Grant left first while the others retreated, giving them space to pass, and they trailed in the other wolf's wake.

She paused long enough to glance at Birch. "Where are we going?"

Though, did it matter? They simply needed to be *away*. Wherever they traveled it simply had to be *not there*.

"Our home base is in North Carolina. You two can recover there."

When Declan didn't growl or stiffen, she figured he was okay with being shuttled off to another state, which meant Abby was fine with it as well. In truth, she simply didn't have the energy to fight.

"What about the director?"

Birch grunted. "He'll be happy to see UH destroyed." The bear shifter waved his hand and then looked to Cole. "Find Foster, and that tablet, grab any other computers they have, and then bring the fucking thing down."

"And Pike?" Cole's voice dropped to a low murmur.

Abby strained to hear Birch's response, but Grant realized she hadn't followed. "Abby? Something wrong?"

Declan released a soft grumble and stepped forward, his head and shoulders in front of her. He held her captive once again, standing between her and any perceived threat.

"I'm fine." She stroked the uneasy wolf and spoke to him. "I'm fine, but tired. Let's go, Declan."

The tablet, the compound, *Pike* . . . could all be handled by someone else.

CHAPTER THIRTY-FIVE

*D*eclan's mouth remained flooded with saliva, the need for flesh still riding him hard. He wanted to tear into his enemies and bathe in their blood. He wanted to show them *all* that they shouldn't touch what belonged to him.

Abby was *his*. Her small hand knotted in his fur, her weight firm against his side. Grant led them through the halls, gun in hand and body tense. Humans littered the ground—some shot, others torn by claws.

Pride and joy twined inside him. His team had done that—his *pack* even if they weren't all wolves. Not just his pack...the closest thing he had to family now that he knew about *him*.

The wolf's feral mind pulled on him, wrenching him away from thoughts of his brother and what he'd done.

Abby gave him more and more of her weight with every step, her slow strides gradually turning into shuffles. He turned his head and gave her a low bark. He swept his gaze over her, seeing the blood and bruises.

Fury—scorching hot and lightning fast—overtook him in that instant. More adrenaline flooded his four-legged form, and the craving for blood—retribution—

doubled. He'd calmed with Abby's presence, but the reminder of what she'd endured snatched away that hint of peace.

Her fist eased, and she ran her fingers through his fur. "Shh...I'm fine."

She wasn't fine. She limped. Some of her skin was purple. *She bled.*

He ached to go back and finish what he'd started in that room.

"Declan?" Grant called out. He flicked one ear toward his teammate while his gaze remained on Abby. "Helo's landing. Let's move."

Declan grumbled and closed his eyes for a moment. His wolf resisted when he fought for calm.

"Declan! Move your furry ass."

He'd show Grant a furry ass, the asshole.

As they finally exited the building, the echoing *thump, thump, thump* of the helo's propeller reached them, overwhelming any other sounds that crept into the space.

Which was why they—*he*—didn't see their attacker until it was too late. Because one moment Abby clung to him and the next...the next she was wrenched away and into another man's arms.

Declan spun with a snarl, muscles tense and lips pulled back to expose his fangs. He growled long and low, the sound escaping before he even recognized who he faced.

Eric Foster held a gun to Abby's head.

He'd kill him. Slowly. Painfully.

"Back off!" Eric's voice wavered. The man's eyes were wide and filled with terror. The muzzle of his gun shook the tiniest bit. In this other hand, he held Abby's tablet.

"Let her go." Grant's rumble rose above the sounds from outside.

"I'm leaving and you're going to let me." A tremble of fear still lingered in Eric's words.

Declan wanted nothing more than to leap onto the human and rip out his throat.

Grant snorted. "Not happening."

Definitely not.

Eric pressed the muzzle tighter to Abby's head. "I'll kill her."

Declan flexed his claws and sank lower, muscles tense and ready to roar into action. One leap. One bite.

"And you'll die before she hits the ground." The slow drawl was followed by the familiar racking of a gun's slide. Movement behind Eric signaled another team member's presence.

"Fucking furries... You think you can just kill me?"

Declan watched the man's eyes, his gaze unwavering. He could almost read Eric's mind as his options flickered through his head. In truth, there wasn't anything he could do to get out of this situation alive. Not. A. Thing.

Declan moved his attention to the gun Eric clutched in his right hand. It let him see the minute tensing of muscles and slight movement of joints. The shot was coming, the human was a split second from putting a bullet in Abby's head.

Declan leaped. Mouth wide and fangs bared, he sliced through the air with his gaze intent on his target. He craved blood—Eric's blood—and wouldn't stop until it flowed down his throat.

Screams. Shouts. Pain. Snap. Pop. Tear.

Blood. Eric's blood. But there was something else. A metallic tang that reminded him of his own scent.

Declan's blood.

He opened his mouth and let Eric's flesh fall from his jaw to land on the once living and breathing human. The body beneath him twitched and jerked—death throes creeping in. Declan swung his head to his right, to eyes landing on Abby slumped to the ground—crying but alive. A quick glance revealed that she wasn't injured. At least, not any more than she had been already.

Tears flowed down her cheeks and he whined. His mate shouldn't cry. He'd killed the man who wanted to hurt her. She should smile.

He stepped over Eric's downed body, intent on getting to her. He'd nuzzle and nip her, show her everything was okay and...

And he found himself flopping onto the ground. Had he tripped over Eric? Sloppy of him. He normally...

Was it harder to breathe? A little. That was odd.

Abby sobbed, her body shaking with the harsh sound, and he lifted his head. He released a soft chuff and mentally growled at the wolf. They could calm their mate better if he had lips instead of wolf's jaws.

Wait, had that chuff come out as a pained whine? No. He wasn't hurt. He'd killed Eric and...

And suddenly there were hands on him. Not just Abby's, but others as well. A firm grip that held him steady when he fought against their hold. It *hurt*.

"Don't die on me," Abby pleaded with him.

Why would he die? He...

"Please, Declan. *Don't die*."

She was being ridiculous, and he'd shift and tell her so. Women were a pain in the ass. Though he also liked her ass a whole lot. He snorted—maybe. He definitely nudged his wolf to retreat so his skin could overtake the fur. But nothing happened. Or rather, *something* happened, but not what he expected.

The world—his world—went black.

CHAPTER THIRTY-SIX

*T*hey hadn't made it to the base in North Carolina. Hell, Abby wasn't sure they'd managed to cross state lines. Bullets. Blood. Death.

She shuddered, and a tear—one of many—slid its way down her cheek. She'd experienced physical pain and heartbreaking loss in her life. It was nothing compared to the agony consuming her now.

Declan had died more than once during the mad flight to...wherever the hell they were. Some kind of medical center—obviously SHOC or shifter friendly. A regular human hospital was too dangerous, their shifter blood too different from humans.

And they'd managed to keep Declan alive.

Abby hadn't taken her attention off Declan from the moment they'd wheeled him out of surgery. Even now she kept her eyes on his chest, watching the rise and fall with his every breath. He'd stopped breathing more than once—first on the helicopter and again before they'd gotten him through the doors to surgery. She was sure it'd happened while he remained under the knife as well.

But he'd survived. He'd rescued her, protected her with his body, and survived. His skin was pale from blood loss.

At least that was what the SHOC doctors told her. She wasn't sure what to believe—or who she could trust. Not really.

Not after Pike—Declan's *brother*—had...Her stomach churned, twisting and knotting with a mixture of anxiety and rage.

She drew in a deep breath, tasting Declan's scent on her tongue, and released it slowly. She pushed some of her worry out of her body with every exhale. It had no place in the room. She had to remain strong. She could shatter into a jumble of sobbing pieces once Declan woke.

And he *would* wake.

Abby gently slid her hand beneath Declan's. The heat of his palm contrasted with the cool sheets against the back of her hand. If he was warm, he was alive. She had to remember that fact.

She leaned forward and rested her head on the soft mattress. She adjusted her position until she could see his chest—count his breaths.

In. Out. He's alive. In. Out. He didn't die. In. Out.

Fear still gripped her though. The terror that if she didn't keep her eyes on him, he'd succumb to his injuries.

Yet twenty-four hours of watching and waiting, twenty-four hours of dread, took its toll. The moment she let herself relax was the moment she lost herself to what could have been.

Her eyes fluttered closed, darkness enveloping her in a midnight blanket. When she opened them once more, *they* had her.

A roar shook the air, the bellow sinking past her flesh and into her bones. Rage accompanied the sound, the scent of fire burning her nose. Beneath that aroma was another— one she identified with ease—Declan.

Declan in pain. Declan filled with fury. Declan...calling to her with every howl and snarl. Other sounds joined—rattling chains, the *drip, drip, drip* of liquid striking tile, and the squelch of cut flesh.

A dim light flickered, blink, blink, blinking until the glow turned steady and illuminated the room.

Yes, she'd been right. *They* had her. No, *they* had *them*. Her and Declan both. They were in that tiled room—Abby secured to that chair once more while Declan hung from chains.

"Declan," she whispered, and she blinked back the tears stinging her eyes. Not tears from her own pain, but from his.

He'd come for her again, except this time he'd been captured. Now she was forced to watch Pike sink his claws into Declan's flesh and—

He screamed. Or did she? She wasn't sure. The shout echoed through the room, consuming the air and surrounding her in the unending cry. She jolted and jerked against the chains, fighting to be free, and...came awake with a harsh gasp.

She sucked air into her lungs, breathing deep, and her cougar sorted through the flavors. The air wasn't filled with the coppery tang of blood but the stinging stench of the hospital.

And Declan. His scent was not quite right—he remained tainted by the poison, but his true flavors persisted. The fabric beneath her cheek was cool while his hand on hers was warm. She drew in more of his aroma, savoring the intricate fragrance.

His chest still moved. Heat still bathed her skin. Abby called to her cat and the beast altered her hearing so she could listen to the rhythmic thud of his heart.

Declan lived.

She drew air in through her nose and held the breath while she begged her racing pulse to ease. Except that inhale brought her hints of someone else's presence. Snake— black mamba. Strong and yet somehow weak at the same time. Fury mixed with joy and a hint of...something.

Abby tore her attention from Declan and sought the source of that scent. She turned her head and found her stare captured by a stranger's. He stood on the other side of Declan's hospital bed, an immaculately pressed suit covering his towering frame. Midnight hair and nearly black eyes coupled with deeply tanned skin gave her a sense of...wrongness. No, it wasn't his coloring so much as it was his smell—the combination of both.

His eyes darkened further until she couldn't even see the difference between his iris and pupil. She felt as if she stared at the devil himself.

Then he smiled and shifted his weight, a dark lock of hair falling forward to curl above his brow. A seductive devil anyway.

"Miss Carter." He tipped his head. "I'm Harmon Quade, the director of Shifter Operations Command."

She should be at ease in his company, right? Because he was the director of SHOC and SHOC had helped her and...

"Mr. Quade."

"*Director*," he corrected.

"Director Quade," she whispered, and swallowed hard. Okay, *Declan's* team had helped her. For some reason, she felt as if this guy would have gladly left her for dead.

"Miss Carter, I—"

The room's door swung inward on silent hinges and the hallway's glow slipped into the room. The light cast the newcomer in a deep shadow, leaving only the newcomer's outline visible. He took one step and then two into the room, his steps heavy and solid on the aged linoleum floor.

She couldn't see his face, but his scent…She knew who'd come to her rescue. Again? Crisp forest, fresh rain, and newly turned earth. They weren't flavors that appealed to Abby's cougar, but the cat trilled with his presence anyway.

Better the devil she knew. "Cole."

CHAPTER THIRTY-SEVEN

COLE

*U*nfortunately, Cole couldn't kill the director for scaring
Abby. He didn't think Birch would let him maim the snake
either, so he settled for glaring at the other male. He slowly
made his way across the sterile room toward the woman
huddled on the right side of Declan's bed.

Abby wasn't *theirs*, but she belonged to Declan, which
meant that—in some way—she belonged to the team. Cole
was part of the team, so...

So, he was trying like hell to justify his feelings toward
the she-cat. The tiger rumbled a warning in his mind.

"Hey, Abby. How are you feeling?" he asked, not stopping his approach until he stood at her side. He eased close
enough for his thigh to brush her shoulder in silent support.

"Tired."

"Agent Turner, your presence isn't required." Quade bit
off those few words, and Abby stiffened.

A wisp of fear teased his nose, joining the other tendrils
of terror and anxiety that clouded the room.

"Funny how I don't care." Cole curled the corner of his mouth up into a small smirk. Just enough to annoy the director. He wanted the asshole's attention on *him*—not the little cougar.

"Maybe you don't understand. I don't want you here." Quade's eyes darkened, his snake coming out to play.

"Uh-huh. Why are you here, Quade?" Cole balanced his weight on the balls of his feet, body ready to spring into motion in an instant. It was never a good idea to relax in the presence of another predator. If he faced off against someone like himself, brute force would get the job done. A snake shifter? He had to be quick or he'd end up with the poison of a black mamba coursing through his veins.

"I'm taking Abby—"

"Miss Carter." Cole spoke over the other man. The team could call her Abby—no one else.

Quade's expression darkened. Yeah, they were having a pissing contest, but he didn't care. The director would attack any perceived weakness. "I'm taking Miss Carter, as well as the tablet recovered at the scene, to the southern field office."

Abby tensed, and Cole reached for her, giving her shoulder a firm squeeze. "Abby remains with her mate."

"She doesn't have a mating mark."

"The lack of a mark doesn't change her status. She's Declan's mate." He gestured at the unconscious werewolf. "Declan's a little indisposed right now, but I can pry his mouth open and force him to take a hunk out of her if you'd like." Cole lifted a single brow in question.

"That won't be necessary." Quade spoke through gritted teeth, the *s* long and drawn out. "I can wait for the debrief. For now I'll take the tablet and speak with Declan and Miss Carter at another time."

"Funny thing about that tablet." Cole scratched the back of his head, playing the good old boy just to annoy the director. "It didn't exactly make it through the op."

Dark scales rippled over Quade's skin, tanned flesh disappearing beneath the black of his snake for a flash before he regained control over his beast. "Excuse me?"

"The tablet was fucked during evac."

"Then Miss Carter will accompany me *now*. I need to know everything *she* knows about FosCo and Unified Humanity."

"See, the thing about it is..." Cole shook his head. "That's not happening."

"Agent Turner—"

"Harmon." A wave of dominance rolled into the room, the newcomer's strength as overwhelming as it was gentle. Birch wasn't a flashy alpha. He didn't beat anyone with his alpha strength unless necessary. He let his mere presence do the talking. "Is there a reason you're bothering my team?"

"Nah, he's not bothering us, Birch." Cole let himself relax—just a little—and was gratified to sense Abby's tension easing. "He's just checking on Declan here. He thought about taking Abby to the field office..."

"But he knows mates don't get separated when one of them is injured. Of course, he offered to wait until Declan is fully healed." Birch took over. His tone was light, but a core of steel lingered in his words. "Though I'm not sure why you want to waste time questioning her. The tablet was destroyed, and her only knowledge is that FosCo wired money to Unified Humanity. There's nothing more she could tell you."

He could mention what they'd downloaded from the Ogilve, Piers, and Patterson servers, but the team wasn't ready for the director to have access to that information just yet. Possibly never.

"I see," Quade murmured.

"I am glad you decided to visit Declan during his time of need, though. It saves me having to e-mail you later." Birch played the good old boy just as well as Cole. "Since you'd decided to suspend us, the team is going to take some time off. Declan needs to recover, and the rest of the team needs a little breather. Plus there's the matter of Pike, as we discussed."

Quade shook his head. "Pike requires further discussion. Right now you need to focus on finding someone to replace Declan. He'll be punished for—"

Abby whimpered, and Cole growled, his tiger taking control of his voice. "Excuse me?"

Birch shot him a dark look—a silent order to shut the fuck up—and then spoke to the director. "Why?"

"He went rogue and absconded with a prisoner. A clear violation of SHOC orders."

The tension in the room doubled, the air thick with the growing need for violence. Birch locked gazes with Quade, the two men staring each other down. Abby cowered, leaning into Cole when yesterday she would have put as much distance between them as possible.

Cole snorted, rolled his eyes, and decided to channel Grant. "Yo, Birch. I know we say he's got a stick up his ass, but maybe it's a dictionary. 'Absconded.' What kind of bullshit word is that?"

Quade glared. Birch kinda glared while he fought the urge to smile. Abby released the breath she'd been holding but remained tense.

"Agent Birch, I will not stand here..."

"So leave?" Cole lifted his eyebrows, and hope sparked in his heart.

Unfortunately, Quade just went back to glaring at him and stayed put.

"As far as Team One is concerned, Declan Reed secured the cougar shifter, Abby Marie Carter, in a secondary location and awaited the team's arrival. At no time did he violate SHOC directives." Birch tipped his head toward Cole. "Agent Turner as well as Agents Grant Shaw and Ethan Cross will testify to that fact."

"Bullshit," Quade snapped. "You expect me to trust a bunch of heartless, mercenary killers?"

"You should." Cole's tiger padded forward. Even if he *was* lying, the cat didn't like being called a liar. His vision changed, altered by the presence of his inner beast. "You should believe us because we *are* a bunch of heartless, mercenary killers. It'd be better for your health."

"Are you—"

"Director Quade." Birch cut the other man off. "I think Declan needs his rest. Grant has compiled the team's field report, including Abby's statement." The team alpha's tone softened slightly while he worked to placate the director. "While her intel is minimal, he's also piecing together the tablet recovered at the scene."

Quade gestured toward Cole. "This one said the tablet was destroyed."

This one. Cole swallowed the growl that threatened to break free. This was one time he needed to step back and let Birch do the talking. He had more experience with these games.

"We don't know the extent of the damages, but you *will* be the first call I make once Grant has finished his analysis," Birch assured the director. "Miss Carter, unfortunately, was in the wrong place at the wrong time."

Quade's stare held a speculative gleam, as if he didn't quite believe Birch. Considering the grizzly was lying out of his ass—that the tablet was toast—he had a reason to be suspicious.

"Fine." Director Quade stomped from the room, bypassing Birch without another word.

Then Cole had the grizzly's attention. "Stay put. I'll send Ethan in to relieve you in a few hours."

Cole jerked his head in a brisk nod, and then he was alone with Abby once more, the curvy cougar shifter slumping against him.

"Abby? You okay?"

She snorted.

"Yeah, dumb question." He chuckled. He was so fucked up. Even Abby's snort was cute. He sighed and shook his head, stepping away from the curvy cougar. She didn't belong to him. She belonged to Declan. He had to remember that.

Cole padded to the other side of the bed, taking up the space the director had left. He snagged a nearby chair and tugged it close before flopping into the seat. He leaned back in the chair with a sigh and turned his attention to his friend's profile.

The lucky fucker. He got his ass kicked—almost died—and he still got the girl. Not that Cole wanted Abby, per se, but…He glanced at her, gaze touching on her blond hair, pink lips, upturned nose, and sparkling eyes. He wanted what she represented. Or at least, what she *could* represent someday.

"Abby?" He kept his voice low, just loud enough to draw her attention.

"Yeah?"

"Declan is your mate." She shook her head as if to deny him, and he snorted. "He's going to wake up territorial as hell. Don't let anyone else put their scent on you, okay?"

"Like you?"

He hadn't exactly touched her with the intent of pissing off his friend, but he wasn't exactly upset about it either.

"Yeah." He gave her a small smile. "As soon as he gets some protein in him, he'll want to leave. Birch is sending you two to his lake cabin. It's private and secluded—no other shifters there. He can finish recovering, and he'll have some time to figure this mate shit out."

She shook her head. "But we're not—"

"Suck it up and quit lying to yourself. He's yours just as much as you're his." And didn't *that* hurt like a bitch.

CHAPTER THIRTY-EIGHT

*D*eclan had been "healing" for two days at Birch's lakeside cabin and he was about to lose his mind. Shifter healing didn't take that long, dammit, and now he was bored as hell.

He needed someone to kill. Someone he was *allowed* to kill. He had plenty of guys he *wanted* to take out—every UH human he could find—but Birch told him he couldn't step off the property. The team had shit to do at the North Carolina SHOC base, and Papa Bear didn't want him stirring up anything new.

Birch also told Declan that if he was so fucking bored, he should quit being a pussy and claim Abby already. Declan hated to admit Birch was right, which made him hate the grizzly even more. As if it were that easy, but it fucking wasn't. Asshole.

Declan stared out the window of Birch's cabin and eyed the mountains in the distance. Normally the forest and mountain areas were for runs—alone or in groups—but maybe he could find a natural grizzly bear and take his frustrations out on one of them.

It'd get him out of the home and free of Abby's tormenting scent. They hadn't shared a bed since their time at Pike's place. It was enough to drive a wolf mad.

Which brought him back to needing to work off some of his pent-up desire.

He let himself imagine hunting a big-assed bear—just for a minute—and then sighed. It'd probably make Abby angry, and for some reason that *mattered* to him and the wolf.

He shook his head and sighed. She'd tossed his nuts in a jar and didn't even realize it.

"Declan?" Her soft voice drifted down the hallway, stroked his chest, and moved lower, giving his dick a nice squeeze.

"Yeah, I'm coming." Not really, but he'd like to—deep inside her over and over. Except that wasn't happening. Yet.

The short hallway led to the central living room, a great room that also housed an open kitchen and a space tucked in a corner with a dining room table and a couple of chairs. Solid wood floors with layer upon layer of sealant filled the area. Pretty and easy to clean. At least that's what he'd been told.

Abby had her back to him, that curved ass swaying from side to side while she danced at the kitchen stove, some random oldies song playing on the radio. The scent of frying bacon and eggs reached out for him, and his stomach growled, the wolf hungry. In truth, he was hungry for Abby, but the beast would take breakfast as a consolation prize.

"Hey," he murmured, drawing her attention, and she glanced over her shoulder. A soft smile curved her lips, blue eyes intent on his. Then they focused elsewhere, traveling down his body in a sweeping caress. "You need help with breakfast?" he asked.

She gave him another heavy-lidded look, pink tongue darting out to lick her lips. Then she had to go and nibble that plump lower lip, and all he could think about was tugging it free and giving her something else to put in her mouth.

A soft breeze drifted through the room, sliding through the kitchen window and swirling around the space. Sure, it brought in the crisp scents of the country air, but it gave him something else, too. The musky sweetness of her desire. The delicious scent of the sweet cream between her thighs, and he wondered when she'd let him get a taste.

His cock throbbed in his jeans, length hardening within the confines of the thin fabric, and that was where her eyes went next. Right to his dick, staring at him as if she was starving and the bacon in that pan wasn't going to do shit to sate her hunger.

She needed him? As much as he needed her? She'd had a great big no-trespassing sign stamped across her forehead from the moment he'd woken in the hospital. She'd kept her distance.

She'd pulled away every time he'd gotten close. It made him realize he'd obviously been good enough for some fun when they were being chased, but now that things were calm, she'd changed her mind.

The wolf kept telling him he was a dumbass and that he needed to nut up already.

"Sweetheart." He moved forward, stalking her as if *he* were the cat. Wolves knew how to hunt, though. How to watch and wait for the perfect moment to pounce. Fuck, he hoped it'd be time to pounce on Abby soon. "You keep looking at me like that, I'm going to take what you're offering."

Abby's face flushed pink and she dropped her gaze to the ground before she spun and refocused on breakfast.

Another gust of wind, another tempting wave of her desire. His threat hadn't diminished her need. Nah, it'd intensified the scent of her yearning. She wanted him—bad.

Declan kept up with his slow and steady tempo until his body was less than an inch from hers. He placed one hand on either side of her, palms resting on the front edge of the stove—away from the flames, but close enough to hold her captive.

He bent down, not touching her, but he was damned close, and murmured next to her ear, "Abby."

She shuddered, a full-body shake that he couldn't miss. "Declan. How do you want…?"

His cock throbbed, and he groaned before nuzzling the side of her neck. He breathed deep, took in the delicious scent of her skin. "Any way I can get you. Beneath me. On top of me. Clinging to me." He kissed a spot of bare skin just beneath her ear and smiled when a tremor racked her body. "While you come on my cock and scream my name."

Abby whimpered and swayed, as if her knees were no longer willing to support her. "Declan, you can't…"

"Can't what?" He could do anything he set his mind to, dammit. Right now his mind was filled with fucking Abby hard and deep.

For-fucking-ever.

"You…we…" She stuttered every other word, and he nibbled her earlobe, making her shudder once again.

"We? We can use this counter? We can use the couch? We can find a bed?" He eased forward the tiniest bit, his body brushing her sensuous curves. Curves he wanted to worship with his hands—his mouth. He wanted to drop to his knees and explore every inch of her lush body. "There are several down the hall to choose from."

Abby shook her head, her hair caressing his skin, and he

was the one who trembled. His balls drew up tight and he rushed toward the edge of release, his body ready to find that ultimate pleasure from a simple tease from her *hair*.

What the hell was wrong with him?

Abby. Abby was wrong with him. Those few moments they'd shared hadn't been enough. He'd never get enough.

"You know we can't."

"I know we *can*," he countered.

Abby sighed, and he nearly groaned aloud. He knew that sound. That was the "we need to talk" sigh.

She placed the greasy tongs on the spoon rest and turned to face him, forcing him to back up a little and give her space. He didn't want to give her space, dammit. He wanted them to occupy the same space at the same time—specifically, with his dick inside her.

"Declan." Another one of those sighs.

Fuck.

"Abby?" He quirked a brow. Maybe if he teased her, he'd get out of some emotional "express his feelings" talk. He'd done enough of that with SHOC-appointed therapists over the last two years.

Same answer, different doctor. *The subject is a sociopath who cares for nothing.*

They didn't get that he cared about something in his life. Things he refused to talk about. Like his brother. Well, before Pike facilitated Abby's kidnapping. Now he only cared about her.

"This..." Now she was on to head shaking. Not a good sign.

"This is something we should take to the bedroom. Great idea," he murmured, and curled his left arm around her back, palm flat just above the curve of her ass, tugging her closer. He'd forgotten the feeling of her lushness, the softness of her skin, and how he reacted to the points of her nipples against his chest. Another signal that she was aroused.

"No."

He hated that word. Normally he simply ignored it because it generally came with "please don't kill me."

With Abby, it was "no, we can't get horizontal."

Dammit.

He sighed and dropped his head forward, resting his forehead on her shoulder. He closed his eyes and tried to block out her scent, the sound of her heartbeat, and the way her breath fanned his shoulder and then drifted down his back. He basically ignored everything about her that made his dick hard.

She squirmed and wiggled, trying to do...something.

"Abby? Just...just sit still for a minute." Maybe a century. Or ten.

She didn't stop, though. Nah, she had to torture him further. Had to wriggle until she had her arms free and wrapped around his shoulders. One hand rested between his shoulders while the other toyed with the hair at the base of his neck. He shuddered and gritted his teeth. He wasn't going to come from a hand in his *hair*. He wasn't some adolescent pup who'd never gotten his dick wet.

"Abby." He added a growl to his voice, dropping it low in a clear threat. Not that he'd ever hurt her, but she didn't know that.

She snorted.

Okay, maybe she did know. Dammit.

"We really, really can't. Not while things are so..." She shook her head, dark strands caressing his heated skin, painting him in her scent. It soothed the wolf—a little—to have that hint of her on his skin. "So in the air."

"Birds are in the air. I'm not a bird," he grumbled.

She chuckled. Here he was, hard as a rock and desperate for her and she *chuckled*.

"No," she whispered. "No, you're not. You're a wolf. A big, bad SHOC agent and..." More sighing, more head shaking. He hated that shit. "And I'm a cougar who has a life somewhere else."

"You seriously think I'm going to let you go back to that number-crunching hellhole? So they can assign you to another company that's in bed with UH?" He pulled away from her, his rising anger doing a lot to tamp down his lust. "Or that I'll let you walk around as if UH doesn't have a target on your back?"

Her lower lip trembled, and he hated himself a little bit. Not a lot, because she needed to understand, but a little.

"Aw, shit," he grumbled, and hugged her tight. Not because he wanted to get in her pants but because she was on the verge of tears. He couldn't have that. "I'm not gonna let anything happen to you. I swear it. We'll figure something out."

"I had a life, Declan. I had a place," she whispered, pain in every syllable and the sting of her emotional agony in his nose. "I only ever wanted somewhere to just be *me*." He rubbed her back, not real sure how to respond, so he kept his mouth shut. "I had it with my parents, and then I was a lone cougar in Alaska, but..." Moisture dropped onto his shoulder, and he wondered who else he could kill for her. Maybe those asshole seals in Alaska. He'd never eaten one. Probably pretty fatty, but he could— "I made a life for me. I was respected. I had a place in the world. It wasn't the greatest, but it was *mine*."

"You don't think you have a place now? Aw, sweetheart..." He hated this heart-to-heart crap, but he'd deal with it if it meant stopping her tears. He pulled away and cupped her cheeks, forcing her to meet his gaze. "I don't know what happened to your parents and I'm sorry for it. As for Alaska, you say the word and that entire herd is gone. The world doesn't need their shit stinking up the air. As for your job, that was just a paycheck."

One tear escaped the corner of each eye, trailed down her cheek, and rested on his thumbs. "But your place? It's right fucking here. With me. Do you understand?"

Abby's chin wobbled, and she shook her head. She was breaking his damn heart.

"You're gonna make me get all emotional and in touch with my feelings." He groaned and sighed. Declan bent his neck and rested his forehead on hers, their stares locked on each other. "From the moment I saw you, you were mine. Not because I wanted in your bed—because we both know I want to haul your ass into the other room and fuck you so hard you can't walk straight for a week—but because you just *were*. Wolf didn't care what had to be done. I didn't know it then, but you were *it*."

"It?"

"You're everything, sweetheart. You want a job, we'll find you one that keeps you away from UH assholes. You want a family, we'll work on making one. Start on this counter if that's what you want. I'm gonna make you so fucking happy, and I don't care who I have to kill to do it. But no matter what, at the end of the day, you're my mate and I'm fucking keeping you."

"Cougars don't mate."

Declan snorted. "Apparently cougars *do*. Your parents did."

Abby shook her head. "My mom was a cougar and my dad was a wolf. They only mated because Dad was old-fashioned and wasn't…"

"Call it old-fashioned if you want, but he wasn't gonna let her go. Wolves find a mate; wolves keep a mate. And then they mark their territory. Make sure every male who even gets a hint of our mate's scent knows she's taken." She was quiet for a second, just staring at him, and he needed her to understand. "Abby?"

"Yeah?"

"You're taken."

Her breath hitched "I ..."

A new scent teased his nose, one that had his wolf wanting to sneeze. "Abby?"

"Yeah?"

"The bacon's burning."

CHAPTER THIRTY-NINE

*B*acon's burning?" As cliché as it sounded, Abby could get lost in Declan's eyes for years—forever. She swayed in place, mind clouded by her fiery arousal and the pulses of need that attacked with every beat of her heart. She took a deep breath, seeking out his scent, and got...a lungful of smoke. Her cat sneezed and she coughed. She pulled away from Declan while she alternated between choking on the clouds of smoke and waving the worst of it off while she transferred the hot pan to another burner to cool.

She shoved Declan aside and raced to the kitchen window. She flicked the latch and shoved the thing open further to let in more fresh air and push the dark clouds *out*.

And Declan...just laughed.

She glared.

He laughed harder.

"Like a friggin' hyena," she grumbled, and passed him again, snatching the dish rag from the counter and wrapping it around her hand before she grabbed the handle of the frying pan.

"Nah, I'm all wolf, sweetheart." He murmured, laughter still in his voice while he reached around her, took the pan from her grip, and nipped her shoulder.

His voice, that nibble, sent a tremor down her spine, the sensation followed by an overwhelming wave of desire. For him and only him. Forever. Even if cougars weren't a "let's get mated" kind of species.

"Declan." She'd somehow managed to turn his name into both a plea and a scold in one.

"'Declan, you're right'?" He slipped his arm around her waist, his solid front to her back. "'Declan, I don't want to live without you'? Or 'Declan, I want to get mated'?"

Abby wanted to throw caution to the wind, to throw her hands in the air and say "screw it," but ...

The cougar told her to shove that "but" up her butt.

Did she want him? More than anything in her life. Mentioning the fact that cougars didn't mate was just an excuse. Some did. Some were driven to find that *one* person and claim them before anyone else could. Her parents had been like that, and since meeting Declan, Abby realized she was like that as well.

He released her and moved to the sink, dropping the sizzling pan while she went to the front door of the small cabin and pulled it open. A cross breeze would get the place aired out and—

And she found herself wrapped in his arms once more, carried to the comfy couch, and he dropped onto the soft cushions, her sitting across his thighs.

"Did you pick one yet?" he murmured, and that talented mouth found hers, teeth nibbling her lower lip.

"Pick what, now?" A sting zapped down her spine, and she melted against his chest, relishing that snippet of pain. Her cat liked it, liked being submissive to the wolf. Though it was quick to point out the submission was only in the bedroom. She was a modern cat, after all.

"I'm right. You don't want to live without me. You want

to get mated." He lapped at her lower lip, soothing the sharp sting he'd caused.

Abby shook her head, trying to clear away the sensual spell he wove around her mind. "No, you don't. You only think you want me." It didn't matter that she craved him more than air. "The thing with UH and your team and Pike..." She hated the way he winced. "You want something to cling to, Declan."

He pulled back, those sparkling blue eyes on hers, and she melted beneath his sensual stare. What he wanted was there, plain to be seen by anyone—everyone.

"Because Pike betrayed me? Betrayed SHOC? Shifters?"

Abby nodded, and he shook his head, but she wouldn't be brushed aside. "You lost your brother, and now you need something to hold on to."

It was why she'd kept her distance. She wasn't going to be used like a comfy blanket and tossed aside when his emotions recovered.

"For a smart woman, you're very dumb."

All right, getting sexy wasn't at the top of her list any longer. Declan tucked a lock of hair behind her ear, his stare turning intent, his teasing smile gone. "I can't claim to know Pike's thoughts, but if he was going to truly betray our kind, the SHOC compounds would have been hit already. That would have been followed by council headquarters. What he was doing there is something he'll have to deal with, but he didn't betray SHOC."

"He betrayed you," she whispered. "And I won't be some substitute—"

"For the love of bloody, rare deer, woman," he growled, and bared his fangs, the teeth growing longer and longer until they resembled the wolf's.

A quick flip found her on her back, Declan hovering above her with his hips snug between her spread thighs. The hard ridge of his arousal nestled along the juncture of her thighs, the hot hardness stoking her arousal once again.

"I'm gonna say this one more time. You listening?" A light dusting of gray fur slid along his jaw, and blue eyes flashed yellow.

Her breath caught, heart racing with a combination of desire and worry. Which made her want him even more. It felt good—this contrast between need and fear.

"Listening?" He growled deeper, his whole body shaking, and his dick vibrated against her center.

Abby swallowed hard and nodded. She was listening. Ish.

"Pike is an asshole. My team can fuck off, and if UH even *thinks* of coming near you again..." His growl intensified, more fur sliding into place. "You. Are. Mine. You run, I'll chase you. You hide, I'll find you. You even *think* about another man, I'll kill him." He rocked his hips, a roll of his hard length along her cloth-covered slit. "Everything that's happened since I met you has been *for* you."

Her body warmed, not just from desire, but from another emotion as well. Caring? Hope? Soft tendrils of love?

That last thought had her freezing in place for a moment. They'd known each other for a handful of days and he was talking about mating and claiming and...

Declan lowered himself, more of his weight resting on hers, and she widened her legs further, wanting him as close as possible. She craved the feel of his soft fur on her skin, craved the closeness that would come from mating.

Mating. Her human mind still balked. Cougars didn't... The she-cat reminded her that her parents *did*. Because her mother was a cougar and her father was a wolf who refused to let her out of his sight.

He looked at her the way Declan looked at Abby. A little creepy, a hint psychotic, but beneath it all was an instinctual need to simply *have*. All of her.

Abby's inner animal told her that it felt the same. It needed Declan.

"I don't know what to say." She cupped his cheeks and lifted her head, meeting him halfway when he lowered his own. She brushed her mouth across his, a caress of soft flesh that she gradually deepened. He took more and she gave it, opening for him when his probing tongue demanded entrance.

He swept into her mouth, and she savored his taste. Abby entwined her fingers behind Declan's neck, firm hold keeping him close while their kiss continued. A brush of his chest on hers, teasing her hardened nipples. The rocking of his hips so his cock taunted her hidden depths. Then the way his hand...He skated it down her side until he reached her ass. He cupped the right globe, gave it a hard squeeze, and then moved on.

He gripped her thigh and squeezed, then pulled and opened her to him even more.

Her whole body shook, her clit twitching and pussy growing heavy with wanting. She needed so much. Him inside her, him claiming her, him...

Abby rolled her thoughts back. Claiming?

Yes, her cat hissed. She wanted to be claimed by Declan, and she wanted to do some claiming of her own.

That realization, the confirmation of her feelings that'd prodded her only a day or two ago, forced her to tear her mouth from his.

"Declan," she gasped, and he growled.

"Mine." He took her lips once again, the kiss turning dominant, punishing. He lifted his mouth and tipped his head, going deeper, taking more. *"Mine."*

On his next change of position, when he next put more than a hairsbreadth between their lips, she rushed out a single word. One that would irrevocably change their worlds forever. One she no longer hesitated to use. "Yes."

"Oh, *fuck no*." A familiar voice, one that belonged to a soon-to-be dead man if Declan's sudden snarl was any indication.

Her mate—or soon-to-be mate—ripped his mouth from hers, lifted his head, and bared his teeth at the person near the door. She had a suspicion, but she hoped she was wrong.

Abby turned her head and released an annoyed huff when she saw who lingered. She'd just gotten her head wrapped around the mating thing and now they were interrupted. "Hi, Ethan." Her attention drifted to the men crowded behind the lion shifter. "Hi, guys."

The four members of Declan's SHOC team waved. Well, Ethan waved while he shook his head. Birch looked everywhere but at her and Declan. Grant simply gave an absent nod as he stomped past them in search of the kitchen because "something smelled good." While Cole stared and wiggled his eyebrows, before asking, "How would you guys feel about a threesome?"

Which officially ended any chance of their mating occurring in the next several hours.

CHAPTER FORTY

*T*wo hours and no sex later and Declan was ready to kill them all. Starting with Birch and his idea that agents should bunk with other team members.

Birch wanted him and Ethan to share a room, as if they were kids needing to learn to play well with others.

"You can fuck right the hell off." Declan shook his head. He ignored Birch's nod as well as Abby's soft squeeze of his hand. "The answer is no."

"What he said." Ethan pointed at Declan, but his attention was on the grizzly. "I'm not sharing a room with those two. Do you know what happened the last time we shared a space and the asshole brought some chick home? I didn't get to sleep for *days*, Birch. They fucked for *days*. You know my cat gets pissy when he doesn't get his sleep, and coffee doesn't do shit for my whiny bitch."

"If you'd stop calling your lion a whiny bitch, maybe it'd stop being such an asshole," Declan drawled, and he tried to pretend Abby's growl wasn't vibrating through him. The asshole just *had* to mention a woman from his past. He wasn't sure which one Ethan was talking about, but bringing up any of them in front of Abby was a dick move.

Even if her growl made his dick hard. Not that he could

do anything *with* his stiff cock with the team hanging around.

"Both of you, shut it." Birch growled low, his deep rumble filled with frustration and menace. The bear focused on Ethan. "The team bunks up. Always has." The glare turned to Declan. "Always will."

"The team hasn't had a mated member before," Declan pointed out. He wasn't having a fucking unmated lion in the same room as his mate. He was only bunking with one person and that person didn't have a dick.

"You're not mated, are you?" Birch quirked a brow, and Declan glared at the man.

"I was gonna take care of that—"

"Gonna isn't done." The grizzly cut him off.

"I'll show you *done*," Declan sneered, and curled his lip. His wolf paced just beneath his skin, hunting for an opening so it could pounce. He wanted to work off the energy coursing through him, and taking it out on Birch was as good an answer as any.

"Okay, then." Abby stepped between him and Birch, her hand on Declan's chest to keep him still. The only thing that saved Birch was the fact that she didn't touch the bear. "Let's just calm down."

A snort came from behind them, Grant strolling forward and joining their small group. They'd been having the same argument so long, Cole had started the grill. Now he shoved a paper plate of food at Grant. This was Birch's attempt at having just a regular, relaxing barbecue.

Though the meat wasn't exactly cooked—just a little seared.

"Just let 'em fight it out." Grant spoke around a bite of his burger. The wolf needed to learn some manners and not talk until he was done chewing. "The winner gets his way."

Birch sighed. "They both want the same thing."

Grant shrugged. "Then let 'em have their way."

"Grant, it's important to—"

"Have a happy, cohesive team in order to effectively protect and care for our kind. We're given a great responsibility as SHOC agents, and we can't betray the trust of our people by fighting among ourselves." Grant took another bite of his burger. "I know. You say that every time." He shrugged and kept chewing. "It'd save you a few minutes to just tell us 'same shit different day.' Save even more if you shorten it to 'SSDD.' We've memorized it; it doesn't need to be repeated." The wolf waved his plate toward Cole standing near the grill. "You know, Cole does the best impression of you." Grant yelled to the tiger. "Yo, Cole, come show Birch how good you make fun of him. Do the happy, codependent speech."

"Children. You're all fucking children." Birch pinched the bridge of his nose, closed his eyes, and sighed.

"With guns." Ethan grinned and rocked back and forth. "Big ones."

Abby sighed. One of *those* sighs. Dammit.

"Sweetheart..." Declan murmured, and placed his hand over hers.

"I thought you were calling her 'baby.'" Cole joined them and stood beside Grant, eating a mostly rare burger, as well. Then the tiger turned to Birch and dropped his voice. "We have to form a happy, cohesive team in order to—"

Birch pointed at Cole. "Shut the fuck up."

Cole shrugged and bent his head to take a bite of potato salad from his plate. Without a spoon. Then his attention came to Declan. "Baby?"

"She doesn't like me calling her 'baby.'"

"Can I call her 'baby'?" Cole waggled his eyebrows,

and Declan's wolf surged. His skin rippled, his beast's nails scraping his muscles and stretching his flesh. He pulled on the animal, yanking and tugging it away from the edge of his control. It was so close, so near to busting free, but a fight with Cole wouldn't solve his problems.

It would make him feel better though, so maybe...

"No, you can't, and if you even think—" His arms stung, fur sliding free of his pores, and a growl built in his chest. One that vanished beneath Abby's soothing caress. She traced circles on his chest, a soft *shhh* escaping her mouth.

"He's just messing with you," she murmured.

"And I'm *just* going to mess with him." Hard. Declan's human half still felt the urge to kick Cole's ass.

"Okay, I think we're getting off-track here. Let's refocus on the problem and discuss what can be done." She laid both hands on his chest. She had to really want to redirect him if she was willing to get back to the "fuck no Ethan isn't sharing a room with us" argument. They'd been having the same one for nearly two hours.

"There's nothing to discuss," Birch growled. "We work as a team, we live as a team—"

"We survive as a team." The rest of them chorused, and Birch growled louder.

"Even after you all find your mates? Have pups and cubs? I mean, sharing a cabin on the lake is one thing, but what about when you're at the home base and waiting for an assignment? How big of a home do y'all plan on building to house everyone?" Abby's soft questions—true confusion in every syllable—silenced Birch. "And where?"

Their leader shook his head. "We're not 'mate' kind of shifters."

"Speak for yourself." Cole spoke around a mouthful of burger. "Some of the other teams have families and crap.

They have houses close to each other, but they each have their own. This asshole is no better or worse than the rest of us, and Abby is willing to overlook the guns and killing and shit." He shrugged. "I don't see why we can't find someone if they're willing to keep an open mind."

"Aw," Ethan drawled. "Cole wants a girlfriend."

Cole swung at Ethan, plate balanced in his other hand while the tiger and lion sparred, trading insults and blows. The four of 'em just watched those two go at each other, alternating between laughing and growling while they fought.

Birch released another sigh—this one bone-tired. "We're not like other teams. We do the jobs they won't. We take the risks that send other teams running."

Grant coughed and spoke low. "Pussies."

"We don't take mates because any-damn-one deserves better than a future cut short by tying themselves to an agent from Team One."

Declan grunted and Grant did the same. Yeah, they did. Declan hoped Abby never realized the kind of wolf she tied her life to and the heartache that might await her down the road.

Abby withdrew her hands, and he slid his arms around her waist, unwilling to let her go far. She turned in his embrace to face Birch, and her next words came out as a soft whisper. "You see yourself as a poor choice, but any woman would be lucky to mate one of your men, Birch. Life is a risk. Mating an agent on Team One is the best mistake a woman can make."

Birch gave her a questioning look, one eyebrow raised. Yeah, Declan wanted to know what she was talking about, too. Or what she was smoking.

"You take orders from SHOC, but you also ignore them

when they go against what you feel is right. You're all loyal to each other—to the point that you were ready to go rogue for Declan...and me." She fell silent for a moment, and he lowered his head, pressing a soft kiss to her crown. "If that isn't happy or cohesive, who cares? You're dedicated to each other and doing what's right. You've done bad things, but you're not bad *people*. You take the jobs others won't because you're better than them."

Grant grunted. "What she said." He took another bite of potato salad. "Does this mean I can get the fuck away from Cole's rank ass?"

"I don't smell!" Cole had one arm wrapped around Ethan's neck.

"Your boots, man! Get some insoles or something. Put those little odor eliminator balls in them. I gave them to you for Christmas and I still have to deal with your stink," Grant called out, and Cole released Ethan, turning his anger on the wolf instead.

"How'd I get a bunch of babies instead of killers?" Birch grumbled.

"Aw, you know you always wanted to be a big papa bear," Declan drawled, and Birch flinched, an old pain flitting across his features. Fuck, he was an idiot. "Birch, man, I'm sorr—"

The bear waved him off. "It's fine. I'll talk to the director. Find us a few options for a home base. See what's available across the country and what it'll take to get us set up somewhere. If we've gotta build six homes from scratch, it'll take time, but maybe we can—"

"Six?" Abby voiced the same question he had. "I thought SHOC teams were five-shifter teams. I don't want my own house or anything." She chuckled, and Declan echoed her, but he didn't take his eyes off Birch.

Which meant he saw the emotions that slipped over his features—guilt, worry, unease, regret...

"Birch?" Declan's wolf added its own hint of a rumble to his voice.

"About that..." Birch hedged.

"Yo, Birch. I didn't realize you'd talked to Dec and Abby about Pike already." Ethan was still bent in half and wheezing, not that Cole let him breathe. "He coulda flown in with us."

"Pike?" Declan's snarl was all wolf. All furious beast anxious to rip out throats and shit on bodies. *"What about Pike?"*

Declan followed the direction of Ethan's gaze across the yard until his eyes landed on what—*who*—had captured the lion's attention.

Pike—brother, enemy, dead wolf walking.

CHAPTER FORTY-ONE

*T*here was knowing that Abby was missing part of Pike's story and then there 'was *knowing* she was missing part of his story. She was still stuck on the first knowing, which was why her anger flared white-hot in an instant.

The man had threatened her, scared her, and hit her. *More than once.*

All while working for Unified Humanity.

Yes, there might be wholly justifiable reasons for his behavior when she'd been his captive.

Unfortunately, now that she was free, standing among shifters who'd risked everything to keep her safe, she kinda...forgot. Just for a moment, just a split second when her human mind experienced a distracting jolt of fear, which gave her cougar a chance to snatch control. The cougar didn't care about anything but the fear and pain. It only remembered the fight to ground Declan, to stop his wolf from taking over completely and turning him feral.

Pike hurt her. Stupid or not, the cougar wanted to hurt him back.

Declan released her, his arms withdrawing, and his wolf's nails caught on the shirt she wore. Already his beast was on the surface and ready to tackle Pike. Abby would simply have to be faster, and her cougar leaped to her aid. Her body strengthened, legs adopting the power of her cat. And the agility.

The agility that let her dart ahead of Declan, quickness that let her duck his snatching grasp, and push of strength that allowed her to leap and pounce on the wolf from twenty feet away.

Snarls and growls came from behind Abby, but she only had eyes for Pike. She struck Pike's chest, sending him falling backward, and she straddled his body. She dominated him, wrapped her claw-tipped hand around his throat until they penetrated his skin, and hissed once more. The coppery scent of his blood hit her nose, and her cougar purred. Pike had drawn her blood, and now she did the same.

Her other half gave her more power, infusing more of her body with the beast's presence. Now she waited. Waited for his retaliation. Waited for him to throw her off and attack. Waited for him to . . .

Well, she sure as hell hadn't been waiting for him to bare his throat. He turned his head aside, gaze on the ground while he also attempted to expose more of his throat. Then . . . a whimper. A whine. A wolf's plea for . . . forgiveness?

No. She shook her head with disbelief, but her cat released an encouraging trill inside her mind. The beast recognized something Abby didn't, but if identifying what the animal saw meant she didn't get to cut Pike into tiny pieces . . .

Well, she didn't want to know.

He made the sound again, more of his neck bared, his head turned as far as he could. Exposed. Submissive.

A stupid freaking *apology,* and now she didn't feel quite so justified in her attack. It was no fun beating up someone who wouldn't fight back. Abby huffed—frustrated and annoyed—before moving to sit beside him.

A hiss reached her ears, the sound purely feline, and she knew one of the others had shifted—Cole or Ethan was delaying Declan. That was the only wolf who'd be fighting to get to her and Pike so hard.

"Don't release Declan!" Birch roared the words, and Pike flinched beneath her.

"Dammit, kid. I told you to stay put until I had a chance to talk to them," Birch snarled. He growled as he approached them, fury in every stomping step, as if he were about to dive after Pike, too.

Well, she wasn't done yet.

"Hold it, Birch." She held out her hand, warding him off. Off-white cougar's nails tipped her fingers—sharp and deadly. "Only one person gets to kick Pike's ass at a time, and it's still my turn. You can yell at him in a minute."

Brass ovaries... she had 'em apparently.

"It's fine. He's right," Pike whispered, and she could see the pain lingering in his eyes. "Birch told me to wait, but I wanted to explain."

"Explain what?" Declan snarled at Pike and then at her. "Abby, get your ass over here."

Instead of moving, she took a deep, calming breath so she didn't try to kick all their asses at once. "No, I'm not. I'm not done fighting Pike. It's still my turn." She glanced at her mate, and Declan looked like he couldn't decide if he wanted to strangle her or fuck her. Abby knew how she'd vote, but only when they got rid of their audience.

"Pike, I'm the team alpha for a reason. I make plans; the team executes." Birch pointed to himself. "I say jump..." He gestured at the team. "They don't have to ask how high because they listened *the first fucking time I gave them an order*."

Abby shifted slightly, wiggling closer to Pike and farther away from Birch. Apparently Birch was slightly miffed at Pike, too.

"He's not on the fucking team," Declan snarled. "He's a traitor. You fucking—" Her mate's eyes blazed with his wolf's presence. *"You gave her to them."*

"You're not team alpha." Birch's glare moved from Pike to Declan. "You don't get a vote."

"I've wondered about that. I think we should be able to vote on shit. Like, when it comes to choosing our base when we're on assignment." Grant was still noshing. "The take-out on the last one was gross. *I* didn't even want to eat at some of the places." The wolf shuddered and then gagged.

And the tension popped *like that*. Grant was intelligent, deadly, constantly hungry apparently, but at his core he seemed like a peacekeeper. Of sorts.

"This isn't a conversation I wanted to have yet." Birch glared at Pike, and Pike winced again.

"I couldn't let Declan think that—"

"That you betrayed me and *my mate*? That I should—"

"Enough." The word whipped through the air, a wave of dominance and pure strength in those syllables. Her cougar flinched, recognizing a stronger shifter nearby. One who demanded obedience.

She generally wasn't an obedient kind of girl.

Birch propped his hands on his hips and dropped his head forward. His shoulders rounded, and the man looked like he carried the weight of the world—beaten and dragged down by responsibility.

The team alpha straightened and stared at Declan. "Pike was freelancing. For me."

More growling from her mate—his amber-eyed gaze moving between Pike and Birch before finally settling on the wolf at Abby's side. "You told them about the house. You're the reason Abby got shot. And then you told them about the island." Declan surged, and Ethan and Cole tightened their holds, pulling her mate back again. "You little shit..."

"He's also the one who made sure she suffered minimal damage while Unified Humanity had her," Birch countered.

Abby wouldn't call it "minimal" herself, but she supposed it could have been worse.

"He told them where to find her in the first place." Declan snarled once more, and both Ethan and Cole struggled to hold him back. "He—"

Birch held up his hand. "On my orders. Everything he did—everything he revealed to Unified Humanity—was at my direction." He rolled his shoulders. "Twitchy, remember?"

"All your 'twitchy' bullshit got us was Abby hurt."

The bear shrugged. "Maybe." Birch tipped his head toward Pike. "And maybe not. That's not a discussion for right now. As team alpha I'm telling you he's our sixth man. The rest will figure itself out."

"As long as it gets figured out before my balls explode, I don't give a fuck," Abby heard Declan mumble, which meant *everyone* heard Declan mumble, and she groaned.

"Declan..."

"It wasn't me." He snapped his gaze to her, eyes wide, the picture of innocence.

More than one of the men snorted.

The snort turned into a cough, which turned into several coughs, and they all looked anywhere but at her.

"All right. So much for a fucking barbecue." Birch clapped his hands. "Let's break for the day. Get settled in your rooms and then do whatever you want. We're having a run in the north quarter tomorrow night. No excuses. Every-one's wearing their fur. You can make fun of me if you want, but it's a damned team-building exercise. We can't have a happy—"

They four men finished it together. "Cohesive team in order to effectively protect and care for our kind. We're given a great responsibility as SHOC agents and we can't betray the trust of our people by fighting among ourselves."

Birch sighed, the men laughed, and Abby just smiled. They were dangerous—deadly—but they were still just men. Ones who liked to laugh, joke, and...

She met Declan's gaze and felt his heated expression all the way down to her toes. She knew he wanted her—she craved him just as much—but beneath that was something she wanted to call...love.

CHAPTER FORTY-TWO

*D*eclan sighed and leaned against the nearest tree, crossing his legs at his ankles. Bark dug into his bare shoulder. On the outside, he appeared relaxed and content. On the inside, he wanted to run across the clearing and snatch Abby away from Ethan, Cole, and Grant's reach. If he didn't mate her soon, he'd kill someone.

But that wasn't exactly "team building." Team destroying, though... That could be fun.

He sighed. Again. Where the hell was Birch? They couldn't get their shit-show into the forest without him.

The snap of a twig, the crunch of leaves, and a gentle wind from the south announced the newest member of their group. One who had him torn in two—alternating between kicking the asshole's ass and whacking him for being so stupid... before kicking the asshole's ass.

"Lazy," Declan murmured as the newcomer stepped into his peripheral.

"Cautious," Pike countered.

He grunted. "I didn't cut your throat last night."

"Because Abby wouldn't let you."

Declan shrugged. It was the truth, after all. The only reason he hadn't done anything to Pike was because Abby had wrapped herself around Declan and fallen asleep the moment her head hit his shoulder. Even now he was certain she'd been faking, but he wouldn't tell her that. He wanted to mate *eventually,* and pissing her off would only delay them *again.*

Quiet blanketed them, two brothers standing side by side, but Declan felt as if thousands of miles separated them. They'd always been close, but now he wondered if it'd all been fake.

Abby's laugh reached out, her pure happiness acting like a soothing caress to his wolf. She was alive and whole. She wanted to be his. He wasn't sure what he'd done to deserve her, but he wasn't letting go. He hadn't done a good job of keeping her safe so far, but he'd do better. He had to. He couldn't live without her now.

"I'm sorry." Pike's voice was low, raspy.

"I know." He did know. The wolf knew, too. That didn't diminish its desire for vengeance though.

Pike slumped, shoulders curved forward, spine rounded. If he'd shifted, his tail would have been tucked between his legs, too.

Declan's wolf growled and shoved. It wanted him to snarl at the pup at their side. Show him the error of his ways. It wouldn't mind killing him either. But Declan kept it back. Not because he wasn't furious, but because Pike was his brother.

"Why?" That was Declan's only question.

"Birch—"

"I'm not asking Birch. I don't give a damn about the grizzly's twitchy bullshit. I'm asking you—*my brother*—why you betrayed me." He shook his head, the pain of his brother's treachery throbbing in his chest.

"You're not the only one driven by the past, Dec." Pike sighed. "You don't have a monopoly on pain."

"You?" Declan snorted, and pointed at Pike. "You left the pack voluntarily after the alpha died. I didn't force you to follow me."

"You mean after you killed the alpha?" Pike hissed. "You're my *brother*, Dec. I wasn't about to let you leave without me."

Declan ignored him. "I've done everything for you—given you anything you've ever needed. What do you know—"

"I know." Pike rasped those two words, his brother's agony more than evident. "I know that before you joined SHOC you'd spend months on a job. You'd come back for a few days and then leave on another. You think I just sat around and twiddled my thumbs while you did that shit?" Pike shook his head. "I had my own life. I had my own experiences with Unified Humanity. When Birch contacted me, I didn't hesitate." His brother looked him in the eyes, meeting Declan's hardened stare without a hint of a flinch.

"I'm sorry things played out the way they did, but the result was worth it."

Declan's wolf snarled and pulled at him, fighting to tear free of his human skin and sink his claws into Pike. "She shielded you."

"I know. I thought she was going to rip out my throat when she pounced." Pike rubbed his neck.

"No, in that room—at Unified Humanity. I was going to..." He ran a hand down his face. He was so fucking tired, and he knew they'd just go 'round and 'round with the argument. Declan *knew* he was right and Pike...fuck. Pike might have been right, too. "You were unconscious, and I was going in for the kill. She jumped on top of you so that I ended up with her neck between my jaws. You hurt her and she still saved your ass."

"I didn't realize."

"Yeah, well . . ." Declan shrugged.

"She saved me twice." A hint of awe filled Pike's tone, and he wasn't sure he liked the way his brother stared at Abby.

"She did." He shook his head. "She's the strongest shifter I know. She's been through so much—growing up and with us—but she's still over there laughing with the team."

"Stronger than you?"

He glanced at Pike, wondering if the kid was joking, but he looked honestly curious. "Killing's easy. Surviving, though, that's hard."

"Declan?" That soft voice, the delicate scent of her skin, and the soft padding of her bare feet on the grassy earth announced Abby's approach—and the end of his conversation with Pike.

They still had shit to figure out, but Declan had calmed enough to put off killing his brother . . . for a little while, at least.

He turned his head and watched her come toward him. She was his, in mind if not in body quite yet. Every curvy inch of her five-foot-eight frame. Every part of her would be his—soon. Fuck, he hoped *very* soon because he thought he'd go crazy without her. Neanderthal him wanted to *own* her down to her soul. He wanted to be her first thought of the day and last just before she fell asleep.

Because he sure as hell didn't want to be the only one going crazy in their mating. She already had him wrapped up in knots to the point that his wolf couldn't think of anything *but* her. Her smiles, her laughs, her kisses, her touches…

"Is everything okay?" She nibbled her lower lip, uneasiness in her expression while she flicked her attention between him and Pike.

"It's fine, sweetheart," he murmured, and held out his arm.

He tugged her close the moment her fingers wrapped around his. Once those curves were snug to his side, he gave her a kiss on her temple. He couldn't trust himself to kiss her anywhere else. Once he got started he wouldn't finish until he was *finished*. He was almost to the point that he didn't care who happened to be standing around watching.

Abby placed her hand on the center of his chest and tipped her head back to meet his gaze. "You sure?"

Maybe he could kiss the tip of her nose and be okay. He did just that and drew in a deep breath at the same time. Yeah, he wasn't okay. His cock went hard with that single hint of her scent, and he closed his eyes, trying real hard not to come in his jeans.

And his mate knew it. She wiggled her hips, body caressing his firm length while she gave him a knowing smirk. Even Pike could tell, his shithead little brother laughing like a damn donkey.

Declan reached out and whacked him in the back of his head. "Shut up, asshole."

"Declan," Abby admonished him. Of course.

"You can't expect me not to hit him. I didn't kill him, did I?" Yet. "Besides, he's my brother. I've been hitting him for more than twenty years. I can't stop now. It'd hurt his feelings."

Abby snorted. So did Pike. Declan had the urge to

glare at them both but settled for Pike. He still wanted to get in her pants and his fangs in her shoulder. Hopefully tonight. He knew the perfect spot just at the bend of the creek, and he'd already warned the team off. That area was a no-paw or -human-feet zone until sunrise *tomorrow*.

That'd give him the rest of the afternoon and all night to sate himself. Or at least take the edge off.

Declan licked his lips, imagining losing himself in her. In his fantasy, she'd shift back to human when they reached the creekside. He'd lay her down on the soft grass and take his time with her. Trace her curves with his tongue before he buried his face between her legs. Cats weren't the only species that liked cream, and he wanted all of Abby's. Then he'd settle between her legs and—

Poke.

Hell, no he wasn't poking. He was smoother than that.

Poke. Poke.

What the—

Poke. Poke. Poke.

Declan shook his head and rapidly blinked his eyes before turning his attention to the small finger poking his chest. "Huh?"

"Birch is here. He wants to get started."

He stared at her a moment more, trying real hard to figure out what the hell she was saying. "Huh?"

A large—familiar—hand whacked him in the back of the head. "Get your mind off your dick. Birch is ready to run."

Declan swung his arm out, fingers curled to form a fist, and aimed for his brother. Who ducked out of reach with a smile and a laugh before he jogged off to join the rest of the team. There was still a small hitch in Pike's step, but a shift would take care of the remaining injuries, putting him back together. At least physically.

"You sure I can't kill him? If I do it in his sleep, he won't feel a thing."

Abby just chuckled and gave him a soft kiss on the chin. He figured that meant no. Dammit.

CHAPTER FORTY-THREE

*A*bby held Declan's hand, his touch a comfort, while they slowly padded toward the rest of his team. She squeezed his fingers a hint tighter, a tremor of unease sliding into her blood, and she pushed the feeling aside.

"Sweetheart?"

She glanced at him, giving him a soft smile. "It's been a while since I've participated in a group run. In Alaska, gatherings were more like group *swims*, and before that, it was with my parents, so..."

"Eh, we're not all that organized. We'll shift, run as a group for a little bit, and then break off. Birch likes to find a cool cave to nap in. Ethan has a favorite rock where he can pretend he's got a pride of pussies waiting to lift their tails. Cole will fish a little in the creek. He just likes us to share the forest when shifted so our animals are familiar with each other."

"And the wolves stick together? You're like a mini-pack."

Declan snorted. "*Pike and Grant* can go run together."

"And us?"

"*We* will go exploring. I'll show you some of my favorite spots." He tugged her close, his hardness—including *that* hardness—pressed to her.

"Your favorite *private* spots?" Heat flushed her face, and a war roused inside her. She wanted to mate him—there was no disputing that—but in the middle of the forest during a run? Did she...?

Declan's eyes darkened, a deep amber replacing the bright blue. His wolf was out, peering at her through his eyes, and she recognized that look. Simply because it matched her own. Yes, the wolf wanted to mate. Now. In the forest. During the run.

Where anyone could come upon them while they solidified their connection.

Abby's center grew heavy and ached, that part of her already eager for his touch. Arousal blossomed and spread, reaching out from her core to consume her body. Her nipples hardened beneath her thin cotton shirt. She hadn't bothered with a bra or panties since she'd have to strip for her shift. They would have been just another layer to discard.

"Yes." He growled the word, deep rumble sending yet another jolt of need down her spine.

"Are you two coming?" Grant called out and then grunted, whispering "asshole" to someone before he yelled again. "I don't mean *coming*. That's later. I meant are y'all gonna strip and shift already. You're taking forever, and my balls are getting cold."

They were naked already? Abby turned her head, wanting to both confirm her suspicion *and* get a peek at the team, only to have Declan place his hand over her eyes.

"It's not cold, asshole. Summer hasn't been gone that long. Turn around."

"Does she want a look at my ass? She just had to ask." Grant's grunt that time was quite a bit louder.

"Turn. Around." Declan growled at the team, and the

texture of his skin changed, the wolf easing forward and taking over.

Abby turned her head slightly and rubbed her temple on his palm, her cat's attempt to soothe their angered mate. "It's fine," she murmured. "I don't care."

"*I* care." He grumbled. "Turn or lose your eyes."

"Do I get a look first? I need a good memory to carry me through the rest of my blind life." Grant had to keep pushing.

Her mate took a step toward the group, and she wrapped her arms around his waist, placing herself between Declan and the team. "Hey. He's just pushing your buttons."

He huffed and puffed—but there were no houses to blow down—and kept his gaze trained on the group at her back. "I'm going to push a button through his skull."

"Can you do that tomorrow? If you blind him now it'll annoy Birch and he's already agreed to let Pike bunk with the others, which means..."

Wolf's eyes met hers. "Alone."

"Yeah." Anticipation stirred her blood and her clit twitched, body anxious for him.

"Mate."

She nodded. "Yeah."

And she wanted it—him—so bad. Nothing else in her life had ever felt so right as being with him. She'd go through it all again—the pain, the fear—if only to end up with Declan once more.

"We turned around," Grant grumbled, though Abby was beginning to think the wolf just liked giving Declan a hard time. This time his words weren't followed by a groan, but a high-pitched whine.

Declan looked past her and then gave her his attention once more. "Strip."

If only they were in a bedroom...

She stepped away and then whipped her head over her shirt and tossed it aside, her shorts soon following, and then the cougar was there.

She embraced the cat, welcoming the animal with open arms and no resistance. Her transition slipped over her in a ripple of fur and flesh, bones and muscles reshaping to turn her into a glorious, golden beast. What used to hurt when she was younger didn't even warrant a flinch, nerves accustomed to the shift. Pale skin became sun-kissed fur, hands and feet turning into paws tipped with deadly nails, and bulky muscle swelled to replace her curves.

She dropped to four feet within a second of welcoming the cat, and Abby whipped her tail back and forth. Then she moved into a stretch, extending her forelegs first and digging her claws into the dirt before rocking forward and stretching one back leg and then the other. Abby turned her head up to the sky, enjoying the warmth, and she breathed deep to draw in the scent of her surroundings.

But her first scent wasn't of the grass or the trees. It didn't include nearby prey, or the aroma of the team. No, the flavors that consumed her were from one wolf—one specific, delicious wolf.

She lowered her head and looked to her left, searching for the source of that tempting aroma, and he was right there—at her side in all of his massive, midnight, dangerous and deadly glory.

A rumbling growl came from behind her, a sound the cat didn't recognize as Declan's, but she *could* identify the species.

Bear. She'd fought bear in the past. Fought and won, and she would again and again. She'd fought to survive in the past just so she could escape Alaska. Now she'd fight to keep the new life she'd only just tasted. A life of happiness even if it was occasionally bloody.

She settled into a crouch, claws firm in the dirt and grass—prepared to launch herself at any threat. She opened her mouth, fangs exposed, and released a long, threatening hiss. One warning was all it would get before she...

Declan chuffed and nipped her ear, the slight sting hardly worth thinking about because the cougar was still trying to understand... Two wolves. A lion. A tiger. A bear.

Oh my?

She shook her head. She wasn't in the wilds of Alaska. She wasn't fighting a polar bear for her life. She was in North Carolina with her mate and his SHOC team. They were going for a run, and then later...

Later she'd mate.

Abby nuzzled Declan in return, assuring him she was fine, and added an extra purr to make sure he understood. She was content. No, more than content. She was happy.

Another growl followed by a huff and she turned a glare on the bear—on Birch. The bear was Birch. The tiger was Cole, while Ethan was the lion. The two wolves... One resembled Declan, only slightly smaller in size. That had to be Pike.

Which meant the pale gray wolf was Grant. Grant with his tongue lolling out, tail wagging, and general look of play covering every inch of him. He was ready for fun, and Abby realized... so was she.

Now.

Abby nuzzled Declan once more, giving him a low, questioning trill, and then bolted for the tree line. Not just any part of it either. She sped across the ground, claws flinging dirt into the air with every long stretch, and she launched herself up and over the group of males. She landed with a *thump* on the other side, sliding sideways for a moment before she righted herself and glanced at the group.

She flicked the tip of her tail, waiting to see who would be the first to break ranks and chase her. With a howl and a leap, she had her answer, Declan's call echoing through the trees, and he grunted when he landed nearby.

The others released their own calls, snarls, roars, and growls in response, but Abby only had eyes—and ears—for Declan. The second his lupine gaze met hers, she was off. She broke into a sprint, cat's agility allowing her to bank right, then left, and then right again. She darted through the forest, embracing her beast while she simply enjoyed the act of running with a group. It was not a normal pack or a pride, but she figured they were better—a growly, grumpy, dangerous-as-hell, badass family.

And she was part of it—them—now. Or would be once she mated Declan.

A sharp nip to her hind leg grabbed her focus, and she shot a glare over her shoulder at the dark gray wolf keeping pace. The others crashed through the brush as well, a widely spread line of deadly predators wreaking havoc on nature.

But the wolf nipped her again, and she hissed at him. She was enjoying her run, dammit. The freedom of warm air in her fur, the breeze stroking her whiskers, and the joy of simply being a cat.

If he did it again, she had half a mind to finish the damn run in the trees. It'd been a while since she leaped from branch to branch as a way to travel—she was a hell of a lot heavier now—but she'd do it. *Just watch.*

The wolf didn't bite her again, though. He *pounced*. He took them both to the ground in a roll of fur and fang, slipping across the leafy forest floor. Soon their momentum gave out and they slid to a stop. Declan held her there, dominating her and yet not, while the rough sounds of the team's race slowly faded. When they were barely more than a whisper on the wind, he released her and hopped back.

Apparently, now he wanted to play—with her.

He bent down, forelegs nearly flat against the earth while his ass remained high, his tail rapidly wagging back and forth. He darted forward and then hopped back. Then he jerked left and right and left again, his mouth open wide and tongue lolling out. He barked at her, two short yips, and pounced on her again.

Or tried. She-cat would take it once, but not twice. She ducked out of his path and prepared herself to run. He wanted to play? He could try to catch her. But this time she'd known what kind of game they were playing.

Though it seemed he didn't want to chase; he wanted to *be* chased. Which was fine. Once she caught him she'd make him tell the team that cats ruled and dogs drooled.

CHAPTER FORTY-FOUR

Declan put on more speed, his longer strides helping him keep ahead of Abby. Even with her cat's natural quickness, he managed to outrun her through sheer reach. It paid to be larger than her agile feline.

He darted left, leaped over the next log, and landed with a heavy *thud*, his gait not faltering. But hers did. A scramble of leaves, breaking twigs, and then a snarl told him she hadn't fared the jump as well as him. He didn't get a whiff of her blood on the wind, which meant her body wasn't hurt—just her pride.

He made a sharp right at the next rock and used the thick layer of leaves to help him spin to face her. He slid in a whip-fast circle, and suddenly he was eye to eye with her, the furious cat glaring at him with frustration and a hint of menace. Oh, his mate wanted to pounce on him. Good thing he *wanted* her to pounce.

He yipped and barked, tail wagging, front legs lowered. He wanted to keep playing—needed her to keep running. Just a little farther. The direction of the wind changed, a hint of fresh water carried by the breeze, and his wolf howled within his mind. Joy overtook the beast, knowledge that they'd soon claim their mate suffusing him.

He hopped left and then right, a sharp bark at Abby that earned him a darker glare and a flick of her tail. Sure, the narrowing of her eyes showed anger, but he knew Kitty wanted to play.

And he had the perfect spot for them to enjoy.

He hopped forward and nipped the air, his teeth audibly clicking together. Then he whirled once more, taking off deeper into the trees. He kept one ear focused on Abby's movements while he kept watch on the rest of the world around them. Sure, the creek was near, but he needed to make sure no one else was in the area, too. If one of those assholes thought they'd get a show...

A sharp jolt of pain tweaked his tail, and he glanced over his shoulder to find a grinning feline just behind him. She'd caught up while he was worried about other males ogling her and she made it known.

Just wait until he got her naked.

The bubbling creek was soon within earshot, the gentle splash of water acting like a siren's call. It lured him forward and he went—gladly. He flew over the last of the forest's shrubs and landed with a grunt on the wet dirt just beyond the line of trees. The moment his paws hit the moist ground, he danced in a circle, making sure he didn't expose his back to the little she-cat.

Abby was right behind him, her golden body easily clearing the brush, and her feline's grace made the leap seem effortless—beautiful. She was solid muscle and fierce power, a powerful cat that rivaled his own wolf's strength. She was a worthy match to his own beast. Size separated them, but the power their beasts held was so very close.

At a glance, anyway. The wolf still wanted to play. He wanted to pounce and roll and see who came out on top... before he made sure Abby was on the bottom.

She paced back and forth, tail flicking, the darkened tip revealing her cat's agitation. Declan was getting ready to agitate her a little more. He wouldn't hurt her, but...

He pounced, jumped across the feet separating them and shoved her sideways. He knocked her off-balance and she stumbled, losing her footing. She rolled across the wet dirt, snarling and hissing with each shift of muscle. He kept pace, joining the tumble until he was sure she ended up beneath him.

Which was when he realized his error. When he realized she was beneath him, all right. And also on her back. She pulled her legs close and then planted them on his chest and belly, shoving him from atop her furred form. Her fierce shove launched him into the air a couple feet before he landed with a bone-jarring *thud* of powerful werewolf muscle and bone.

Embarrassed werewolf muscle and bone.

I am alpha wolf. Watch me get my ass handed to me by a cat.

A cat who thought she was hilarious and quickly rolled to her feet before breaking out into some awkward feline dance. He could practically hear her thoughts. "Neener-neener, look who's a wiener."

He'd show—

Abby pounced next, taking *him* down in a pile of claws, fur, and fangs. She nipped his shoulder and curled her nails around his legs. She tangled them in his fur, as if clutching him close even as she fought to push him away. Then he felt it, the shift of muscles and the subtle change in her force.

She wanted to be on top and his wolf...wasn't opposed to the idea. It meant she could do most of the work while he simply—

She nipped his ear and he yelped, her fangs pinching the

thin skin and zapping him with a spear of pain. Dammit. While he'd been imagining her riding his human form, she'd managed to pin his mangy ass. Stupid wolf.

The wolf didn't argue but reminded him that he was thinking more with his cock and balls than his brain. Her ferocity made him crave her, and if Declan didn't understand that...

Yeah, Declan's human mind understood.

He understood and decided that it was his turn to regain control. Those feline eyes were a little too happy about getting him on his back, and he simply couldn't have that.

Another roll, another change of position, but this time he didn't follow the quick move with a snarl. No, he cooed, whimpered, and whined. He lapped at her muzzle and nuzzled her jaw, wanting her pale skin and two-legged form to return. He licked her once more and then pulled back. He met her stare and tipped his head to the side in question, wondering if she wanted the same as him. They had privacy. They had each other.

And then they'd have a mating.

Her cat mirrored him, the angle of her head the same as his, and he lowered his nose to rub it on hers. He whined again, rubbing his snout on her lower jaw once more before meeting her gaze again.

Her purr began low, almost inaudible, but quickly grew in volume. It increased until it vibrated through his whole body. A sound of contentment, happiness...willingness? Her gaze darted up and down the bare banks of the creek, and he pictured what she saw. They were at one particular, sharp bend. An area that curved so tightly that they were out of sight from anyone up or down the creek. It was a private, yet exposed place.

And so help his team if they intruded.

Declan retreated, easing back so she was no longer pinned beneath him. Then he went further, not stopping until she was out of his reach. He didn't want her to feel pressured, but damn ... he wanted her.

The wolf retreated, giving way to his human body. Naked. Exposed. Anxious for her cat to let go already.

"C'mon, sweetheart," he murmured. "We're alone. Wanna make you mine."

She gave him a questioning trill, a soft roll of her cat's tongue, as if to ask him if he was sure.

"That I want you? Or that we're alone? I'm sure about both." He padded to the edge of the cool, gently flowing water. "Gonna rinse off this mud, and then I'll see about licking off every drop of water on your skin. How's that sound?"

That earned him a purr, a delicate sound from a dangerous beast, a contrast that made him want her even more. She was a contrast, softness that made him want to take care of her. At the same time, she retained a fierce strength that made him feel sorry for anyone who faced her. It was easy to kill. It took a lot to survive.

And she had. Through everything life threw at her, she'd survived. She'd overcome the worst. Now he only wanted to give her the best.

After he sank his fangs into that pretty shoulder and marked her so one and all knew she was taken.

Abby's shift was effortless, a flowing retreat by her cat and a gentle emergence of her human form.

"Abby," he murmured, and held out his hand, waiting for her to make the next move. He knew he didn't deserve her—not after the life he'd led. But if she'd let him, he'd take her and never let her go.

"Declan"—she took one hesitant step and then two— "what if ... ?"

"I'll kill 'em."

Her lips quirked into a tiny smile that had an extra dose of need sliding into his blood. "You threaten to kill your team an awful lot, but I haven't seen too much of that going on."

"You just have to bust my ass." He shook his head and kept his gaze trained on her. On the sway of her hips, on the subtle bounce of her breasts while she approached. The moment her hand touched his, he curled his fingers and enclosed her hand with a firm grip. He wasn't losing her now that he had her in his grasp.

Declan tugged, and then he had that damp body flush with his own, and her tempting scent surrounded him, blocking out all other aromas in the area. She was wet for him already, anxious for his possession. Her need spurred his, desire stirring in his balls while his shaft hardened.

Her hips wiggled slightly, just enough to caress his quickly hardening dick. She smiled wide, lips pulled back to reveal a hint of her cat's fangs. Then she bent her head and scraped a single fang over his chest.

"Fuck," he rasped, cock reacting to her whisper, her tease. "Abby, I won't be able to control myself if you tease me like that. I'll lose it, and I want to make this good for you. If you…"

She repeated that scrape, and Declan was man enough to admit that he whimpered.

"Just being with you will make it good," she said.

The wind picked up. It swirled around them, bringing forward more of the flavors of her arousal. Hot. Slick. Salty musk.

He ached to taste her, touch her, fuck and claim her.

Declan lowered his head, resting his forehead on hers. "Gonna rinse this sand off you, and then I'm going to claim you. Got that?"

"Better get started, then." With those teasing words, she tore from his arms and darted to the water's edge.

She splashed into the low waters with a joyous laugh, one that was so lighthearted and carefree that it washed away more of the darkness in his heart. She'd been brushing away those spots minute by minute, hour by hour. Even as he killed, it was on her behalf so dark stains on his soul never formed.

If he had a purpose, if it was for her, he didn't suffer. Further proof that she was his and his alone.

With a growl, he followed, baring his fangs and adding a snarl. The chilled water lapped at his heated skin, but it couldn't diminish his desire. Not when her hands slid over his body.

He did the same, tracing her form, exploring her with a desperate touch. He wanted to learn all of her. He wanted to know the meaning behind every sigh and each moan. He was desperate to understand what each groan meant and exactly what could be done to make her shatter in his arms.

And when he washed away the last streak of mud, he knew it was time. His wolf spurred him into action, encouraged him to sweep her into his arms and cradle her against his chest. He turned and strode to the water's edge and worked to ignore her tempting lips wreaking havoc on his neck and chest.

Abby nibbled his wet flesh, tugging on his skin and nipping him with her cat's fangs. She released a soft whine and wiggled in his arms, the feline asking for more. More than he'd give to her. Soon.

"There's a blanket over here with our name on it. Once I lay you down, you won't be getting up again for a while."

CHAPTER FORTY-FIVE

*A*bby didn't think she'd want to get up for a long, *long* while. And then his words penetrated her passion-glazed mind.

"You planned this." She murmured the words against his shoulder, then licked away the nearest drop of water.

Declan snorted. "Can you blame me?" His deep tenor slid through her and caressed her spine from inside out. "I want you to be mine, but we're surrounded by the team twenty-four seven."

She grinned and nipped his shoulder blade, licking away any sting as soon as she was done.

His pace slowed, and she lifted her head from his shoulder, turning her attention to her surroundings and the plush blanket resting on a sun-dappled patch of grass nearby. A few colorful pillows added to the alluring picture, along with a basket she hoped contained food...for later.

For now she wanted to gorge herself on Declan.

He lowered to his knees in a smooth move and then laid her on the soft blanket before taking his spot beside her. They remained close, his heat searing her nude body, yet she still had room to look her fill.

"Can't stand having those unmated males near you." His

words were gruff and low. Almost so garbled she couldn't understand him, but the message came through.

"They weren't ever going to take me from you." Abby lifted her left hand and caressed his biceps, stroking him from elbow to shoulder and then across his collarbone before slipping behind his neck. "From the moment you caught me, I've thought of nothing but you."

That was only a tiny lie. She'd thought about pain and death, too, but Declan had always been at the top of her thoughts.

His eyes darkened, a deep amber overtaking his vision. "No one will ever hurt you again."

She ran her fingers through the hair at the base of his skull, soothing the growling beast. "I know."

"No one will take you. No one will scare you." More of the wolf came out, his obvious fury still present.

"I know." She tugged, but he didn't budge, so she pushed to her elbow and went to him instead. She inched closer and brushed her lips across his as she brought their bodies together. His thick hardness nudged her hip, proof of his desire.

For her. Only for her.

Her core ached, her own body making its need known. She wanted him just as badly, wanted to be possessed and taken by him. Their hearts beat in time, their souls calling to each other, and their bodies were desperate to tie their futures together.

Now.

"Mate me, Declan. Mark me so everyone knows I'm yours," she whispered against his mouth, carefully slipping her fingers from his hair. She ghosted the tips over the flesh at the juncture of his shoulder and neck. "And I'll make sure everyone knows you're mine."

He shuddered, and his length twitched, throbbing, while a drop of moisture escaped the tip to decorate her skin. He was on edge, not far from finding that ultimate bliss.

A bliss they needed to discover together.

"Abby…" All he said was her name, but there was so much more in his tone. A warning and a plea in one.

She hooked one leg over his, sliding her knee higher and foot along the back of his thigh. She opened herself more and more to him, not stopping until she was wrapped around his hip, heel coming to rest at his lower back.

"Come to me, Declan." She nipped his lower lip, but he remained motionless.

"We…" He shook his head. "I'm…" The cool scent of his doubt drifted to her, suffusing her with the flavors of his emotions.

"Perfect for me." She gave him a gentle, openmouthed kiss. "Everything I've ever wanted." And another. "My mate."

He shuddered once more, and she sensed his control faltering. He acted like a demanding, grunting male who wasn't about to give her a choice, but he still fought to give her a chance to deny him.

As if she ever would.

Abby tightened her grip just enough to hold him, to pull him atop her when she rolled to her back once again. This time his hips settled between hers, skin to skin, bare hardness nestled to her slick heat. He shuddered with the new, intimate contact and she did the same, that single touch enough to push her near the edge of release.

Declan stared down at her, eye color flickering between amber and blue, his two halves battling for supremacy.

"Claim me, Declan Reed." She forced herself to remain immobile, to cease teasing him and give him a chance to move away.

"Last chance to run, Abby. Once I make you mine I won't let you go."

He growled the words as if they were a threat, and it sent a tremble of need dancing over her nerves.

She quirked her lips in a soft smile. "And once I make you mine, *I* won't let *you* go."

She rolled her hips, rubbing her slick, bare center along his firm length. She shuddered with the caress, the feel of his veined shaft stroking her intimate flesh, and whimpered as the pleasure gathered inside her.

"Fuck." He spat the curse and shifted his hips, that hardness changing position while he lifted away from her. He stared down at her body as the head of his length nudged her opening. "You're so beautiful. So perfect." He rolled his hips, gently sliding no more than an inch of his cock in and out of her.

The shallow penetration drew moans from deep within her chest, her whole body aching for more, aching for him. And then he gave her exactly what she craved.

Declan didn't stop with his next thrust, didn't cease penetrating her in a slow, tormenting slide until their hips met. "So mine."

Abby moaned deep and grasped his shoulders, the cat's claws emerging to scrape at his damp flesh. "Ahhh!"

Her sheath rippled and squeezed him, trembling around his thick, pleasurable invasion.

"Tight. Wet." He adopted a steady pace, a gentle glide of his length in and out of her center. The rough and tumble assassin made love to her, his passion a series of gentle rolling waves.

Not the rough, feral passion she'd expected from him.

She met his stare, and the reason was quickly visible in his eyes. He worried for her, worried about her response to his rough need.

"Declan, give me all of you." She scratched his back, knowing she left bright red lines in her wake. "Everything."

"Abby." His eyes seemed to glow, his wolf tugging at the end of its tether.

Next she broke skin, piercing the hard flesh of his shoulders with a small prick. "You won't hurt me. You never could."

She met his every thrust, bodies moving in a gentle glide and careful passion. She tightened her grip on his shoulders and lifted herself from the ground, then captured a bite of his flesh between her teeth. She bit down, not piercing him but showing him she was just as much an animal as he was. She had a cat inside her. A cat that was desperate to be his.

"Mate me." She murmured the two words against his chest and then repeated the harsh nibble. "Take me or let me go."

It was the push he needed, the final nudge that sent him over the edge into the uncontrolled passion she craved.

"Mine." The voice was Declan's, but the harsh rasp and growl was all wolf. The wolf who refused to let her go. Good thing she wanted to stay.

Abby fell back to the blanket and let Declan take control. She allowed herself to be swept away by his punishing pace, by the bliss he gifted her with each and every flex and relaxation of his muscles. His thrusts increased in power and rhythm, the slap of their bodies echoing through the clear forest air as they both sought release.

A release that would soon come. Her body shook, nerves alight with impending ecstasy and overwhelming pleasure. Her sheath rippled and squeezed his long length and hard thickness. His veined shaft caressed the most intimate part of her, the head stroking her G-spot with an accuracy that drew cries from her with every thrust and retreat. She sobbed his name, begging and pleading for more and more from him.

And he gave her what she craved. His pace turned into a punishing race, their fight to the ultimate pleasure increasing with every beat of their hearts. She whined, begged, and pleaded for more, aching to reach the pinnacle with Declan at her side.

With Declan inside her.

He gripped her hip with one hand, holding her steady and forcing her position to alter just enough to...

"Declan!"

Enough to give her G-spot a hint more pressure, to give her a hint more ecstasy that had her hurtling toward the edge. She stood at the brink, at the delicate line between need and possession.

"Give it to me, Abby." He growled and bared his fangs, the long white lengths of his wolf's teeth shining brightly with the sun's rays. "Now."

He wanted her—all of him wanted her—and she was prepared to accept him.

Accept and take him.

She released the thick leash she had wrapped around her heart long ago, during her life of turmoil and pain, and let it fly free of her body. Now she embraced Declan, drew him to her chest, and accepted every battered and bruised inch of his soul. He was her mate.

Hers.

With that acceptance, she cried out his name, head thrown back and shoulder exposed as the ultimate pleasure overtook her. It suffused her blood, stroked her nerves from inside out, and stretched to possess every inch of her trembling body.

Then he gave her more, he gave her everything. Declan

struck in that moment, in that very second she flew off the cliff of pleasure. A vicious pain tore through her, the jolting stab of agony breaking through the rising pleasure. But only for a moment. Only for a split second that stole her breath while he gave her what she'd craved for so many years. Fangs sank through flesh, teeth tearing into skin and muscle until he'd bitten as deep as he possibly could.

And he remained there, his body still drawing out her final release, his teeth in her shoulder and his mouth sucking at the wound he'd caused. Her cat roared in joy, the beast purposefully refusing to heal the damage. It had more important things to do. Such as copy Declan's actions.

Just as soon as she was done coming. Her orgasm continued on and on, his every thrust and every suckle spurring the ecstasy to rise higher and higher. And she embraced it. Embraced the pleasure and the pain and the extra pleasure the pain gave her. Her body tingled and throbbed with the overwhelming joy, with the maddening, ultimate relief until . . .

Until his strokes faltered, until his rhythm stuttered and he whipped his teeth from her shoulder. Blood and saliva dripped from his lips, the ferocity of his beast right beneath the surface of his skin. Wolf's eyes met hers, nothing but the beast in his gaze while he whispered a single word.

"Abby."

He wanted it—wanted to be claimed—now. His body was there, dancing on the precipice just as she had. He held himself back, watched and waited for her, and she couldn't help but give him what he craved.

Her cat rushed forward, fangs dropping in an instant as she rose and struck. Between one heartbeat and the next, blood filled her mouth, the bitter, coppery fluid pouring from his wound and sliding over her taste buds. Hints of his animal's muskiness and the man's pure sweetness flowed down her throat, coating her from inside out just as...

Just as his hips jerked once, twice, and with the third, he froze. His hips remained flush to hers, his roar filling the air while his seed filled her body.

The cat purred and chuffed at the idea, at the thought of carrying his cub or pup. It made her grip him tighter, pull him more firmly against her center so she didn't lose a drop.

Abby slowly withdrew her fangs and lapped at the wound, licking away the trickling droplets that swelled along the wound. Now they could never be separated.

Ever.

Declan slipped out, and she whimpered with the loss just as Declan groaned. His breathing came in harsh pants, his chest heaving and brushing her breasts with every inhale. Finally he fell to the side with a groan, dragging her close as he dropped to the blanket. She curled against him, body slick with sweat and coated in his scent.

"Damn," he wheezed, and lifted his head, kissing her forehead. "Just..." He inhaled deep and slowly breathed out. "Damn."

Abby hummed, unable to say anything just yet. She would. At some point, she was sure. Just...not yet. For now she wanted to glory in the feel of his damp body on hers, the aroma of their passion, and embrace the knowledge that she had a mate. She had one person dedicated to her and her happiness just as she was dedicated to his.

No matter what the future held, they had each other.

A bellowing roar split through their content quiet, the bear's fury followed by a chorus of barks, and then came a lion's objection as well.

So, they had each other and his SHOC team.

"I'm gonna kill 'em," Declan slurred, a hint of a growl

in his threat, but she knew he was just as drowsy from their lovemaking as she was.

"After." She sighed and snuggled closer.

"After?" He tightened his hold with a hum.

"Uh-huh. After a nap. And then after you claim me again. Maybe after you claim me twice." She nuzzled his chest and then relaxed with a sigh. Yes. A nap and a couple more rounds of claiming sex sounded like a very, *very* good idea.

He squeezed her tight and hauled her atop him, tugging until they were nose to nose. "Wolf has never wanted anyone other than you, Abby." He lifted his head slightly and brushed his lips across hers in the softest of kisses. "He never will."

Declan looked at her with smoky eyes that promised her the world. The same way her father had always looked at her mother.

Everything was okay—everything would *be* okay. At least until Unified Humanity decided to strike again. For now she'd take her joy—and Declan—and hold both close to her heart.

EPILOGUE

It looked like Birch was going to let Declan's post-mating glow last only until eleven. He'd roused Declan and Abby fifteen minutes ago—ordering Declan to get his furry ass moving. Now the team alpha had a look in his eye that said the team was about to be smothered by a load of Unified Humanity–Shifter Operations Command bullshit.

Declan held his mate close, one arm firmly around her waist, while she sat across his lap. He hadn't let her get more than an arm's length away once he'd gotten his fangs in her pale flesh. The wolf finally had her, and the beast wasn't about to let her escape.

The team sat around a table on Birch's back deck—the *entire* team. Which included Pike. Pike, who made sure his ass was next to the team alpha and as far away from Declan as he could get.

Abby had told Declan he couldn't kill his brother. He wondered if she'd let him rough him up a little though.

"Now that the happy couple has joined us," Birch drawled, "here's where we stand."

Grant raised his hand. "I'm sitting. Does that mean you want us to stand? Is this gonna be like church with all the praying and the 'please rise, please be seated, amen' shit? Because if it is, I'm gonna need a sandwich."

Birch sighed. "Fuck my life."

"Abby, will you make me a sandwich?" Grant flashed what Declan could only describe as "sad puppy" eyes.

Declan growled low, his wolf prowling and anxious to pounce on the male who dared ask his mate for anything. "Grant..."

"I wouldn't mind a sandwich," Ethan added.

"Potato salad, maybe?" Cole put in his own order.

"My mate is not cooking for anyone." The deck vibrated, and his roar echoed across the lake, the still water shimmering with the sound.

Abby stroked his chest, her small hand tracing circles on his pecs, as she whispered, "Shh...Calm down."

And as it always seemed to do, his wolf calmed with her touch.

"I called it. She's a dick whisperer," Pike murmured, and that had Declan's fury rising once again.

Declan ignored his brother's whisper and kept his attention on the team alpha. The quicker Birch spoke, the quicker he could drag Abby back to bed. "What's going on, boss?"

The team alpha took a deep breath and released it slowly. His gaze touched on each of them, attention even landing on Abby as he sought out the rest of the team.

"Quade is no longer a threat to Abby."

Cole snorted. "He never *was* a threat to Abby. One of us would have killed him if he'd tried to go after our kitten."

Declan's wolf bristled at the nickname, and he let a low growl escape his throat. "Cole..."

The tiger waved him away. "Down, boy. Bad dog."

"The director," Birch growled between gritted teeth

while he glared at Cole, "is under the impression that Grant was able to piece the tablet back together and part of the data was recovered. It reveals exactly what Abby reported—FosCo wired money to Unified Humanity. He's withdrawn his request to speak with her in light of that as well as the fact that she's now fully mated to a SHOC agent."

At least Declan wouldn't have to waste time killing Quade now.

"You going to share your 'twitchy' feelings with the class?"

Birch ran a hand through his hair and then gripped the back of his neck, massaging the muscles. The wind changed direction, a gust that snared Birch's scent and blew it in their direction. Declan pulled apart the different flavors, quickly identifying each one...including the last. The one that had his stomach clenching and his heartbeat stuttering.

"Aw, shit," Ethan mumbled.

"That bad?" Grant whined.

"Motherfucker," Declan growled.

Cole groaned. "I need to order more C-4, don't I? With or without notifying SHOC?"

Abby frowned, brow furrowed, and her attention drifted across the team before returning to Declan. Her sparkling blue eyes were clouded with confusion. "What?"

"Birch doesn't get worried, but right now he's worried."

"Concerned," the grizzly snapped, and curled his lip, flashing a fang.

"*Concerned*, then," Declan drawled, rolling his eyes.

Birch curled his lip a little higher before speaking again. "Over the last several years, tips about Unified Humanity and assignments to take them out from headquarters have tapered off."

Declan nodded. They had lessened over time. "Because we've been making a difference." Pike snickered, and he shot his brother a dark glare. "Something to share?"

Pike remained silent.

"There's someone inside SHOC feeding information to Unified Humanity. That same person is limiting what information agents receive."

Declan's heartbeat stuttered, and his lungs froze. Abby shuddered in his arms. He pulled her even closer, tucking her head against his shoulder. The others . . . weren't happy.

To say the least.

"What the fuck?"

"Fuck that."

"No fucking way."

Birch held up a hand to silence them all. "I had my suspicions, which is why I sent Pike in to UH." The grizzly nodded at the other wolf. "Pike gave me—us—the tip on FosCo. Our arrival, Abby's discovery, and SHOC's response prove there's someone on the inside feeding intel to Unified Humanity."

"Who?" Declan wanted to bathe in their blood and feed their bodies to natural predators.

"We don't know," the grizzly snarled. "Yet. Foster's death meant we couldn't get any info from him, and he was the closest link between SHOC and UH. The traitor is safe—for now. He—"

"Or she," Ethan grumbled, and everyone focused on the lion with narrowed eyes. "What? Why are you looking at me like that?" He frowned at them all. "The chicks in the pride do the heavy lifting and conniving. Never met a bigger group of feline bitches in my life. They will tear your shit up and smile while doing it. Just sayin'."

Birch picked up where he left off. "He *or she* is out of

reach right now, but FosCo wasn't the only big business wrapped up in Unified Humanity. Pike gave us another name—a name that won't go past our team until we figure out what the hell we want to do next."

"We?" Declan raised his eyebrows in question.

"We." Their team alpha gave Grant a blank stare. "We're going to talk about a democracy since going against UH while there's a traitor in SHOC might end up with some of us six feet under."

"Sweet." Grant punched the air. "First order of business, I want to be in charge of location selection for all future operations."

"Grant," Birch snapped, and the wolf immediately straightened, any hint of a smile vanishing from his expression. "This isn't the time for fun and games. We do this, we do it knowing that shit is gonna keep getting flung at the fan and we're the fucking fan that's gonna end up covered in it."

"I'm in." Abby's voice didn't waver, and she straightened in Declan's lap. "I know I'm not an agent, but if you're taking votes, then I'm in."

"Abby," Declan murmured, wrapping both arms around her and pulling her close, but she wouldn't have it.

"No." She brushed off his hold and turned to face him. "Unified Humanity needs to be stopped. If there's someone inside SHOC helping them succeed...we—you guys— have to do this." His mate lowered her head, soft forehead pressed to his own while she whispered. "There can't be any more children like me, Declan. Not if there's something that can be done to stop them. Can you imagine another child out there in a burning house? Praying for their lives while they're locked in a cupboard? The fire..."

"Shhh...sweetheart." He cupped her cheeks and brushed

away her tears. Declan lifted his head and let his gaze sweep the others, satisfied when they all gave him a brisk nod. "We'll do what we can to stop them and find the traitor." He directed his next question to Birch. "Where are we looking first?"

"Foster supplied the cash to Unified Humanity. Thanks to Pike's intel, we're going after the brawn next. We're hoping that will lead us to the brains. Somewhere in there, we'll find out who in SHOC is blocking us at every turn." Birch leaned over the table, gaze intent. "Take some time to get your head on straight because once we're back on deck, things are gonna get real ugly, real quick. This shit ain't gonna be easy."

Declan grinned, and the team spoke as one. "But it sure as fuck is gonna be fun."

Dangerous, too, but at least he'd have Abby at his side. He could face anything as long as he had her in his life... and in his heart.

Read on for a peek
at Cole's story in
TIGER'S CLAIM,
coming in Autumn 2018.

CHAPTER ONE

Cole figured Birch wouldn't appreciate him blowing up a mansion overflowing with humans.

After Cole got out of the building, of course. No sense in killing his own tiger-shifting ass, after all. He only wanted to take out the humans who were desperate to see all shifters six feet under. They'd conveniently gathered in one place. Almost like they were asking to be turned into crispy critters.

It'd give him a chance to test the new charges he'd devel—

"Request denied." A low growl from Birch—man, the grizzly was cranky—filled his ear. The team's newest com device was tiny as hell—developed by his werewolf teammate Grant—and crystal clear. Unfortunately.

Cole lifted his glass of bubbling champagne to his lips and pretended to take a sip to shield his mouth as he spoke. "Did I say that out loud?"

"Nah," Ethan—the only lion shifter on the team—drawled. "You just have that 'let's bring this building down' look in your eye."

Cole grunted. "I always do."

He specialized in explosives, after all. It'd been too

damned long since he'd watched anything disappear in a scattered wave of fire and concrete.

Two women wrapped in sequins and glittering jewels slowly strolled near, their gazes stroking him from head to toe. The blonde licked her red-painted lips, while the brunette gave him a look that promised a good time.

Yeah, he looked damned good in a tux if he did say so himself. He hated the penguin suits, but they had their uses in this kind of setting. They went with the polished floors, sparkling chandeliers, and millionaire crowd.

He lowered his glass and tipped his head to the women. "Ladies, good evening."

The blonde wetted her lips, an obvious tease. The brunette's mouth tipped up in a small smirk, and a glint of desire sparked in her eyes. He forced himself to appear interested when all he wanted to do was toss them both through the nearest window.

The only reason they were here at this Unified Humanity event was because they hated shifters.

"I don't think we've met before, Mr...." The brunette's voice trailed off in obvious question.

"Turner." His lips curled in a smile. "Cole Turner."

"Bond. James Bond." Grant's deep voice—the pain-in-the-ass werewolf—reached him through the com. "Lame, man."

Cole continued as if the jerk hadn't spoken in his ear. "And you lovely ladies are?"

The brunette held out her hand first. "Olivia Walters."

He gently grasped her fingertips and brought her hand to his mouth, brushing a soft kiss to her knuckles. "It's a pleasure."

In more ways than one. She was beautiful to look at— even if her father was an evil monster. More important, she was the first step in getting close to said evil monster. It'd only taken him four months of coming to these blasted hoity-toity parties—rejoining the old-money class he hated—to finally get invited to a Walters gathering.

Cole released Olivia's hand and turned to the blonde. She was pretty in an understated way, and it didn't take him long to realize nibbling her lower lip wasn't meant to entice him. Her hand trembled as she held it out for his.

Huh. A *nervous* murderer. *Interesting.*

"Charlotte—"

Olivia nudged Charlotte away, the woman's hand dropping from Cole's before his lips had a chance to brush her skin. "Cole...Can I call you Cole?" Olivia didn't wait for a response. "Are you associated with the Turner Group?"

Cole parted his lips and drew in the surrounding scents. His tiger padded forward from the back of his mind, anxious to help so they could get the hell out of there. He tasted each flavor and easily identified them. Excitement. Anticipation. *Arousal.*

Gross.

"I am." *Unfortunately.* He flashed her his most disarming grin and fought to suppress the churning in his gut. He hated his connections to the Turner Group, but they were undeniable and—right now—useful. "I'm the youngest of the Turners. My older brother is the president. The rest fall in line after him."

Olivia giggled as if he'd said the most amusing thing in the world, and he fought the urge to roll his eyes. "And what do you do for the Turner Group?"

Cole winked at her. "I'm the independently wealthy black sheep of the family."

Even if he had black-and-orange striped fur instead of wool.

"I've always enjoyed spending time with the naughty ones."

"Olivia," Charlotte broke in, and Olivia shot a glare at her friend. "Your father is looking for you."

Olivia gave him a smile. "I'd love to finish this conversation later. If you're not here with anyone, perhaps we can find each other again."

Grant snorted in his ear and singsonged, "The chick wants some tiger dick."

"The night is, happily, my own." He winked.

She stepped closer, fingers skating down his lapel. "Excellent," she purred. "I will see you later this evening, then." With that, Olivia slowly turned away from him. "Come along, Charlotte."

He kept his gaze on the two women, watching Olivia slice through the crowd with practiced ease while her little friend scurried in her wake. A waiter drifted past, and he reached out, snagging another glass of champagne.

Cole brought the glass to his lips and spoke to the others. "I don't stick my dick in crazy."

"The crazies are fun, though." Ethan sighed. "They're real freaky. You don't know what you're missing."

"Grant, identify the girl's friend," Birch said, as if they hadn't ever been talking about fucking. Like always. "Put together a file. Charlotte seemed to like our boy."

Cole slowly made his way along the outer edge of the crowd and turned to face the wall, gaze on some overly expensive—probably priceless—piece of shitty artwork. "She seemed like she'd piss her panties if I talked to her."

"I thought you were into that." Declan—the recently mated wolf on their team—just had to open his mouth.

"Nah, that's your brother," Cole murmured, and returned to his slow meandering.

"Don't knock it till you try it." Pike, Declan's brother, spoke up.

Before that moment, Cole didn't imagine their team could be quiet all at the same time, but...yeah. No one had a response to that, it seemed.

"Pike. What the fuck?" Disgust laced Declan's words.

"Declan, don't judge. Remember what the psych said when you asked about how you like to tie Abby to a tree?" Pike's words were followed by Declan's growl. "He said your kink is not my kink and that's okay."

"Grant." Birch sighed. "Do you have that data on Charlotte?"

"Working on it. This conversation is funny as shit though. And did I mention I'm out of soda? 'Cause I'm out of soda." That wolf and his junk food.

Their team alpha's low growl—a real one that told them to shut the fuck up—silenced them all.

Cole took advantage of that bit of quiet. He drew his tiger forward to make his hearing even more sensitive. He listened to the murmured conversations as he drifted past one group after another.

He hated the entire scene—trophy wives, pompous executives, and bratty daughters hunting for a rich husband. More than one looked at Cole like he was rich husband material.

Rich? Yes.

Husband? A mate, maybe. Someday. A day far from right now and only after he found someone exactly like...

Like a woman who was already mated to one of Cole's teammates, which made her off-limits.

He was an asshole, not a homewrecker. Even if he did feel a pull toward a certain cougar shifter.

Cole listened to the discussions with half an ear, gaze

traveling over the people he neared. He mentally went through Grant's research, identifying the humans he came across.

Net worth of...forty million. The next person was only twenty-five million. There was a woman who'd married well whose husband had died early. She was worth a hundred fifty million and had Walters closing in on her.

Yes, Walters needed money—a lot. It was only a matter of time before he believed Cole was the one to give it to him.

Olivia wandered up to her father just before he reached the widow, and the two exchanged a few whispered words.

"Looks like she's telling Daddy about our boy," Birch murmured, and Cole grunted.

Yeah, when James Walters cut Cole a quick glance before he refocused on Olivia, Cole knew he was their topic of conversation.

Cole took another sip of sparkling champagne. "Time to play hard to get."

There was no sense in making it easy on Walters. Rich men were used to having to pander to *richer* men. Cole had triple the net worth of anyone else in the building. Easily.

He changed direction and carefully cut through the crowd, passing off easy smiles whenever someone looked his way. He lost himself among the penguin suits and glittering dresses, allowing the humans to swallow him in their presence. He kept a sedate pace, weaving between people until he finally reached the opposite side of the ballroom.

He turned and leaned against the cream-colored wall, taking another sip of champagne. The shit was nasty. What he wouldn't give for a beer.

"How's Papa?" Cole murmured.

"He left the widow, and it looks like Daddy and daughter are hunting you," Declan answered.

"Good." He'd stay put for a little while. Just long enough for them to catch sight of him before he changed position once more.

Except... All it took was a single flash of color—a cream gown with touches of red—that drew his attention from his mission. It drew him to *her*—a stranger with long red hair, sparkling green eyes, and kissable lips.

She was gorgeous. She was tempting. She was... a shifter?